A Rewrite in New York

Holly Lipovits

Playlist

Drive ♡ The Cars

That's So True ♡ Gracie Abrams

I Love You, I'm Sorry ♡ Gracie Abrams

7 Things ♡ Miley Cyrus

Here We Go Again ♡ Demi Lovato

Silver Springs ♡ Fleetwood Mac

Close To You ♡ Gracie Abrams

Feels Like ♡ Gracie Abrams

Mystical Magical ♡ Benson Boone

Pretty Boy ♡ Alex Sampson

Can't Fight This Feeling ♡ REO Speedwagon

You're So Vain ♡ Carly Simon

I Need You ♡ Billy Squier

For every heart that believed in second chances, may you find the love that never asks you to shrink—especially within yourself.

A Note to the Reader

This novel touches on themes of infidelity, emotional manipulation, emotional gaslighting, and grief. I know how heavy these can be. If you find any moment too difficult, I hope you'll trust your limits and skip ahead. Zoe's story will still be here when (and if) you're ready.

Thank you for letting me share this piece of my heart.

A Rewrite in New York

Chapter 1

The cursor blinks back at me in disgust. My brain has turned to mush, and no one wants to take any helpings. My eyes dart across my laptop screen as my vision blurs slightly from exhaustion, and my fingers tremble while they hover over the keys. Since I am in my last semester of college working on my master's in creative writing, you would think I'd have the creative flow to be able to write my story.

It's just a story. I've written hundreds of them. Is it because I'm afraid of the spotlight all over again? Sure, I've had trouble reading my stories in front of class during workshops, but that didn't mean it wasn't any good, right?

I sigh and tip my head back, staring at the stick-on stars that glow above me. Yellows and oranges and pinks clutter my vision. I close my eyes and suck in the cool breeze that hits my face from the cracked window. The smell of fall tickles my nose and wraps around my neck like a scarf. It is that time of year again: fall. The *Gilmore girls* theme song echoes in my head just like every year before. I nuzzle into my sweater and look outside.

The sunset oozes its colors as if painting the sky—reds, yellows, oranges, and pinks. They all blur together into one masterpiece.

Small clusters of faint stars paint the sky and I hear laughter below. Kids yell at their parents to buy them snacks and goodies. Dogs bark and cars honk their horns.

It's just another evening in Cleveland.

I smile at my reflection in my laptop's screen. My burnt orange hair flops just above my shoulders in a bob-style haircut as strands of my wispy bangs flutter above my eyelashes. I opted for a reddish lip stain that, I think, makes my blue eyes pop. Plus, it makes me feel pretty. Tiny gold hoop earrings hug my earlobes.

I grasp my laptop and close it. Maybe I need new scenery for some inspiration. Or maybe I'm just procrastinating? Certainly not. Never heard of her. I shove my laptop, notebook, and pens in my New York City tote bag and walk out of my bedroom.

I smile down at the tote bag. I picked it up in New York after a little detour with my parents years ago. We were on our way back home from my second cousin's wedding in Boston. My mom pushed me to buy a souvenir, but as a pre-teen, all I wanted to do was go home and sleep after walking for hours through the bustling city. At the time, it was just a souvenir, but now it feels more like a little reminder that the city has been tugging at me ever since.

Our two-bedroom apartment isn't the kind of soulless, gray-on-gray luxury place TikTok influencers pan across, unless iced coffee stains and stacks of paperbacks suddenly count as chic. It's a quaint, cozy twenty-two-unit building nestled just up the street of the charming and bustling downtown area. It's walking distance from the arts university, a park with a lake, my bank, the library where I spend every waking hour (especially Saturday nights, because what else am I going to do?), and the cutest shops and restaurants to boot, like The Bean, my favorite place in the world. Except libraries and bookstores, of course. They have a soft spot in my heart too.

We got lucky with the apartment being rent-controlled, especially after I decided to leave my previous job to pursue my master's full-time. My best friend and platonic soulmate, Tish, works full-time at a bar in town and covers most of the rent thanks to the amazing tips she receives, while I pursue freelance writing and editing gigs to cover the utilities. I'm grateful to have a best friend who understands and supports my passions and dreams.

Tish is snuggled up on the couch with my fat tuxedo cat, Ollie. I love our small apartment—it's home. The walls are white and covered with small twinkling lights near the ceiling. A small portable fireplace sits beneath the mounted TV, and abstract paintings by my mom hang all around. A couple of bookshelves filled to the brim with books and trinkets stand next to the patio door. Vintage forest green chairs, a yellow sunburst couch, and my favorite lounger really tie the place together. The kitchen is tiny, but at least it has a dishwasher along with retro black and white tiled floors and a cozy bistro-style table for two.

Tish looks up from watching TV. Her sandy blonde hair sits on top of her head in a messy bun that glistens against the faint sunset glowing through the curtains. Her bright green-apple eyes light up when she sees me and her naturally blushed lips curve into a smile.

"Hey, Zoe. I thought you were busy writing for your last class?"

I shrug and tap my tote bag slightly and smirk.

"This writer needs some inspiration, so I'll be heading out for a little bit before it gets dark." I stand and kiss her head, booping

Ollie's black nose as I make my way to the door. "Call me in case you need anything."

And with that, the apartment door closes behind me as Lorelai Gilmore begging Luke Danes to give her coffee for the hundredth time tickles my ears.

Chapter 2

The clanking of dishes makes my eyes dart back and forth from the extended line of impatient customers to behind the counter in the café. The dish boy couldn't be any louder. It's not his fault. I should have brought my headphones. And of course it's unusually busy for a Thursday night. Normally the college kids are in their dorms studying for their exams the next day, or coming up with excuses to email the professors as to why they can't come in.

I don't have any clothes to wear and need to wash my laundry.

There's no parking in any of the parking garages.

I just ran a marathon, and my legs don't want to work.

The Bean, tucked between charming brick buildings, glows with the last rays of sunlight as if it's trying to soak in some vitamin D before the night shift. Outside, a few trees are dropping leaves like they're auditioning for a fall catalog, and colorful mismatched tables line the sidewalk.

Inside, the air is thick with the aroma of freshly ground beans and the occasional hiss of the espresso machine sighing at the end of a long day. Rustic wooden tables and overstuffed chairs are scattered around, inviting people to settle in—either for serious work or to pretend they're working while eavesdropping.

Places like The Bean always make me think of that spontaneous trip through New York—all those little cafés hidden within all the high rises. Even just passing through, I felt like I belonged in one of those corners, curled up with a notebook and my eyes glued to the pages of a book.

I take my usual cozy table near the corner and set everything down, making my way to order my usual: white chocolate mocha iced coffee with extra whipped cream. Pure heaven, I swear.

I look around the café, admiring the ambiance this time of year. The sunset filters through wide windows, casting everything in a warm, golden light that makes even the worn-out textbooks look romantic. A few people are typing away on laptops, while others relax with a book or gaze out the window like they're pondering life's big questions (but probably just deciding between a muffin or a cookie).

Maybe I should try to be like them. Maybe I shouldn't try too hard at writing this story thing and just do it. Don't focus too much on the structure or sense of it right now. I just have to get it all out on paper and call it a day. I bite my bottom lip and glance around. I did tell myself I needed some new scenery, but maybe this is too much? Or maybe I'm just overthinking.

Just like I set my previous relationship up for failure... by overthinking every little thing. Or maybe it was already doomed. Nonetheless, overthinking is practically my second job.

♡

We were high school sweethearts. I know, cliché, right? Everyone seems to be these days. We were practically inseparable. He'd pick me up every day on the way to school, and we'd make out behind the gym. I'd leave cute notes with a stain of my pink lipstick or favorite vanilla lip gloss in his locker. He had seemed too perfect... until he wasn't.

Over time, he began growing fussy, anxious, as if he were on edge every minute of the day. Little things bothered him, like when I'd try to hold his hand or kiss him. He'd yank my hand out of his way as if it was smothered with germs or look the other way like he didn't notice me.

Then my overthinking really hammered around my brain. It started small, like replaying conversations in my head late at night, trying to decipher if he meant something different when he said, "I'm really tired, I'll call you tomorrow." I'd lie there, wondering, was he actually tired? Or was he losing interest?

Soon, it became bigger things. If he didn't respond to a text right away, I'd spiral. *Is he with someone else?* I'd text again. *Hey, just checking in... did you see my message?* When he'd finally reply, I'd jump on him with questions. *Why didn't you respond sooner? Were you too busy? Is something wrong?* It all seemed silly.

I could see his patience wearing thin, though he tried to hide it. His words were tight with frustration. "No, nothing's wrong. I was just at work, like I said."

But instead of letting it go, I'd press on. "Are you sure? Because it feels like you're pulling away. You used to message more, you used to—"

"That's in your head," he'd cut me off, his sigh loud and clear through the phone. "I'm here, I'm showing up. But it's never enough, is it?"

And he was right. It was never enough, no matter what he

did. I was so caught up in trying to read between the lines, trying to anticipate what could go wrong, that I created the distance I feared. I questioned everything—his tone, his timing, his choices. If we had plans and he was even five minutes late, I'd feel that gnawing anxiety clawing at my chest, convincing myself that it was a sign of something bigger.

"Is everything okay? Why didn't you text when you were on your way?" I'd ask the moment he arrived, tension already filling the air before we'd even started the evening.

He'd rub his temples, his patience clearly waning. "I was driving. It's five minutes. Can't we just enjoy the night?"

But I couldn't let it go. "It's not just tonight. You've been distant for weeks. You don't call as much, you're always busy. I don't know... it feels like something's changed."

It was exhausting—for both of us. I was so afraid of being blindsided or abandoned that I never let myself fully trust him, and in the end, that's exactly what happened. I pushed him away with my constant need for reassurance, turning something that could have been good into a self-fulfilling prophecy of failure.

Eventually, I found out what I had feared all along—he was cheating on me. It was like everything I'd been anxious about, every overthought text, every question, was suddenly justified. But not in the way I had hoped. The signs I had been searching for, the "pulling away" I had sensed, weren't just in my head. It was real.

I'll never forget the day it all came crashing down. He had been acting strange for weeks—more distant, avoiding eye contact when we were together, and brushing off my attempts to connect. I had convinced myself I was just overreacting, like I always did, but deep down, something felt different this time.

One evening, he left his phone on the counter while he stepped out for a smoke. (Him being a smoker was a red flag. I don't smoke, and find it horrible, so why did I date someone who did?) Normally, I'd never touch his phone, but something about the way he'd been guarding it lately made my heart race. I knew it wasn't right, but I needed to know. I opened his messages, and there it was—a whole string of conversations with someone else. *Vanessa.* Flirty, intimate texts, things I hadn't heard from him in months. They'd been seeing each other for weeks.

I remember my hands shaking as I scrolled through the messages. My stomach twisted into knots, and it felt like my chest was caving in. I couldn't breathe, couldn't think. All the things I had been obsessing over—his late texts, his distant behavior—it was all right there in front of me.

When he came back inside, I was still standing there, phone in hand. He froze, knowing exactly what I had found. "It's not what it looks like," he started, but the panic in his eyes told me everything I needed to know.

"How long?" I asked, my voice barely above a whisper. Though inside, I was screaming.

He hesitated, then finally admitted, "A few weeks."

I don't remember much after that. We argued, of course, but my mind was a blur. All I could think was how I had sensed this happening, how my overthinking wasn't just some paranoid fantasy—it had been real this time. But that didn't make it any better. It didn't change the betrayal, the heartbreak. It only made me question myself more.

I ended things that night. I couldn't stay with someone who had lied to me for so long. I called my dad as tears streamed down my face, my voice trembling with uncertainty. I asked him if I could come home and stay with him and mom for a while. He said yes in a second.

But walking away didn't bring me the closure I had hoped for. Instead, it left me with a fear I can't seem to shake—what if this happens again? What if every future relationship ends the same way, with me overthinking until I drive myself mad, only to discover I was right to be afraid?

♡

A voice echoes near, cutting through my thoughts. I look up at the girl in confusion.

"Excuse me, sorry, but we are closing in 15 minutes."

I nod and feel my voice tremble. "Oh, sorry. I understand, thanks." I swallow and blink away the tears that almost make an entrance.

My thoughts had gotten derailed and I'd hit a dead end. I close my laptop slowly and exhale the breath I was holding. To think I thought James was different, and yet he was just another villain with a mask on I couldn't remove. Or perhaps didn't want to remove.

I shuffle my things together and toss out the last of my iced coffee. The café is nearly empty except for a few people sitting outside under the blue striped awning. The bell above the entrance chimes as I step out into the cool fall breeze. Autumn is my favorite time of year, particularly September. The smell of s'mores tickles my nose, and I smile. Maybe Tish will enjoy some s'mores. I walk toward the dollar store nearby to pick up the necessities.

I didn't end up writing much more of my story, and the new scenery only helped so much. But I think that's okay. I still have time. It's not due for a few weeks, so I think right now it's time for me to relax and take a step back.

I think now is time for a little me time, and that's *always* okay.

Chapter 8

Ollie plops himself on my lap, making himself at home as his purrs/wheezes (being a hefty 25-pound cat, he more so wheezes these days) warm my body. I take my half-filled glass of wine and clink it with Tish's. It's much needed girl's night as we nestle on the couch about to watch my favorite movie, *Ghost*.

A platter of graham crackers, giant multi-colored marshmallows, and mini Hershey's chocolate bars lay on the coffee table beside a box of pepperoni pizza. The twinkling lights near the ceiling hover over us as the lights change colors from pink to blue to orange to green. Tish had the portable fireplace warming the place before I arrived, for which I am forever grateful.

"Oh my god, Zo. I haven't thought about James in forever. Literally *forever*." She takes a bite of pepperoni pizza and shakes her head, moving her gaze to me. "You aren't thinking about getting back together with him, are you? I swear, I will personally hunt him down myself and kill the man with my bare hands."

I tilt my head back in laughter. "No, no, nothing like that. I was just at The Bean earlier and my mind must have wondered, as it usually does. James was, well, an *asshole* to say the least."

Tish nods in agreement. She sips her wine and smirks. "A big asshole. The biggest asshole known to man. But sweetie, you know you'll find that someone special, right?"

I smile at her enthusiasm, appreciating her unwavering loyalty. "Yeah, I know," I say, swirling the wine in my glass. "It's just that sometimes I wonder if I've gotten so used to being on my own that I wouldn't even recognize that someone if they were right in front of me."

Tish raises an eyebrow, setting her slice of pizza down. "Zoe, trust me. You'd recognize it. That spark? That magnetic pull you can't ignore? It's undeniable." She leans closer, eyes gleaming. "Besides, you're a romantic at heart, even though you deny it."

I let out a soft laugh, feeling the familiar weight of Tish's words settle over me. She isn't wrong. Not entirely. Maybe there is still some of that hope lingering somewhere beneath all the armor I'd built up. The part of me that believes in the ridiculous, sappy kind of love like in our movie.

"Maybe," I say, half-shrugging, "but right now, I'm good where I'm at, you know? It's been kind of nice just focusing on myself, not worrying about someone else's drama. Or, I don't know, waiting for the other shoe to drop."

Tish sips her wine, nodding thoughtfully. "I get that. But don't just close yourself off, okay? There's a difference between enjoying your independence and building walls that are too hard to tear down."

I consider her words, staring into the deep red of my wine. Since James, I have probably done more wall-building than I want to admit. But the thing is, these walls keep me safe. They keep me from getting hurt again. Still, there is a little voice inside me that wonders... *What if I'm missing out?*

I shrug, trying to brush off the heaviness of the conversation. "We'll see. I'm still focusing on finishing this last semester of college, and then I am free!" I grab the TV remote and let the movie begin. "But for now, I'm content with pizza, wine, and watching Patrick Swayze try to pretend he doesn't know how dreamy he is."

Tish laughs and smiles, grateful for the shift in mood. "Fair enough. But if some tall, dark, handsome guy happens to trip and fall into your life, promise me you won't push him away just because it's easier to stay in your comfort zone."

"I promise," I say with a grin, raising my glass. "To pizza, wine, and sappy rom-coms."

"And to keeping your heart open!" Tish adds, raising her glass higher.

We clink our glasses together, and as the movie starts, I feel the weight of the conversation slowly lift. Maybe I don't need to rush into anything. It's okay to take things one day at a time, to enjoy the little moments like this.

Ollie shifts in my lap, letting out another wheezy purr, and I scratch behind his ears absentmindedly. Tish is right, as she usually is. I don't need to force anything, but maybe... just maybe... it is time to start tearing down a few of those walls and stripping away some of the armor.

♡

As if the universe is plotting my life out for me or has a thing for karma, my phone pings underneath my pillow. My entire soul wakes to the sound at just past 1:30 in the morning.

I blink myself awake and rub my eyes. Dry drool coats the corners of my mouth and sweat oozes down my back underneath my oversized t-shirt. My phone's screen nearly blinds me as a text notification from an unknown number hovers on the screen.

Hey, you. Been thinking about you. Why don't we catch up sometime? I'd love to meet up. I miss you.

My mouth goes dry as I read the message again, slower this time.

Then I look at the number. I freeze.

My heart suddenly races and scratches its way to the surface of my chest, pounding to break out. A familiar jolt hits, something between panic and disbelief. I don't even notice my phone slipping from my hands until it hits the floor with a soft thud.

It's him.

Chapter 4

"Shut. Up." Tish clutches her hands around my phone, her green eyes wide and mouth agape. "This can't be real, Zo. Literally when we *just* spoke about him last night, too." She shakes her head back and forth and examines the screen again. "Fucking James!"

I swallow and my nostrils flare a little. "Does the universe hate me, Tish? I mean, does it really hate me? Maybe my life is just a game for its entertainment."

Maybe it's not the universe being cruel. Maybe it's just me, always daydreaming too big. Or, better yet, overthinking too hard. Half the time when I picture the life I want, New York sneaks in: loud, messy, buzzing. It's as if part of me is already somewhere else, chasing stories that, in a way, don't exist here. But apparently James still does.

Tish chuckles, her laugh jolting me out of my wandering thoughts. She hands me my phone as she grabs her coffee off the counter and leans against it. "I'm sorry, babe. I don't mean to laugh. It's just kind of funny though, right? Like he decides to reach out to you now, of all times. But on a serious note... the nerve of the guy! I mean really, the damn nerve after all he put you through."

Her words slowly diminish as my mind wanders back to the night we last saw one another.

♡

It was one of those early winter evenings where the chill seeped through your bones despite wearing layers. Under the flickering overhead lights, James and I stood in front of our apartment building, the silence between us louder than any goodbye.

I can still hear the words that tumbled out of his mouth, their weight pressing down on me like a stone. *"I just… can't do this anymore. It's not you, it's me. It's Vanessa. Zoe, I'm sorry."* As cliché as it sounded, it still stung. The way he said it—detached, as if he was already gone, as if I was just a minor inconvenience in his life he needed to shed. Of course he cheated on me with someone who looked like a discount version of a reality TV star.

I remember standing there, staring at him, waiting for him to say more. To explain, to fight for us. But he didn't. He just turned and walked away, leaving me standing alone in the biting cold, feeling as frigid as the air around me.

♡

"Tish…" My voice cracks a little as I come back to the present, gripping the phone in my hand. "I don't think I can do this."

Tish looks at me, her expression softening. She sets her coffee down and crosses her arms. "Listen, he broke your heart once. He doesn't get to do it again. You don't owe him anything. Not a response. Not even a second of your time."

I nod, staring at the text. James's name glowing on my screen feels like a ghost from the past haunting my present. My thumb hovers over the message, but I can't bring myself to fully open it and acknowledge it with a read receipt. "What if he's changed? What if he's sorry?"

Tish rolls her eyes and lets out a short, dry laugh. "And what if he hasn't? You can't live in the land of 'what if,' babe. Trust me, I did that once, and it doesn't end well. Remember Ethan?"

"Yeah…" I trail off, vaguely recalling Tish's own complicated past with a guy who kept coming back into her life just to disappear again. Just to use her for sex and throw her to the curb.

"Exactly," she continues. "You deserve better than someone who'll drop you and then come back whenever it suits him. He doesn't get to play the 'what if' card anymore." She leans in, lowering her voice. "You're stronger now. Remember that. And let's not forget that he cheated on you with someone whose idea of style was wearing sweatpants with a sequined top. I mean, who does that?"

I let out a shaky laugh, my mind still racing. "But what if he actually wants to make things right? What if he regrets leaving?" My voice is almost a whisper now, like admitting it out loud makes it more real. My mind can't help but wander backwards, back in time to when every little thing I'd try to help James with would turn to chaos.

♡

I stood in the kitchen of our small one-bedroom apartment, staring at the brown paper bag on the counter. James had rushed out as a crinkled orange t-shirt stretched over his torso and brown work pants. He'd been muttering about deadlines for the contractors and meetings with the new guys. I knew he'd forget something.

Sure enough, his lunch sat there, neatly packed, just like it always did. I sighed, grabbing it and slipping on my slippers. He'd be stressed if he didn't eat, and I hated the thought of him going hungry, even if he barely acknowledged the effort I put into these little things.

James was already nearing the elevator, his black thermos spilling coffee over the rim. "James!" I called, jogging after him. "You forgot your lunch!"

He stopped abruptly and turned to face me, his eyes sharp and cold. The way he looked at me made my stomach twist, but I kept going, holding out the bag. "I didn't want you to forget. You've been so busy, and I thought—"

"What the hell, Zoe?" he snapped, snatching the bag from my hand. The force made me take a step back. "Do you ever think? I'm already late, and now you're chasing me down like some... some clingy housewife. I don't have time for this!"

I blinked, stunned by his words but trying to keep my voice steady. "I just wanted to help. And to remind you about dinner tonight with my parents..."

His face darkened instantly. He took a step toward me, his hand twitching at his side like he was about to do something— something I didn't want to believe he was capable of. My body reacted before my mind could catch up. I flinched, raising my arms to shield my face, the paper bag crinkling in his hand as he gripped it tighter.

He froze, his hand dropping to his side, but the anger in his voice didn't soften. "Jesus, Zoe. Don't be so dramatic. You act like the whole world revolves around your feelings. Just stop making everything harder than it already is."

I lowered my arms slowly, my face burning with a mix of fear and humiliation. "I... I'm sorry," I whispered, my voice trembling.

"Yeah, sure," he muttered, already turning away. "Just stay out of my way, all right?"

I watched him walk off, his shoulders tense, the lunch I'd packed crumpled in his hand. My chest felt tight, like I couldn't quite catch my breath. I wrapped my arms around myself, standing there in my pajamas as he hurried to the elevator, disappearing as it closed.

A part of me knew, in the deepest corners of my heart, that this wasn't love. Not the kind I deserved. But I buried that thought, just like I always did, and turned back toward the apartment, trying to shake the sinking feeling that I'd already lost myself.

♡

I lie down on the couch, letting my head rest on Tish's lap as her fingers massage my scalp, the thing she knows helps calm my nerves. Tish shakes her head slowly.

"It's not about him. It's about you. Do you want to let him back in, knowing what he did, or is this possibly about closure you didn't get?"

I stare at the screen again, the unopened message taunting me. My heart races as I remember the good times—the late-night drives, the lazy mornings in bed, the way he'd make me laugh until my stomach hurt. But then, just as quickly, the pain returns—the silence that followed his departure, the unanswered texts, the cold finality of his words.

"I don't know," I whisper. "I don't know what I want."

Tish places a hand on my shoulder, her voice gentle. "Take your time, Zo. You don't have to decide anything right now. But remember, the universe doesn't hate you. If anything, I think it's just giving you a chance to show how much you've grown."

I nod, my fingers finally moving, locking the screen without opening the message.

"Maybe... I'll think about it later."

She smiles softly. "And until then, we have brunch plans, remember? Eggs Benedict and mimosas are way better than stressing over some guy. Plus, they won't judge you for your life choices. Just pure deliciousness."

I can't help but laugh. "You're right. Brunch over boys."

"Always," Tish agrees with a grin, taking a sip of her coffee. "Now, let's go, because if my stomach growls one more time, James won't be the only one in trouble. He might find himself on my 'People Who've Wronged Zoe' list, and trust me, it's a long list."

"Is there a cut-off for that list? Because I'm thinking about adding my laundry pile," I say, gesturing dramatically toward the mountain of clothes in the corner of the room.

Tish snorts. "That one might take top priority."

"I'll say," I reply, laughing as we head out the door.

♡

As we step into the new café in town, The Works Café, a blast of warm air hits us, tinged with the aroma of roasted coffee beans and something sweet. Tish wrinkles her nose slightly as she scans the décor, and I can't help but agree with her unspoken sentiment. It's far too trendy for its own good—industrial-chic gone awry.

Exposed brick walls are adorned with abstract art that looks like someone let a toddler loose with a paintbrush and a can of neon spray paint. The tables are a mix of reclaimed wood and metal, and the chairs squeak a little too loudly as customers move them. A giant chalkboard menu hangs over the counter, offering a bewildering array of options: avocado toast with pomegranate seeds, gluten-free pancakes drizzled with agave syrup, and something called flaxseed waffles, amongst other hipster-coded options.

"Who comes up with this stuff?" Tish mutters, eyeing the menu with disdain. "Do we really need a recipe for toast? I mean, I can make it at home without the theatrics."

I chuckle, trying to hide my own skepticism. "At least they're trying to be different. Just think of it as an adventure. Who knows? We might discover a hidden gem… or just a really overpriced plate of disappointment."

We make our way to the counter, and I catch the barista's eye—an overly enthusiastic guy with a bright green apron and a man bun that looks like it belongs at Coachella. "Hey there! Welcome to The Works! What can I get started for you?"

"Um, I'll just have an avocado toast with an iced blueberry latte," Tish says, glancing at me as I continue to browse the overwhelming menu.

"I think I'll pass on the artisanal toast. I'll take an iced vanilla coffee and a banana nut muffin. Please."

He nods, oblivious to the sarcasm, and sends our orders to the kitchen. As we wait, my mind drifts back to my life choices. I have a little bit more free time now, with the semester almost over. I should be working on my short story, but a nagging part of me wonders if I should be looking for a full-time job again. My freelance work paid the bills, mostly. I just feel bad for relying on Tish to cover the rest.

I shake the thoughts out of my head. I need to focus on finishing that draft. It's halfway done, and I'm so close to putting the pieces together.

"What's the word count on your short story right now?" Tish asks, pulling me from my thoughts as we step aside to wait for our order.

"About halfway done. But right now it feels like I'm stuck," I admit, crossing my arms. "I just don't know if I should dive into a job search or just finish the damn thing first."

Tish rolls her eyes dramatically. "Job search? First I'm hearing about this. I think you can just focus on school, sweetie. You're almost finished! Plus, your freelancing has been keeping you busy, right? You know you can count on me to help out, so don't even be thinking about jobs this and jobs that."

I chuckle and look around the café in all its hipster, big coffee cup and pierced barista glory. "I can't even imagine writing here. The last thing I need is someone trying to discuss the nuances of gluten-free baking while I'm trying to create a world with characters who don't care about trendy diets."

"Exactly! And who knows, you might accidentally slip in a character who's a disgruntled barista. 'And then the barista threw a muffin at the clueless customer,'" she mocks, flailing her arms in exaggerated frustration.

"Now that sounds like a plot twist worth exploring," I chuckle. "You're right. I need to focus on this story. It's due in two weeks, and I can't afford to mess it up now."

"Good call. Just don't let the café distract you. Let's get our food and find a corner where we can pretend the world doesn't exist."

We find a small table in a corner, and moments later one of the servers lays down our plates. Tish immediately takes a hesitant bite of her avocado toast topped with pomegranate seeds.

"Okay, this is... unexpectedly good," she admits, eyes widening.

"Don't even think about it. I'm not going to let this place win me over," I huff, eyeing my muffin like it might explode.

"Just one bite!" she pleads, waving a piece of her toast in my direction.

With a reluctant sigh, I lean over to take a nibble, my expression shifting from skepticism to surprise. "Okay, fine! But I'm still mad about the entire vibe of this place. I just know they have live music on Wednesdays, and I will not be dragged to that."

The taste of the toast invigorates me, a welcome distraction from the looming deadlines and the complex emotions swirling in my mind. Maybe this café isn't so bad after all, even if it doesn't hold a candle to our usual spot.

"So once we're done here, what's your plan? Finish the story?" Tish asks, wiping crumbs from her hands.

"Definitely finish the story," I reply, leaning back in my chair. "I just need to find a way to keep my creativity flowing without being overwhelmed. And I know you said I don't need to worry, but maybe I'll consider a part-time gig somewhere low-key, like a library or a bookstore."

"Ah yes, the literary haven. Where you can sip coffee and pretend to work while actually writing your masterpiece," Tish smirks, raising her coffee in mock toast.

"Here's to avoiding adulting as long as possible!" I raise my coffee, clinking it against hers, laughter bubbling up between us.

Chapter 5

My last job wasn't the best. I worked for a magazine, Cleveland Magazine, almost immediately after obtaining my bachelor's degree. I wrote several articles and interviewed many local small businesses and artists who had made something of themselves.

While I enjoyed the job, it wasn't enough.

I felt like it lacked any room for growth and advancement. Sure, I was working on a part-time basis, but that didn't mean I couldn't add more to my plate. Even when I asked to be placed on more projects and write longer pieces, I was shut down, and probably because I was part-time there and a full-time student.

But that was the past, and this is the present. It's hard not to focus on the present, because if I don't, I miss out. And yet, here I am, being pulled back into the past. I'm not looking for a blast from the past moment.

I glance at my phone, the message from James still unopened, still lingering in my thoughts. I don't know whether I want to bring him back into my life. And that's the scary part: if I brought him back into my life, I would simply be going backwards, right? And who wants to do that? Would you go back to an old job in a toxic-ass environment where you were treated like a mere number? Hell no.

I sit in a chair at the laundromat up the street in town. A yawn escapes from my mouth that makes my whole body shake with sleep. It's late on a Wednesday night and the laundromat only has a few stragglers doing their washes before the weekend, when it's bustling day and night.

I stare through the little window of the washer. The colors seem to absorb one another as if creating new colors only the rainbow heard rumors about. The thumping from the machines echoes from my chest to my feet. Every machine has its own piece to play in the orchestra. Every thump, pat, shake, and shimmy flows through the building, showing off what they'd been working on. The large round lights above me illuminate the entire inside, giving off a soft warm ambiance. Signs scatter and devour the walls: *Change machine for customers only! Last load at 8:30 P.M.!* Pocket change jingles and chimes quietly.

And yet, for one reason or another, I'm glad I came here tonight. Here's to the new scenery I was looking for yesterday. Maybe this one will help.

I tilt my head back and sigh. After a little break, I really need to finish this story. I shake my head and redirect my thoughts to my laptop.

Another yawn escapes and I lightly tap my laptop keys, the cursor yet again blinking at me as I stare at my half-finished short story. I have a few weeks left to finish, but it's now or never. I take a deep breath and begin typing.

What seems like eternity later, my washer beeps at me, letting me know it's time to switch loads. I place my laptop down on my chair and move my clothes to one of the dryers against the wall. I load the quarters in and tap my options. I let out a sigh and smile to myself. I just need a few more paragraphs, about a couple of pages, and I'm finished.

The entrance to the laundromat slams shut as another straggling patron makes their way to a washer. I glance up after finishing a sentence. A presence lingers behind me, heavy and familiar, though I don't recognize it at first. The feeling prickles at the back of my neck. I catch movement in the reflection of the dryer door—a tall figure, broad shoulders, a mess of wavy brown hair.

His warm skin is working for him, that's for sure. His clothes are simple, yet stick out: a baggy black hoodie, khaki pants, and white Converse.

Damn, he is one handsome man.

The man turns my way as he heads to take a seat after loading his clothes in the washer. And that's when my heart drops somewhere around my knees, and I feel like a cartoon character who's just seen a ghost. My breath hitches. The air thickens, my chest tightening as if bracing for impact. A strange weight settles in my limbs, making them sluggish, unwilling. I tell myself to move, to turn and confirm what I already know, but it takes a few extra seconds before my body finally obeys. When I turn, my eyes meet his, and the world lurches sideways.

James.

The air leaves my lungs in a sharp, almost inaudible gasp. A pulse of heat rushes through me, followed by an icy flood of something I can't name. My hands grip the edge of the dryer, my fingers curling into the cool metal to anchor myself in place. My body screams at me to move—to leave, to run—but my legs won't budge. Curiosity holds me in place, pinning me like a bug beneath glass.

He seems equally surprised, his eyes widening as they lock onto mine. For a moment, time stretches, and the world around us fades into a hazy blur of laundry cycles and folding tables. My heart races as a cocktail of emotions surges through me—confusion, anger, nostalgia, and a flicker of something else I can't quite place.

Damn, his text. I never replied to his stupid out-of-the-blue text.

I bite my lip and feel myself shrinking behind my laptop, rustling my hoodie over my head. His voice oversteps my forever overthinking thoughts.

"Zoe?"

His voice is uncertain, testing. I don't respond right away, my heart slamming against my ribs. The weight of the past crashes into me all at once, pressing against my skin. I should leave. Just grab my things and go. But instead, my voice betrays me.

"James... hi."

His name feels foreign in my mouth, like something I should have long forgotten.

"I—uh," he stammers, running a hand through his hair, a familiar gesture that used to make my stomach flip. He clears his throat. "How are you?"

I curl my hair behind my ears and look up at him. Such a simple question, and all I need to do is give a simple answer. "I'm doing good. Really good. How are things with you? Bizarre seeing you back in town."

He presses his lips in a fine line, a smile creeping onto his face. "Guess I can say the same. I'm actually back in town for a short business trip. Just finished my second book." He pauses for a moment as if hesitating over the next set of words. "It's called *And Then There Was One*. Apparently, it's the newest addition to the *New York Times Bestsellers* list. I don't know, I'm just the writer."

My stomach twists. Of course he wrote another book. The literary darling, always landing on his feet when he doesn't deserve to. Meanwhile, I'm here, my laundry tumbling in a dryer, my short story unfinished. My heart thuds with a mix of pride and annoyance. Memories flood my mind—nights spent dreaming about a future together, whispered promises under starlit skies, and then, the crushing weight of betrayal when I discovered he had cheated.

I force a smile, though my face feels tight. "Wow, James. Congratulations."

He chuckles and nods, slowly leaning in. "Thanks. Look, not to be blunt, but Zo, when were you going to reply to my text?"

Zo. The fact he thinks he can still call me that after all these years. How original, trying to be charming. It's giving *ick* instead.

I dance my fingertips over my phone laying on the seat next to me. "Oh. Right. Your text. I guess I've been busy lately, with school and all. I must have... forgotten." I shift in my seat a little as my palms feel sweaty and numb at the same time. This cannot be happening. Am I actually having a conversation with James? The James who broke my heart and stomped on it a million times and then some? The James who left me for another woman who, by the way, looks like a knock-off Jessica Simpson? I look up at him and force a smile, trying to mask my tangled feelings.

He looks down and shuffles in place. And I notice the nervousness oozes off his body. Why is he nervous? He has no right to be nervous. I do, not him. Not the man, excuse me, *boy*, who decided he no longer saw me as beneficial for his life anymore.

"No, it's okay. I'm sorry for asking." And then looks up at me. "I know this is technically the second time I'm asking, being we just ran into each other again, but would you want to meet for coffee? I'm in town for another week and leave next Saturday."

Coffee? Is he seriously asking me to get together for coffee? Coffee is where people meet up for a business meeting, for catching up on life. I don't owe him coffee. My mind races, weighing the pros and cons like an overly cautious accountant. On one hand, a chance to reconnect over steaming mugs (though mine would be iced, obviously) and perhaps relive some of the warmth from our past. On the other hand, am I ready to dig up the ghost of our relationship? A relationship that was destroyed by his infidelity and lies?

"Uh... coffee? I'm not sure," I mumble, the words tasting sour on my tongue. My laundry still needs drying, but I feel as if I can barely breathe through the air thickening around us. I shake the spiraling thoughts from my head and stand up. I grab my laptop and notebooks and shove them into my tote bag. This isn't the time to answer that. I need time to think... a lot of time. He can't just ask me to meet up for coffee after all this time. Who does he think he is anyway?

"You know what, James. I'm so sorry, but I have to head home. My cat Ollie is probably sitting by his empty food bowl, giving me the saddest little stare like I've abandoned him forever. Can I think about this coffee thing and get back to you?"

He inches toward me and closes the gap between us, his arm reaching my free hand. I feel my heart trying to make a run for it. My chest feels tight and my vision blurs at the sight of him. "I–I'll get back to you. I have to go."

The door clasps shut behind me and I make my way toward the apartment, toward Tish, toward my safe place. The crisp fall air makes my body shake and tremble as it slams into my face.

That's when I feel something wet sinking into my scarf. I'm crying. My vision is blurry from crying. I wonder why I am wasting these tears on him. Tears he doesn't deserve. Tears he doesn't even know about.

Chapter 6

The door clicks shut as I make my way into the apartment. The warmth from the portable fireplace hugs my body as I take off my boots, scarf, and coat. Ollie is laying in front of it, literally inches from it, soaking in all of the warmth and savoring it as if leaving none for the rest of us.

The smell of buttery and salty popcorn swarms my nose as I shuffle toward Tish. She's sitting on the couch as *Gilmore girls* blares from the TV. It's practically a permanent rerun in our apartment, the kind of background comfort we never really get tired of. She shifts her head toward me, sensing I am not feeling like myself. She's good at this stuff.

"Whoa, did something happen?" she asks, her voice soft and laced with concern. "You look like you've seen a ghost."

I groan and sprawl out on the couch, lying my head on her lap. Her fingers brush my hair and softly massage my scalp. She really does give the best head massages without even trying. My voice muffles against the blanket. "I ran into James."

Tish freezes, and I can practically feel her eyes widening as she processes. "The James who stomped on your heart and left you for that Cameron Diaz look-a-like?"

"Jessica Simpson look-a-like, but, yeah, that one," I mumble, rolling over so I can stare up at the ceiling instead. My eyes are stinging, and I blink hard trying to keep it together. I take a deep breath, my voice trembling. "I ran into him at the laundromat. Like, out of nowhere. I haven't even replied to his stupid text, and suddenly as if falling from the sky, there he was."

Tish doesn't say anything right away. She just keeps massaging my scalp, her fingers softly combing through my hair in the most comforting way possible. It's the kind of care that allows you to fall apart completely.

"Oh, babe," she says, her voice full of sympathy. "That's a lot. How are you feeling?"

I let out a shaky breath. "I don't even know. I'm more confused than anything. He's back in town for some book thing and it's 'apparently on the *New York Times Bestsellers* list.' Like, who just blurts that out? And so nonchalantly, as if he forgot what he did to me..." My voice trails and I nuzzle deeper into the couch on Tish's lap, my body absorbing the warmth from the fireplace.

Tish snorts. "James and his 'look at me, I'm successful now' vibe. Classic. He makes me sick, Zo. Sick." She pauses for a beat. "So after everything he put you through..."

Her voice trails and I know what she's referring to. I shake my head, still unsure. "I honestly don't know if I want to meet him. He hurt me, Tish. Like, really hurt me. But seeing him tonight... it brought up all these feelings I thought I'd buried. And now, I don't know what to do. He even asked me to meet up for coffee."

She sighs and reaches for the wine bottle sitting on the coffee table, twisting it open with a satisfying pop. "Let's hit pause and not focus on him right now. We shouldn't give him any more thought than he deserves—not that he deserves it at all. You're almost done with your short story, right? You've got to celebrate the small wins, sweetie! You're about to finish your last assignment for your last class. That deserves a toast."

I smile weakly, sitting up as she pours us both a glass, the deep red liquid swirling in the dim light. We clink our glasses together and I take a long sip, feeling the warmth spread through my chest. It feels good, even if just for a moment, to think about something other than James.

"To small wins," Tish says, giving me one of those looks that makes everything feel just a little bit easier. "And to whatever decision you make about that coffee meet up. Whether you meet him or not, I'm here for you. You know I'm always here for you."

I nod, grateful for her support. "And I so appreciate and love you for it." As the warmth of the wine spreads through me, another realization hits me, cold and sudden. "Oh my god... my laundry."

Tish raises an eyebrow, her head tilting to the side. "What about your laundry?"

"I left it," I groan, slumping back into the couch. "I literally ran out of the laundromat in the middle of the conversation with James. My clothes are probably sitting in the dryer right now, getting all wrinkly and cold. Why am I like this?" I slowly drag my hand down my face.

Tish bursts out laughing, nearly spilling her wine. "You didn't! You just abandoned your laundry? And your ex? Again, literally."

"Yeah, yeah," I say, rolling my eyes, but I can't help but laugh too. "Just left them both in the dust. Priorities, right?"

"Laundry can be dealt with tomorrow," she says, still chuckling. "Right now, focus on finishing your story."

I nod, feeling the weight of the evening begin to shift. As much as this whole James situation is messing with my head, there's still one thing I can control: my writing. The one thing that hasn't let me down, even when everything else is spinning out of control. Like literally, why is all of this happening? I didn't sign up to be on a reality TV show or corny Hallmark movie.

♡

Later, in my room, the quiet settles around me like a blanket. The soft sound of my laptop's hum fills the space, and the pale moonlight filters through the curtains, casting silver streaks on my desk. I stare at the blinking cursor on the screen, my nearly finished short story waiting for me to give it life.

My phone sits on the desk next to me, taunting me. James' message is still unopened. It's like a tiny weight, just sitting there, pulling my attention away from the task at hand. Should I meet him for coffee? Should I even reply? He even asked again in person. My brain is stuck in a loop, playing out a thousand different scenarios, none of them feeling right. Thankfully he hasn't tried to reach out since I left. Like Tish said, I shouldn't give him any more time of the day any more than he deserves.

I bite my lip, forcing myself to refocus. The story. *Finish the story first, Zoe.* James can wait. Forever.

I start typing, my fingers flying over the keyboard, the words pouring out of me faster than I expect. It's like all this James drama is giving me more motivation than anything. It's nearly complete and only needs a page or so more. Each sentence feels like a release, a step away from the tangled mess in my head.

And then, finally, after what feels like hours, I type the last sentence. With that, I'm finished. I did it. I sit back in my chair, staring at the screen in disbelief. It's really done. Relief washes over me, filling me with a strange sense of accomplishment that pushes all thoughts of James to the back of my mind—at least for now.

I quickly proofread and then log into my school's class management website to submit my story. The little rainbow cursor spins for a moment until the page refreshes. Big bold words appear on the page: CONGRATULATIONS! YOU COMPLETED YOUR LAST COURSE! While it excites me that I am finished, it also feels surreal. I have been in school for six years now, the beginning a little wobbly, unsure of what to do with my life. I completed my bachelor's degree and now I completed my master's. It's all over, after what felt like a million years.

Sure, my professors have to grade everything and post final grades, but I am done. I have completed college (almost), obtained my master's degree, and hopefully with some positive energy, I will continue to make my dreams come true.

For tonight, I've finished something important. Something that's mine. And besides James popping back up in my life, this is definitely something I can control.

Chapter 7

My laptop dings as an email notification appears from the corner of the screen. My vision somehow doesn't recognize it, as my mind is elsewhere. Elsewhere as in the whole seeing-James-at-the-laundromat fiasco yesterday. My stomach does a front flip and my heart shakes in my chest just thinking about it.

You don't just show up like that. This isn't a Hallmark movie, this is real life. I have priorities and things to do. I shouldn't even be considering replying to James. Why should I bother with him just because he decided to walk into the laundromat in my town all high and mighty? Who does he think he is?

I climb out of bed and change into leggings and an oversized Friends sweatshirt, throw my bob up in a tiny pony, and tug on some fuzzy Mickey Mouse socks. I trot my way to the bathroom and wash up. My mind shouldn't even be able to have the ability to think about James. And yet here it is, controlling my little brain with thoughts galore on James.

I exhale deeply, my nostrils flaring with anxiety. Maybe I need to take a step back and take a breather. Yes, James did a horrible thing, and yet, maybe somehow the universe is telling me to grab onto some closure, like Tish suggested? But in all seriousness, do I really need closure? Is it worth meeting him again to chit chat over coffee, especially after what he did? Sure, it's not like he killed a person, but it certainly feels like he killed my heart.

It feels like he killed my ability to open up again if I'm being honest.

I shake my head and head over to my desk, opening my laptop. I pull up my inbox and at the very top is an email from my professor. I tilt my head in wonder. As soon as I see the subject line—*Your Story Submission*—my heart flutters. Hopefully he finally graded it. I click it open, and the words jump out at me, glowing on the screen like some kind of prize I didn't know I was competing for.

Good morning, Zoe,

Apologies for the Saturday email! Congratulations on completing your master's! I've just finished reading your story, and I wanted to personally thank you for submitting such an impressive piece of work. It's rare that a story grips me from the first line, but yours did.

I think it has real potential, and I would love to send it on your behalf to Poets & Writers *magazine for publication consideration if you're open to it. Let me know within the next week.*

Warm regards,
Professor Hopkins

I can't help but jump out of my chair and do a little happy dance. Ollie jolts awake as I grab his paws and shake him. He's obviously not entertained, but I appreciate the alertness. I sit back into my chair, still smiling like an idiot, and read the email again, just to make sure I didn't hallucinate it in my still groggy post-*Gilmore girls* state.

I grab my phone and text Tish, who is out with her mom for a long overdue girl's day before her shift at the bar.

Guess what? Professor Hopkins wants to send my story to Poets & Writers *magazine!!*

Moments later my phone pings, sharing that Tish has texted me back. I appreciate the fact that whenever she is busy or wherever she is, she finds a way to get a hold of me.

NO WAY!! AAAAAH CONGRATS!! I will be coming back soon with mimosas to celebrate!!!

I can practically hear her squeal through the text, and it makes me laugh, the kind of belly laugh that you didn't know you needed until it spills out of you. I close my laptop and lean back, staring at the ceiling. This has got to be the best news I've received in a long time. I feel... accomplished. Truly accomplished. Like I really made it through this semester, even with all the craziness—the writing deadlines, the emotional turmoil of running into James, the whole existential crisis of being on the edge of graduating. But right now, it all feels worth it.

I head out of my bedroom and grab my tote bag with my wallet and phone. It's been chillier as the days go by, so I wrap my chunky red scarf around my neck. I'm craving a small celebratory coffee. No, I'll make it a large. Who knows, maybe it'll even be on the house. I can't help but crack another smile as I head out the door.

And then I realize I still have to pick up my laundry. Ugh.

♡

The morning air coils around me like ribbon, sharp and fresh against my cheeks as I step out of my apartment. It's the kind of fall morning where the sky is an impossibly clear shade of blue, with only a few clouds lingering like cotton candy puffed up by the breeze. The kind of day where you can see your breath if you exhale slowly enough, wisps of vapor fading into the cool air. The leaves rustle softly beneath my feet as the trees shed their autumn coats, splashes of orange and red dotting the sidewalks beneath them.

I snug my hands underneath my sweatshirt sleeves, my fingers instinctively seeking the warmth as I make my way down the street. The aroma of faintly damp leaves and something sweet— maybe cinnamon sugar—tickles my nose. I let the chill soak in, hoping it'll shake off the weird fog that's been hanging over me since last night. I need to clear my head before I can deal with any more James-related thoughts, and there's only one thing that can help with that.

I finally make my way to the café, The Bean. The one and only café in my heart. The bell jingles as I step inside, and the scent of espresso and vanilla hit me immediately. It's warm here, the hum of conversation soft and inviting, mixing with the quiet clinks of mugs and plates. It's Thursday and the line isn't too long, thank goodness, so I quickly order my usual. Something about the rich sweetness and the coolness of the cup always feels like a peck from Jack Frost. The perfect antidote to mornings like this.

As I wait for my drink I glance out the window, watching the early risers shuffling by with scarves wrapped tightly around their necks, the wind tugging playfully at their coats. I let my mind wander for a bit, replaying the events of last night. But every time I think about James my chest tightens, and I quickly push the thoughts away. I swallow the lump that's formed in my throat and take a breath. He isn't worth it. This time, now, in this very moment, is mine. *Don't let him ruin it.*

I shake my head and the barista's voice digs its way through my thoughts, handing me my drink. I take a sip, the white chocolate coating my tongue and sending a little spark of contentment through me. For a brief moment, everything feels normal again. Just me, my coffee, and the familiar hum of the town waking up around me.

I head toward the laundromat, my mind drifting back to James again as the normalcy evaporates. I shut my eyes tightly and shake him out of my thoughts. His face, his voice, the way he'd asked me to coffee like we were two old friends catching up. And the worst part? The way my heart had fluttered, just a tiny bit, at the mention of his stupid book, like I wasn't still furious with him. I hate that I still care, even if it's just a little.

When I finally reach the laundromat, the morning light is slanting through the windows, casting long shadows across the empty machines. The air is warmer inside, but it feels sterile compared to the cozy buzz of the café. The machines hum in their quiet, constant rhythm, and I can hear the faint clinking of loose change bouncing in someone's dryer from across the room.

The place is mostly empty, save for an older man folding towels in the corner alongside a woman who must be his wife, smiling and bumping her hip against him to the music. He smiles and takes her hand, pulling her toward him. She leans against him, and they dance. Elvis's voice tumbles out of the speakers singing "Can't Help Falling in Love." The towels left unfolded and the clothes still sitting in the hamper.

I smile at them, feeling my heart ache at their happiness. Yet I feel happy for them too. To be able to grow old with someone for that long, to crave their presence, their smile, their hugs and warmth. To be so in love with someone your heart longs for them through disagreements and arguments, even fights. That is true love.

And yet, I feel a ping of sadness. Sure, I am young, 28 years old. But I sometimes crave, only a smidge, for that kind of love, that kind of companionship. It's rare, and when you find it, you must grab onto it and hold it and never let it go.

My thoughts are tugged back to reality when someone walks through the door, their orange hamper covered in bright stickers and purple duct tape. I walk around the rows and search for my laundry when something bright pink smothers my vision.

My pink hamper.

It sits next to the snack-filled vending machine alongside the last dryer on the wall next to the restrooms, neatly positioned like it's been waiting for me. In this town, people don't mess with what isn't theirs—half the time you can leave laundry overnight and it'll still be here in the morning. My heart does this weird little jump, and I stop mid-step, staring at it. The clothes—my clothes—are folded. Not just stuffed into the hamper in a rush, but perfectly folded, like they've been handled with care. My socks are even paired up.

I feel my pulse quicken as I approach it, the quiet hum of the laundromat seeming louder now, like it's building to a crescendo.

The little white note catches my eye, sitting on top of my clothes like a cherry on a sundae. My fingers tremble slightly as I pick it up. The paper crinkles under my touch, and I unfold it, the words jumping off the page in familiar handwriting.

Zoe,

You left in a hurry last night and figured I'd fold your laundry for you. No need to thank me—consider it a peace offering, or maybe just good laundry karma. About the coffee... If you're not interested, I get it. I won't push. I'll be around until next Saturday, so no pressure. Take care.

James

I stare at the note for a long moment, letting the words sink in. James. James folded my laundry. Why does this feel like such a betrayal to my pride? And why does it make my heart twist in that strange way, the same way it used to when he'd surprise me with thoughtful little gestures back before everything went to hell?

The coolness of the paper seeps into my fingertips as I read the note again. *Laundry karma?* What even is laundry karma? I want to laugh at the absurdity of it, but there's this heaviness in my chest, this weird cocktail of emotions swirling around—anger, nostalgia, maybe even a little bit of gratitude, though I hate to admit it.

I run my fingers along the edge of the paper, feeling the texture of his handwriting as if it carries more weight than it should. And the laundry... folded so neatly, like we are still us. Like he hadn't shattered everything with his stupid lies and the stupid affair.

The memory stings, the betrayal still fresh even though a few years have passed. I clench the note in my fist, crumpling it a little before slipping it into my jacket pocket. My eyes drop to the neatly folded pile of clothes, sitting there like some weird monument to what we used to be—orderly, thoughtful, maybe even a little tender. It's ridiculous, but for a moment, I feel like this pile of laundry is mocking me. *Look how nice things could be, if only you'd let me back in.*

"Yeah, no thanks," I mutter under my breath, shaking my head. I take a long sip of my latte, letting the chocolatey goodness distract me.

There's a nagging voice in the back of my mind. He wants to meet for coffee. Should I? It feels like stepping into a minefield, where one wrong move could blow up everything I've worked so hard to forget. It feels like I keep asking myself this same question. My brain warns me to stay far, far away from this mess, but another part of me—the part that's apparently still holding on to some tiny shred of curiosity—wonders if maybe I should go. Maybe I deserve some kind of closure. Or at least an explanation for why he did what he did, if there even is one.

I bite my lip, staring down at the pile of orderly folded shirts and socks like they hold some kind of answer I can't quite reach. What would meeting him even accomplish? Would it help, or would it just drag me back into the hurt and confusion I once felt?

I sigh, my breath puffing out in the sterile air of the laundromat. Outside, the wind rattles the glass doors and I catch a glimpse of the sky through the windows—an expanse of pale blue scattered with thin wisps of clouds, the kind that look like they've been painted with a soft brush. It's a crisp autumn morning, the kind that smells like change and makes everything seem just a little more possible. The leaves on the sidewalk are doing that slow, lazy swirl, dancing along with the breeze like they've got nowhere to be. Oh, if only my life could be that easy going.

I shake my head again, trying to clear the fog of emotions that have settled in. Right now I can't afford to get lost in the past. I've got my laundry, I've got my day to get through, and I've got way more important things to focus on than figuring out what to do about James.

Tucking the note deeper into my pocket, I grab my pink laundry hamper, holding it tight like it's an off-beat, fragile connection to something I'm not quite ready to let go of, and head for the door. I clutch my latte with my other hand, taking slow sips.

The chilly autumn breeze rushes in as I step outside, brushing against my cheeks and waking me up to the present even more than the latte. The air smells like freshly baked pastries and damp earth, that classic fall combination that always makes me feel oddly nostalgic, like I'm in some kind of indie movie montage.

The perks of living in a small town.

And yet, my mind starts to wander into the unknown, and my overthinking takes over. My fingers grasp onto the edges of the hamper just a little tighter as I slowly place one foot in front of the other.

Chapter 8

As my thoughts tumble together like the swirls of leaves and crisp air around me, I walk toward the bistro tables in front of The Bean just next door. I need a moment to think, or better yet, talk to someone about this. Like my mom.

I settle myself in a chair. Other tables are filled with couples and students focusing on their laptops and phones. It's always the go-to place for when Tish and I need a good cup of joe or fresh scenery, or just a place to unwind and chill.

I set my hamper and latte down on the table and grab my phone out of my tote bag, my fingers automatically tapping my mom's contact. I call her before I can second-guess it. There's something about talking to my mom that always makes things feel clearer. Maybe it's her steady wisdom or her relentless optimism—or maybe it's just the fact that she's Mom.

The phone rings twice before her familiar voice, warm and light, comes through the speaker. "Zoe, what a surprise! How are you doing, honey?"

I can already picture her sitting at the kitchen table, drinking her third cup of coffee for the day and watching one of those renovation shows where people always decide to knock down a perfectly good wall. Or maybe she's busy painting another abstract piece for one of her art shows.

"Oh, you know, the usual adulting task of laundry. Well, picking up laundry. Forgotten laundry, I should say."

"What's 'forgotten laundry?' Don't forget your mother is old."

I smirk at her question because it sounds funny when someone else says it. "I just forgot my laundry at the laundromat last night. That being said, you'll love what I'm about to tell you next, Mom."

"And what's that?"

I take a deep breath and bite my bottom lip. "I actually ran into James last night."

There's a pause on the other end before she replies. "James? Ooh, you mean *James* James, don't you?"

"The very same," I say, rolling my eyes.

"Oh, wow," she says, dragging the words out like she's absorbing the shock. "And how do we feel about this?"

"Confused." I blurt it out faster than I expected. "It feels like some cosmic joke. And now he wants to meet for coffee. It's just... surreal, you know?"

My mom hums on the other end, probably sipping her coffee thoughtfully. "Well, you know what I always say about second chances."

I smirk, thinking about her and Dad. They were the definition of messy back then—proof that love alone isn't enough to keep two people together.

♡

Their marriage started to unravel when Dad's work consumed his life. A once-attentive husband, he morphed into someone who missed birthdays, family dinners, and even milestones like my high school graduation. His job as a corporate attorney demanded so much of him that it felt like he had nothing left for us.

Mom, ever the optimist, tried to hold things together. She planned date nights, sent him reminders of anniversaries, and even left him little notes of encouragement in his briefcase. But Dad's absences spoke louder than her efforts.

I was twelve when I overheard their worst fight. "I'm tired of coming in second to your career, Joseph," Mom had said, her voice trembling but firm.

"And I'm tired of feeling like nothing I do—*providing* for this family—is ever enough for you!" Dad had snapped back, his frustration palpable.

They separated six months later. Mom moved us to a smaller house across town while Dad stayed in the family home. It felt like a death in the family, that separation. I hated how quiet Mom seemed at dinner and how Dad's messages and phone calls felt forced and obligatory.

But something shifted years later in my first year of college. Dad had left the corporate grind for a smaller, less demanding role. Still an attorney, just at a smaller family firm. He'd started showing up, not just to my events, but to the things that mattered to Mom. I remember the first time I saw them together again. My college graduation four years later. Dad handed Mom a bouquet of yellow roses, her favorite, and when she took them, their fingers lingered just a second too long.

It wasn't instant, their reconnection. It took time, therapy, and a willingness to confront years of hurt. But they found their way back. They've traded the chaos of their earlier years for a quieter kind of love, one built on compromise, forgiveness, and the lessons of their past.

♡

"Yeah, yeah, I know," I reply, bracing myself. My mom loves a good redemption arc. "You gave Dad a second chance, and now your marriage is better than ever. Like almost happily ever after better. You do know that you two are annoyingly cute these days?"

She laughs, and I can hear her smiling. "Yes, but I wouldn't trade it for the world," she says with a proud little huff. "Look, sweetheart, I'm not saying you need to take him back or anything. It's entirely your choice. But you should at least hear him out. And if you get a bad vibe, you walk. But maybe he's grown, changed. People are allowed to change, evolve into better versions of themselves."

"I don't know, Mom," I sigh, kicking at a particularly crunchy pile of leaves. "What if it just drags me back into all that hurt?"

"Oh, you'll know," she says simply. "I know how you are with your overthinking. It gets the better of you, you know that. Don't close the door before you even open it."

I chew on my bottom lip, contemplating. "You really think I should meet him?"

"That's up to you," she says. "Just trust your gut. You've always been good at that. And you're stronger now than you were then."

Her words hit me, not like a gut punch, but like the gentle reminder that my mom has always been my biggest fan, whether or not she liked the people I dated. "Yeah... I know, Mom. Thanks."

"That's my girl. Keep me posted. I love you, sweetheart."

"I love you too, Mom. And thanks. I'll talk to you later."

I open the text from James and immediately begin typing out the words before I can overthink it any further. *Hey. Okay, let's meet for coffee. Wanna meet at The Bean next Tuesday, 10:30 am?*

I hit send and let out a long, exaggerated sigh, like I'd just agreed to go on a game show where the prize is emotional chaos.

♡

When I get back to the apartment, I'm greeted by the sound of giggles. Tish is sitting at the table, her phone in one hand and a glass of orange juice and champagne in the other. She looks up and smiles, holding up her glass in glee. "Guess who's back from girl's day?"

I jokingly tilt my head in wonder. "You?" I say with a grin.

"Me," she agrees, lifting her glass. "But more importantly, guess whose short story is getting published?"

I laugh and grab a glass. "Mine. It's pretty amazing, isn't it?"

We clink glasses, and the bubbly fizzes as I take a sip. The champagne makes my nerves feel a little lighter. "I also, uh, decided to meet with James."

Tish raises an eyebrow, her glass pausing mid-air. "So you're really doing this, huh?"

"Yep. I had a talk with my mom, and you know how she has a way with words. Figured I'd at least hear him out," I say, trying to sound more confident than I feel.

She puts her glass down and gives me a serious look. "You know I'll support whatever decision you make, but just... be cautious, okay? I know you, Zoe. You've got a big heart, but you've also got some major history with him.”

I nod, appreciating her concern. “I know. I’ll be careful.”

“And if he gives you any weird vibes...” She makes a dramatic cutting motion across her throat, “...you run. I’ll even come pick you up, scratch that, rescue you if you need it. We’ll run off into the sunset with mimosas in hand.”

I chuckle, feeling a little more at ease. “Deal. But for now, let’s toast to my publication. *Almost* publication.”

We raise our glasses once more, the clink of the crystal echoing through the apartment.

♡

I shuffle myself over to the couch with my laptop in hand, making myself cozy on the lounger near the portable fireplace. I can feel the warmth as it nuzzles against my feet, simmering up through my body. Ollie is lying on his back, belly up as if roasting himself against the fire. He’s a spoiled cat, that’s for sure.

Tish is out working at the bar, raking in all the tips she deserves. It’s just me, myself, and I this evening, and that’s all right by me. Plus, it’s giving me some time to catch up on deadlines with my freelance work from earlier this week.

The light from my laptop screen illuminates my face and jolts my body awake after a rough morning of laundromat fun. My mind immediately races to the thought of James. I’m glad I took my mom’s advice and decided to text him back, hoping for some closure in some way. It still feels strange he shows up out of nowhere, especially the day after he texted. It’s as if he planned this whole thing out... and maybe he did? Although it wouldn’t make sense, he couldn’t have known I would be at the laundromat of all places. And yet I still feel a weird vibe that this perhaps was planned. Planned by the universe, maybe.

I shake my head and dart my eyes back to the screen, opening my email to write Professor Hopkins back. I formally accept his offer of publishing my piece in the magazine, thanking him for the recognition. It's not every day you get your short story published in a national magazine read by fellow bookworms and writers from all over. My heart does a little happy dance in my chest.

My wine glass clinks against my laptop as I take a sip. The bubbles dance down my throat as it warms my body throughout, making me feel a bit more relaxed. Ollie lets out a contented purr from across the room, and for a moment, I consider asking *him* for advice. He's seen me through plenty of boy drama. But alas, his wisdom is limited to when his next meal will arrive.

As I'm about to open my editing workspace for my freelance work, a ping from my phone distracts me. It's a text from James. I take a deep breath, my heart fluttering like it's auditioning for a role in a cheesy rom-com. I glance at the screen, hesitant but curious.

Sounds good. See you then, Zo. I'm really glad you agreed to meet.

I stare at the words for a moment longer than necessary, my mind already concocting possible scenarios for our upcoming coffee rendezvous. Will it be awkward? Tense? Or maybe—against all odds—pleasant? *Ew.*

Ollie, still stretched out in front of the fireplace, gives a dramatic stretch before lazily rolling onto his side. He looks at me with those big, green eyes, blinking one at a time as if to say, *Human, none of this matters. Feed me.*

I turn back to my laptop, determined to focus on work. There's something therapeutic about the click–clack of keys as I write, but tonight my mind is restless, darting between thoughts of James and everything else in my life. The thought of him still nags at me like a loose thread I'm too nervous to pull.

My phone pings again. This time it's Tish.

How's solo time going? Any more laundry misadventures?

I chuckle and quickly type back:

Laundry's safe and sound. No wrinkles either. Just me, Ollie and some wine. Oh, and James texted back. Coffee is on for next week.

She responds almost immediately.

OMG! That's great! Or terrifying. Both? Be prepared for me to give you a pep talk when I get home, babe.

I send a reply. *Definitely both. And please, I'll need all the pep talks.*

I can already imagine her bursting through the door later with a new bottle of wine and the gospel according to Tish. Tish has been my ride-or-die through every phase of my life since middle school, from bad boyfriends to failed attempts at making home-made sushi.

I try to push James from my thoughts again and focus on my writing. But even as I settle into the creative zone, I can't help but think of the "what ifs." What if it's all just a big waste of emotional energy, and I walk away feeling as confused as ever?

Ollie lets out another sleepy purr, and I glance over at him, grateful for his nonchalance. In his world, everything is as it should be—warmth, comfort, and food at predictable intervals. No ex-boyfriend drama, no existential crises over coffee dates.

"Maybe I should just be more like you, Ollie," I say softly. "Simple. Content."

Ollie doesn't bother to acknowledge my musings this time, too busy living his best cat life. But maybe there's something to be said for simplicity, for focusing on the things that make life good right now. Like the soft glow of the fireplace, the comforting weight of my laptop on my legs, and the sweet promise of a quiet night ahead.

I stretch out on the lounger, slightly closing my laptop for a moment. Next week can bring all the complicated stuff—editing, deadlines, coffee with an ex—but tonight, I think I'll just enjoy the peace of a night in, accompanied by Ollie's gentle snores.

Chapter 9

I jolt awake as my alarm beeps through my sleeping state. Crusty drool hugs the side of my mouth as I feel the warm sun through the window. I must have left it open last night, the chirping of the birds is louder than usual.

And to think I don't drink often. But perhaps with all that life has been throwing at me, I had a good excuse.

I slip off the side of my bed and stretch my arms above me, feeling my back crack and the softness of the plush carpet between my toes. I stumble toward my dresser and glance at my phone already in my hand.

It's 9:55 a.m. on Tuesday. While only a few days have passed, it feels like the whole James fiasco just happened. And it still is, because I literally have to meet him at The Bean in thirty-five minutes.

That means fifteen minutes to get ready, fifteen minutes to agonize over why I am agreeing to this, and ten minutes to show up fashionably late and pretend I am cool, calm, and collected.

It was years of radio silence, and now this. Meeting him at The Bean felt more surreal the closer it got. A week ago, he had practically fallen out of the sky—well, more like into the laundromat, but same thing, really. I hadn't seen him in years, not since that spectacularly awful breakup when I found out he was doing more than just lying about our future together. Oh, and now, just my luck, he suddenly wants to apologize. Again.

James had appeared out of nowhere, just standing there with a laundry basket like it was the most normal thing in the world. I remember staring at him, trying to process what I was seeing. The man who had once been my everything. The man who had broken me. He looked different—older, yes, but also... polished, like the years had added layers to him that I hadn't expected. His sudden appearance after years of silence was unsettling. And now here I was, about to meet him again.

I bite my lip and stare at the mirror. I begin to open the drawers and hover my hands over my clothes. What does one even wear to meet an ex? Something that says, "I'm totally over you," without looking like I'm trying too hard. And then my thoughts stop in their tracks.

Shit.

Am I over him? After the late nights talking away with Tish and throwing up my feelings over wine and ugly crying, I find myself still unsure if I'm even over him. Perhaps it was the Friday night dates at the movies, or dinner at a fancy restaurant, or laying on the grass at the park under the blanket of stars as he caressed my hands as I laid my head on his chest...

I shake my head and pull on my oversized college sweatshirt, my favorite mom jeans, and high-top pink converse, and throw my orange hair up in a small half-up half-down messy bun. I look at myself in the mirror once more, and wince. I scoop up silver hoops and slip them on. I need to scrap these thoughts and pitch them in the trash. Of course I am over him. I mean, he is a cheater. And they say once a cheater, always a cheater.

I make my way into the kitchen and the smell of bananas and strawberries overwhelm my nose. Tish is making her usual smoothie before her morning run. She twists the cap of her portable blender and smiles at me. "Up and at 'em this morning, aren't we?"

I groan and grab my tote bag off the counter. "I would prefer to be sleeping in this morning cuddled with Ollie but alas, it's Tuesday."

"Tuesday?" Tish asks as she tilts her head in question.

"Tuesday. 10:30 this morning. Meeting James 'to talk.'"

Her eyes widen a bit and she pats me on the shoulder. "Oh, girl. I totally forgot, sorry. Good luck today, yeah? Promise to text me you didn't get kidnapped by some perv instead, please." She sips some of her smoothie. "I'm off for my run. Love you!"

I smirk at her and nod. "Yeah, I promise. Love you too."

I grab my keys off the hook near the front door and head out. I may have agreed to meet James, but that doesn't mean I'm going to enjoy it. And neither should he.

♡

With plenty of time considering The Bean is just a walk up the street into town, I decide to take a longer route through downtown. The streets are quiet this time of day, save for the occasional hum of cars in the distance.

It's a crisp Tuesday morning, the kind that teeters on the edge of autumn and winter, where the air has just enough bite to make you pull your coat a little tighter. I stuff my hands into my pockets as I start to walk, breathing in the cool air that carries the faint scent of fallen leaves and damp pavement. The trees lining the street are mostly bare now, with only a few stubborn leaves clinging to the branches, fluttering like little orange and brown flags.

As I walk, my thoughts bounce back and forth, trying to figure out how I feel about seeing James again. The last time we'd spoken—really spoken, not like the other day—had been just a few years ago, back when everything had fallen apart. The lying, the cheating, the eventual breakup that left me reeling. And now, suddenly, he is back. He said he's changed. He said he wants to apologize, to clear the air. He even said he had written a book—a bestseller, no less. It all felt so… convenient.

But maybe I do need closure, or whatever people call it. Maybe this is the chance to finally put it all behind me.

The Bean comes into view as I round the corner. A place I love. And yet, thinking back, it was a place we had both loved, back when we were together.

I can already see people inside, sipping their drinks, heads buried in laptops or lost in conversation. I feel a twinge of nervousness in my stomach. It's just coffee. It's just James. *You'll be fine.*

I stand outside for a moment, hesitating at the entrance. The chilly air kisses my red and nearly numb cheeks, reminding me that I can't stand here forever. I take a deep breath, push the door open, and step into the warm, welcoming buzz of the café. The familiar hum of the espresso machine and the soft murmur of conversation envelopes me, and for a moment I am comforted by the normalcy of it all. I scan the café, face after face, a blur one after the other.

And then I see him.

I do a double take. James is sitting at a small table near the window, the same spot we used to sit together. His brown curly hair is nestled under a crimson baseball cap. He is wearing a basic white t-shirt and a brown leather jacket, probably one and the same I bought for him years ago. It appears slightly faded with a few patches on the arms. His long fingers embrace the large cup as steam smothers his face. I can see his eyes darting back and forth as he reads a book.

His deep blue eyes flicker in my direction. Our eyes meet. My stomach flips and flops all over, and I suddenly regret the second cup of coffee I had this morning.

He stands up when I approach, offering a tentative smile. "Hey, Zoe."

"Hey," I reply, trying to sound casual, though my voice betrays the nervous energy swirling inside me.

He gestures to the chair across from him. "I got us a table."

I pull the chair out and take a seat, grateful for the chance to sit down and stop fidgeting. We sit in an awkward silence for a moment, the kind where you're both too polite to jump into the heavy stuff but too aware that it's hanging there between you. He bookmarks his book and closes it shut. His eyes meet mine once more.

"I'm really glad you came," he says, his voice softer and yet more raspy than I remembered. "I know this is, well, probably weird for you. It's weird for me too."

I shrug, managing a small smile. "Yeah, it's a little weird."

He nods, like he understood exactly what I meant. "I just—there are some things I need to say. I've been thinking a lot about the past, about us, and I realized that I never really gave you a proper apology for what happened."

His words hang in the air and I can feel the weight of them pressing against me. I wait, not sure if I should speak or let him continue. I don't trust my voice not to crack.

"I was a mess back then," he went on, his fingers tapping lightly against the edge of his cup. "I made a lot of mistakes. And I know I hurt you. I never should've lied to you. And the cheating... I've regretted it every day since. I don't expect you to forgive me. But I just needed you to know that I've changed."

I stare down at my own cup, swirling the coffee inside, watching the ice cubes clink against the cup. I find it funny, maybe even charming, that he ordered my usual as if he still knows me like the back of his hand. I dip my finger into the whip cream and lick it off.

And then I remember he is still here, in front of me, staring at me as I eat the whip cream. A smile forms at his lips, showing off his imperfect gap-in-the-front smile. I bite my lip and shrug. "What can I say? I've always been a sucker for sweets." I feel myself smirk and look up at him. "You remembered my usual, so, thank you."

James nods. "No problem. But Zo..." His voice trails and suddenly, his fingers dawdle over mine. The warmth of his hands sends a shock throughout my entire body. "I can honestly say that I have changed. For the better, I think. And, well, I've worked hard over these years to become that better person that you always saw in me. The one that's less messy and... angry. I guess I just wanted to say that."

His words sliver their way through my thoughts. *I have*

changed. People always say that, don't they? But how much do people really change? Or was it just that time has passed, and maybe now the mistakes don't seem as fresh? Mom said people are allowed to evolve into better versions of themselves. He's saying the right things, and I don't believe any of them.

"I appreciate you saying that," I say after a few moments, my voice quiet. "I appreciate the apology, James. I do. It means something. Honestly, I don't know what it means exactly, but... it's something." I sip my coffee and graze my fingertips against the cup. "But I am unsure what to really do with it. After all, it's been a while."

He smiles, a small, tentative smile. "I understand. I just had to say it. Because I genuinely mean it. But I guess I deserve that."

I look up at him. His blue eyes like crystal orbs floating in space, sparkling as gold flakes. His freckles splatter perfectly on his warm skin. I have to control myself and try not to drool over him. He's my ex, he shouldn't mean anything to me. Especially now.

The music in the café surrounds us like a group hug. It's full of the hustle and bustle of cups clattering about as the espresso and ice machines create their own tune. A spoon clatters, and I glance over at a nearby table where a couple is laughing, heads close together, caught in some private world of their own. The café is busy with life on this Tuesday morning. Laughter and conversations drift through the air, mixing with some kind of soft indie music—the kind that's just loud enough to make the place feel warm and full, but quiet enough that you can still hear the world happening around you.

His apology means something, but I'm not sure if I should believe it. Maybe it's due to our broken history? Maybe it's due to the fact that after all this time, James shows up out of nowhere and is trying to fix things with us. And maybe that is why his words are so hard to cling on to and believe. I just don't have it in me to believe him. Not yet. Over time, maybe? But right now, it's too soon. Right now, it's too weird. And maybe it's too much.

Then, like a sudden thought crossing a page, I remember something he told me what feels like ages ago at the laundromat, even though it was just last week. "So," I say, nudging the conversation toward safer waters, "you're a bestselling author now?" My mouth curves into a smile, something genuine blooming from my otherwise wary expression. "That's... wow. It's amazing, James. I'm happy for you, really."

He chuckles, reaching up to rub the back of his neck, a hint of pink blooming across his cheeks that makes him look almost like the James I used to know, the one who laughed too loudly and blushed too easily. "Yeah, thanks. It's crazy, right?"

Despite everything, a swell of genuine admiration rises in me. I knew he was talented—maybe more than he even realized—but seeing him do something like this still feels surreal. It's like finding out your childhood pet has been moonlighting as a minor celebrity this whole time. I shake my head, grinning despite myself. "It's really great. Congratulations."

He glances down at his coffee cup, fingers tracing the rim, his smile soft and almost shy. "Thanks." He pauses, looking back up at me, his gaze steady. "And what about you?" There's something warm in his eyes, something I almost recognize.

A warmth grows in my chest, catching me by surprise. "Actually, I'm getting a short story published in *Poets & Writers* next month."

His eyes light up, his smile growing a little wider, a little more familiar. "Zo, that's amazing. I always knew you'd make it as a writer. I mean, I was the one who always told you to submit your writing, remember? And now look at you."

I can feel a soft blush creeping up my cheeks. His words—whether they're what I need to hear or just something I want to believe—feel like an old favorite song playing on the radio, one you've heard a hundred times but still turn up. For a moment, I almost forget the heartache that brought us here.

But then, like a quiet whisper, a little voice reminds me not to get carried away. Just because someone says something nice doesn't mean they'll stay true to it. He did insist on reminding me he was the one who "told" me to submit my work back then. Can he be more full of himself?

And then he looks at me, really looks at me, with that quiet, searching gaze that used to make me feel like I was the only person in the room. "You know," he says softly, "I never really stopped thinking about you."

My heart stumbles, and I can feel it—a pang I'm all too familiar with. It's as if my body is trying to react while my mind is desperately trying to play it cool. *Here we go*, I think, bracing myself.

"I mean it," he continues, his voice softer, more careful. "I've thought about you a lot. About what we had, and what I threw away."

His words hang in the air between us like a cloud that's threatening rain, thick with memories and regrets I haven't let myself touch in a long time. Part of me wants to believe him, to be flattered that I've lingered in his mind like some kind of haunting melody. But there's another part of me—the more guarded, cynical part—that knows better. Missing someone doesn't always mean you're ready to make things right.

"I don't know, James," I say finally, my voice even as I steady myself. "A lot of time has passed. Things are different now. *We* are different now, you know?"

He nods, looking down at his hands, fingers resting on his coffee cup. His expression is hard to read, a mix of resignation and something that might be sadness. "Right, no, I get that," he murmurs. "Maybe I wanted to see if there was still something here."

I look at him, studying the familiar angles of his face, the way his brow furrows when he's deep in thought. There was a time when I would have given anything to hear these words, to believe in second chances. But now, sitting here, I realize that whatever we had might be better left as a memory—a beautiful, painful lesson.

"I don't know what you're hoping for," I say softly but firmly, meeting his eyes, "but I think it's better if we leave the past where it is. Things take time to simmer, even if it's days, weeks, or months. It takes time. And to be frank, I'm still hurt by what happened. You don't just quickly move on and let something like that go."

He holds my gaze for a long, searching moment, and something flickers in his eyes, a glimmer of understanding mingled with something else—maybe regret, maybe acceptance. After what feels like forever, he nods, slowly. "Yeah. Yeah, no, I understand. You have every right to feel that way, Zo, truly."

The conversation drifts after that, slipping into safer, softer topics. We talk about work, about daily life, about the things people discuss when they're trying to keep the peace. When the clock ticks toward noon, I feel the weight of the morning settle into my bones, and I know it's time to go.

"I'm glad we talked," he says as we stand by the door, sunlight spilling around us like a spotlight on a stage we've stepped away from. "And, for what it's worth, I really am sorry."

I take a deep breath, a small, forgiving smile tugging at the corners of my lips. "I know... I think," I say, a soft warmth in my voice. "Take care, James."

And in an instant, I feel his lips on my cheek. The warmth of them coats my skin, sending a shiver down my neck. The familiarity makes my heart skip a beat and rattle in my ribcage. My brain is screaming at me to run, and fast.

But I can't move. I can't feel my feet and legs anymore. It's like he's put a spell on me to prevent me from fleeing. My heart shouldn't be beating like this. He doesn't deserve anything from me. And here I am, letting him peck my cheek like he's Prince Charming, whisking me away on his high horse to his big castle for a newfound happy-ever-after.

I finally pull my senses together and whip my face the other way. I don't want to give him the satisfaction just because he kissed my cheek. I don't know what he's trying to pull, but I'm not having any of it.

He doesn't get to do that. He doesn't get to think that that's okay. Without another word, I put one foot in front of the other, pulling my scarf around my neck a little tighter, feeling the weight of the morning settle around me like a layer of armor that both grounds and frees me. I'm going to need all the armor I started to pull off back on to protect my entire being from him.

The cool September air curls around me. The sky is a pale, washed-out blue stretched like a canvas above the quiet hum of the street. My thoughts jumble his words together, like trying to solve the last word search clue. They echo in my mind like a melody you can't quite shake. It wasn't the clean, neatly wrapped ending I'd imagined, the kind of tidy farewell you'd read about in novels. Especially with that stupid kiss on my cheek. Instead, it was a little messy and a lot unresolved, like a chapter that refuses to close and might just need to be left unfinished.

Was this the closure everyone talks about? This meet up with James felt like just that, though—unfinished. But is there anything to truly finish? Sure, there's the fact that he mentioned he couldn't stop thinking about me after all this time, but in a way, was he merely holding onto what used to be? Like living in the past?

And yet, maybe this was the perfect closure to that chapter. Maybe it was a good thing I agreed to meet with him, even if it was mostly him doing the talking. He was the one who wanted to get together anyway.

I clench my jaw and shove my hands in the pockets of my jeans, absorbing his words. I reach the end of the block, pausing to look back one last time.

The café door swings shut, hiding him from view. I turn back to the street ahead, letting the breeze carry away the last remnants of his voice and the now faint touch of his lips on my cheek.

What an asshole.

Chapter 10

I walk toward the apartment down the quiet sidewalk as the cool fall breeze blows around me. I gather my scarf around my neck as my tote bag dangles at my side, and I suddenly feel something cool on my face. It's not the cool breeze, but watery. After few more drops I notice the sidewalk and street are darkening with rain.

I pull my umbrella out (good thing I actually decided to use my big girl money to buy one) and open it above me. I yank my phone out and call Tish. I know she's probably on her toes about how it went with James.

"Hey, babe! How did it go with James? I need details like, now."

I press my lips together to prevent myself from smiling. "I think it went pretty good, Tish. I mean, until he had the nerve to peck my cheek and tell me he hadn't stopped thinking about me and—"

Tish interrupts me midsentence. "Wait, wait, hold up. He *kissed* you? And told you he hasn't stopped thinking about you? *Seriously*? What did he say? No, back up, what did *you* say?"

I roll my eyes and laugh, making my way toward a bench. "Yes, seriously. He said he missed me. But you will be proud of me, because I didn't let that suck me in and get all emotional. I told him it's best to leave the past in the past. And, well, he actually agreed."

A few minutes of silence pass until I speak up again. "Um, Earth to Tish?"

"I'm still here, sorry. I needed a minute to soak all that in. I just have to say that I am immensely proud of you, sweetie! I mean, damn. You spoke up and didn't cave in. But I have to ask... do you actually feel good about how it went?"

I feel myself nodding, knowing full well she cannot hear a nod. "I think so. I mean, I still have speculations, but honestly, Tish, I think this was the closure I needed. Maybe he came back into my life, very briefly I might add, for this reason. I just wish he didn't kiss my cheek."

I hear her laughing. "It's giving desperation, Zo. All I want is for you to be happy, that's it. So anyway, what are you up to now? Did you want to meet up in town and do a little shopping? I'm near the apartment anyway. My legs feel like jelly from the run, but I am feeling energized."

"That sounds great! I'm still right in town across from the post office. I'll wait here if that's easier?"

"Oh, yes! Perfect. I'll see you in a few."

♡

I lean back against the bench, the rough wooden slants poking at my spine. But they aren't bothering me. The crisp air once again softly feathers my face as the aroma of coffee and pumpkin spice envelopes my nose. I tap my pink Converse against the sidewalk to the beat of the soft music playing from the speakers hidden beneath the bushes behind me. It's a smooth jazz followed by piano keys. The town is ever so cozy this time of year, always so magical and mysterious in a way.

Oh, yeah, mysterious indeed. I'm still baffled by the fact James decided to show up in my life when I thought things were just getting figured out: graduating with my master's, picking up with more freelancing projects, and I have my first short story getting published in a literary magazine. And boom. James just flies in from nowhere and is all *I'm a New York Times Bestsellers author, la de da.*

My eyes dart in front of me as I realize Tish has been staring at me for a few minutes now, I'm sure. "Oh, shit. Tish, sorry. When did you get here?"

She chuckles and lifts me from the bench, hugging me tighter than usual. Her body is damp from her walk but her Barbie-blonde high ponytail is still perfectly intact. She's wearing purple and black leggings with a purple sweatshirt that has a cute white ghost across the front.

"Mm, about two minutes ago? I noticed you were lost in thought so I didn't wanna interrupt. You're still stuck on James, aren't you? I know you better than anyone, so don't even try to lie."

I look at Tish, her bright green eyes dancing with concern, and I let out a small laugh, shaking my head. "No, it's not just James. I mean, yes, he's been on my mind, but it's everything. The job, the story, and now this unexpected meeting. I guess I'm just a little overwhelmed, you know?"

I glance up at the sky again, clouds shifting in a lazy waltz, re-minding me of the uncertainty swirling inside me. The rhythm of the town around us hums with life—the distant clink of coffee cups, the soft chatter of pedestrians, and the rustle of leaves being pulled to the ground by a playful gust.

She swings her arm around me and kisses my cheek. "Well, ya got me, 'kay? If you ever feel overwhelmed, you know I'm just a phone call or text away. I know you're going to be okay. Life is just funny like that, you know? Things just happen when you least ex-pect it, probably to keep you on your toes. And yet you're doing so well, babe. Your first story is about to be published in a literary magazine. That's huge! And you made that happen by just writing. So, in conclusion of my tirade, you are amazing and deserve the world. Now," she points her finger toward the new bookstore that just opened in town, "let's go explore this new bookstore. I know you have probably been dying to go in, am I right?"

I smile, and hug into her. "Thank you, Tish. I needed that little push. And yes, it's been on my mind since last week and I have been crying on the inside ever since."

"Well, let's get a move on then!"

Tish grins and drags us toward the bookstore, The Literary Café. The entrance window nook is freshly shelved with new re-leases (I am eyeing Emily Henry's *Funny Story* and putting it in my mental book cart) along with strings of lights that jump from red to blue to purple. The sign above the store blows in the wind as if waving us in, inviting us into a whole other world.

A welcoming hum of warmth and chatter seeps out from be-hind the glass door, mixing with the earthy scent of freshly brewed coffee that practically floats us inside. The moment I step in, I feel wrapped in coziness. The walls are painted with dandelion yellow and a bright sky blue. Brown bookcases line every wall, packed with books in every color and size from crisp new novels to weathered classics. Small tables and chairs scatter around, some hidden in nooks and corners, offering intimate little spots to get lost in a story. The table closest to the front of the store nestles wrapped blind date books with the plots in bold writing across the fronts.

The lighting is warm and low, glinting off the golden-embossed titles on spines as if the books are quietly glowing. There's a counter to the left where a barista is pouring a caramel-colored stream of espresso into a cup, and right beside her is a small display of stationery—quirky pens, tiny notepads, and leather-bound journals calling out to be picked up and scribbled in.

"Oh, I'm home," I breathe, feeling my heart do a little happy dance. I'm already making mental notes of the sections I want to explore, from the fiction shelf near the corner to a cluster of poetry books that seem to be whispering my name.

Tish smiles at me and tilts her head toward the coffee bar. "I'm going to grab myself some coffee. Want anything?"

I shake my head. "I'm okay. I'll be exploring the poetry section and notebooks. No promises on not buying any!"

She laughs and heads toward the barista.

My fingers hover over the spines of the books, feeling the softness of each one, all of them oozing with a magical story to tell. And suddenly I can feel a sense of pride in myself. This could be me one day. I could have someone picking up my book on this very shelf and clutching it like it's the last one. To think my short story will be published next month. I mean, mine, out of all of them, was picked up. I still can't believe it. I mean, sure, my professor sent it on my behalf, but still. I feel so honored that I could cry.

Tish reappears next to me with her coffee in hand and takes a sip. "This is definitely good coffee. And who said small bookstores were lame and going out of business? This place seems great."

I nod and stroll past the fiction books, admiring the colorful spines and the earthy smell of the pages the books seem to release. I stumble upon the bright and vibrant covers of my favorite authors, Emily Henry, Abby Jimenez, and Emily Giffin, practically whispering for me to pick them up. Each spine feels like an invitation to dive into someone else's world, to step into lives both familiar and thrillingly unknown. There's something electric about this section—the stories of love, heartbreak, self-discovery, and transformation that resonate so deeply with anyone who's ever searched for meaning in the chaos of modern life.

I walk along the shelf, my fingers grazing the cool, polished spines, and pause to pull out *Funny Story*. The cover is a burst of color and whimsy, promising a story filled with humor and heartache, the kind of book I'd devour in a single night, lost in the pages until morning light filters through my curtains. As I flip through the first few pages, a line catches my eye. One that speaks of the beauty in life's smallest, most fleeting moments. It reminds me of the coffee shop where I'm standing, the simple pleasure of my favorite drink, and the warmth of this bookstore wrapping itself around me.

There is a short stack of baskets near the aisle, and I immediately grab one, knowing myself well enough to know that I'll end up buying out the entire store. Then my eyes land on a copy of *Daisy Jones & The Six,* and I can't resist. I put both copies in the basket and grab one of Abby Jimenez's books as well, *Yours Truly*. It's been on my reading list for ages, so figure why not treat myself a bit. I call it a celebratory purchase.

I then walk toward the back of the bookstore where all of the stationary items reside. I can't resist—stationery has always been a weakness of mine, a small luxury that feels like self-care with each pen, notebook, and sticky notes I collect. The sight of them makes my heart flutter. The table is perfectly arranged, as though each item has been deliberately placed to call to anyone who passes by.

Soft light from a nearby sconce glints off the glossy covers of notebooks, which are stacked neatly in a pyramid. They range from compact, pocket-sized journals to larger, hardcover notebooks bound in linen and leather. The colors are subtle, soothing—there's one in a dusty rose with an embossed floral pattern, another in a deep, velvety navy blue, and even a few with delicate gold foil designs that gleam invitingly.

A small stack of loose-leaf notepads rests beside them, each page adorned with whimsical illustrations of coffee cups, ink bottles, or tiny cats curled up in balls of yarn. I run my fingers over the smooth, cool covers, feeling the slight texture of linen under my fingertips as I pull a journal from the pile. It's a beautiful notebook bound in soft sage green leather, embossed with a delicate leaf pattern in the corner. The pages are a warm cream, faintly lined, and thick enough that I can tell they'd hold ink without bleeding through. I can already imagine filling it with sketches, snippets of dialogue, or the fragments of poetry that always come to mind late at night. I place it in my basket along with the books.

I notice a shelf filled with pens and pencils, markers, and

brightly colored gel pens. I pick up a deep burgundy-colored pen with a fine point, twirling it between my fingers as I imagine the way it might glide across those cream pages.

I glance over at Tish, who's busy browsing a stack of romance novels, oblivious to my detour into the stationery wonderland. It feels like I'm purchasing a little piece of inspiration, something that's just for me, to carry with me on quiet days when I need a fresh start or a place to capture my thoughts—which are always tumbling through my brain.

As I approach the cashier, the barista smiles, clearly amused by my enthusiasm as I place the items on the counter. "Good choice," she says, eyeing the notebook. "Those are handmade by a local artist—they're as beautiful as they are durable. People always tell me they feel like they're writing in a work of art."

I smile, feeling a small thrill at that idea. "That's exactly what I was thinking," I reply, glancing down at the embossed cover. "It feels like the perfect place to capture whatever comes to mind."

With my purchase tucked securely into my bag, I head back over to Tish, who's now juggling three books and grinning at me. "You bought something, didn't you?" she teases, glancing down at the slight bulge in my bag.

"I couldn't help it," I say, smiling. "This place is like a little slice of heaven. And I just know that notebook is going to be exactly what I need for capturing ideas and... well, who knows what else."

Together, we find our way to the cozy seats by the window, the excitement of the bookstore buzzing around us, and I feel an over-whelming sense of contentment. I realize that I hadn't thought about James the entire time we browsed and explored the store. I guess that's a good thing, considering I'm feeling pretty much over him. After meeting with him, and talking to Tish, and just listening to my inner voice, what's done is done. Why keep giving it more thought than I already have?

Just as I'm settling into my chair, my phone vibrates in my pocket, pulling me back to the present. I pull it out, glancing down to see a new email notification from *Poets & Writers*. My heart skips a beat as I open it, reading through a message from someone named Ben.

Dear Ms. Donovan,

My name is Ben Cartwright, and I am the Acquisitions Editor at Poets & Writers. *While I usually do the recruiting and scouting for writers, it appears Mr. Hopkins submitted your story from your MFA creative writing program. I have to say, it's been a thrill to read. I haven't read anything like this in quite some time, and my boss praised it as well. She would like to meet you and talk more about it. That said, I wanted to personally reach out with some very exciting news. Your short story is all set to be published in our next issue!*

As we approach the release, I wanted to offer my congratulations and let you know that your story resonated deeply with everyone here at Poets & Writers. *We'd love to hear more about your inspiration behind it, and perhaps we could set up an in-depth interview to discuss your journey as a writer. Once again, congratulations on this wonderful accomplishment!*

Best regards,
Ben Cartwright

I feel a wave of excitement wash over me, the words "exciting news" and "wonderful accomplishment" ringing in my ears like a melody. I can hardly believe it—it's really happening. I look up at Tish, a grin spreading across my face.

"Tish," I breathe, holding up my phone. "It's officially official. Next month, my story will be in *Poets & Writers*."

Her eyes widen, and then, without warning, she pulls me into a hug so tight I nearly drop my bag of books. "Oh my god, yay! Now it's totally real!"

My mind reels, and I read the email twice, then three times, looping over in my brain like a scratched-up record. I feel as if my feet are barely touching the ground. My heart flutters in disbelief, pride, and—yes—overwhelming joy.

Chapter 11

The sun sets just before eight p.m., and Ollie is snuggled near the fireplace as the warmth heats the entirety of the apartment. It always feels like he's stealing the heat rather than sharing it with us. I smile to myself as I plop my bag of newly purchased books and stationery on the kitchen counter alongside my tote bag.

"I'd say that was the most successful spontaneous shopping trip we've had in a while."

Tish brushes out her ponytail and smiles. "Absolutely. And you deserve it, babe! I mean, look at all you've accomplished in such a short time. Have I told you how proud I am of you? And how happy I am for you?"

I smirk and roll my eyes as I grab wine glasses from the cabinet. "Only on occasion, but thank you." I pull the last bottle of wine from the fridge and raise the now filled glasses to Tish, and we clink.

"To success, and the many *bookish* adventures that await my best friend, Zoe! Here's to the lifelong writer, the natural bookworm, and the brilliant storyteller you're becoming. Congrats, girl. You deserve every bit of this."

I smile and sip the wine. It soothes my throat. The warmth seeps into my chest, spreading a cozy, soothing sensation that pairs perfectly with Tish's words. I smile, savoring the moment, letting myself really feel it.

"Thank you, Tish," I murmur, setting my glass down as my fingers graze the sleek cover of one of my new books. "Honestly, this all of this feels surreal. Like maybe it's all just part of a dream. But you know what? I think I'm going to call it a night and start one of those books. See you in the morning?"

She shakes her head, sipping the last of the wine in her glass. "Gotta early day tomorrow at the bar to help with prep since I took a personal day today. Sorry, babe. We'll catch up in the evening I'm sure. You relax for the night." She strides past me, kisses my cheek, and heads to her bedroom.

I smile and say goodnight, making my way to my bedroom. My room is a blend of warmth and gentle chaos—books spilling off the shelves, stacks of notebooks with scrawled-on pages, and random mementos from past trips and moments, each little item a part of me. I place the newest additions to my collection on the edge of my bed, feeling a rush of excitement as I admire their spines, already envisioning them on the shelves. I can practically smell the fresh pages, the stories waiting within each one ready to whisk me away.

After arranging the books on my shelf, I settle onto my bed with *Funny Story* by Emily Henry in hand. I get myself cozy and suddenly remember I haven't replied to Ben's email from earlier. I put the book back on the shelf and grab my laptop, pulling up Ben's email. His words, still fresh in my mind, hum with excitement and possibility. My stomach flutters as I think about meeting with him to discuss my story, feeling for the first time that maybe someone out there truly believes in my work. I start typing, fingers flying over the keys.

Hi Ben,

Thanks so much for reaching out! I'd love to schedule a time to chat more about my piece. Let me know when your boss would like to chat and I'm sure I can make it. I've also attached my phone number in case that makes it easier to coordinate. Looking forward to it!

Best,
Zoe

I hit send, the thrill of putting myself out there leaving me both exhilarated and a little vulnerable. This meeting could change everything—it feels like a huge step, like my words are reaching out beyond the safe confines of my small, familiar world.

A few small knocks from my door break through my thoughts. Tish emerges from the other side with a large white envelope in hand.

"I checked the mail earlier before my run, and totally forgot that something came for you." She hands me the white envelope emblazoned with my college's name across the top in elegant, bold letters. My heart skips a beat.

"Oh my god," I whisper, staring down at the envelope in awe. Could this really be...?

"Come on, open it!" Tish's voice is practically vibrating with excitement.

With a deep breath, I carefully tear open the envelope, pulling out the thick, cream-colored paper inside. My heart pounds as I read the words. There, in the most formal, beautiful script, is my master's degree. *Master of Fine Arts in Creative Writing*. The official seal gleams on the page, a symbol of all those sleepless nights, the countless edits, the struggle of pouring my heart onto every page. I run my fingers over the text, feeling happy and overwhelmed all at once. This is it. This is what I worked so hard for the past two years.

Tish squeals, her arms wrapping around me. She pulls me into a tight hug, laughing with joy. "Aw, you got your degree!"

I blink back a few tears, a knot of gratitude and disbelief building in my throat. "Thank you, Tish. Really. I wouldn't have made it without you."

She grins, nudging me playfully. "Of course you would have. You're brilliant. You're an amazing writer." She then shoots straight up off the bed and heads over to the door. "Oh, hold on a second. I know the plan was to head to bed, but I can't help myself now. I'll be right back."

She disappears briefly and returns with a small wrapped box, pressing it into my hands with a grin. "I've been waiting for this moment," she says, almost giddy. "Open it!"

Inside the box is a stunning set of fountain pens, each one elegant and unique, the metal caps smooth and cool to the touch. Midnight blue, forest green, and burgundy—each one feels like an invitation to write. And they all have my initials engraved in gold, *ZMD*. Nestled alongside them is a vintage-style picture frame with intricate, gold filigree around the edges.

"Tish, this is incredible," I murmur, running my fingers along the pens and imagining the stories I'll write with them. I hold up the frame, envisioning my degree resting within it, a daily reminder of this journey.

"Now it's official," she says, smiling. "You're a writer, Zoe. And that frame—perfect spot to showcase your diploma, don't you think?"

I nod, my chest warm with gratitude. "Thank you. For everything."

She brushes it off with a wave of her hand, but her eyes are bright. "All right, now, tomorrow might be an early day, but we're celebrating properly. Takeout from Golden Lotus and some more wine to toast to your success."

♡

As we wait for the food, the room fills with laughter, familiar banter, and plans for the future. Our conversations flow like the wine, each sip smoothing out my nerves, each laugh making me feel lighter. When the food arrives, we dig in, the aroma of sesame chicken and fried rice and veggies mingling with the wine, filling the room with warmth and the feeling of celebration.

Tish raises her glass again, a mischievous glint in her eyes. "To the future best-selling author."

I laugh, cheeks warm from both the wine and the sentiment. "We'll see about that," I reply, but in my heart, the dream feels just a little more possible.

Our conversation drifts to my upcoming birthday. I'll be twenty-nine in December, just three months away. It doesn't feel real. I still feel like I just turned eighteen, and sometimes I still feel that young.

As Tish leans back into the couch, her glass of wine perched precariously on her knee, she gives me a look that I've come to recognize—half scheming, half sincere. "Zoe," she says, dragging my name out like it's the opening act to a particularly grand performance. "We have to do something big for your birthday this year. Twenty-nine is practically thirty, and thirty is, like, peak sophistication."

I snort, nearly choking on my sip of wine. "Sophistication? Is that what you were going for when you tripped over your shoelaces on the way to the bookstore?"

"That's called being relatable," she shoots back, waving her glass dramatically. "And don't change the subject. This is about you. What do you want to do for your big day?"

I shrug, setting down my glass so I can reach for another scallion pancake. "I don't know. Dinner? Cake? Maybe a nap?"

Tish gasps, clutching her imaginary pearls. "A nap? On the cusp of your thirties? You're turning twenty-nine, not ninety-nine. I hope you know how lucky you are that I'm here to save you from yourself."

I roll my eyes but can't help smiling. "Look, I just want something low-key. No surprises, no big plans. Maybe something like me, you, and delicious takeout pizza."

Tish narrows her eyes, a mischievous glint flickering in them. It's the kind of look that usually precedes her most harebrained schemes. "Fine," she says, a little too quickly. "We'll keep it low-key. No surprises. Totally chill."

I squint at her, sensing danger. "You promise?"

"Promise." She raises her glass as if swearing an oath.

Despite my instincts screaming otherwise, I nod. "Okay, good.

No surprises." I don't believe her one bit. She giggles and falls back onto the bed. I can't help but laugh. I reach for our glasses and set them on my dresser. "Okay, we have a wine problem."

She rolls her eyes. "Wine problem? Who's she? Never heard of her."

I chuckle. Knowing Tish she's probably already making a mental party planning list as we speak.

Chapter 12

The next morning seems to come faster than my thoughts can. I groan as I stretch my arms above my head and flutter my eyes open to the brightness that devours my room. My eyes settle on my golden picture frame and notice my diploma already placed in it. I smile and realize Tish must have put that together. I truly don't know what I'd do without her. I open the blinds, push them up, and open the window just a tad. The fresh morning breeze soothes my puffy face, and I breathe it in, smiling to myself.

I really did this. I did the whole college thing by myself, and with no one pressuring me to finish or pushing me to graduate. I set a goal in mind and followed through. I'm not used to all this success, but I guess you can say that I could get used to it.

My drawers creak open as I pull out a pair of socks and smother them over my feet. I change into a pink sweater with red hearts and a pair of mom jeans. My fingers dawdle over my small jewelry box sitting by my mirror, and I plop on a pair of pearl studs. I then make my way to the bathroom and wash up, brushing my hair out as the loose curls flop just above my shoulders.

Oh, shoot. Ben.

I grab my laptop and settle on my freshly made bed. I log into my email, and my heart skips a beat as I see Ben's name in my inbox. I quickly pull up the email, barely able to contain the sudden wave of anticipation coursing through me.

Hi Zoe,

I'm thrilled you're up for meeting. I was wondering if we could make this a bit more special and meet in person in New York? We'd love to give this feature the attention it deserves, and I think it'd be an excellent opportunity for you to meet some people in the industry as well as those on the editorial team.

Poets & Writers would be more than happy to cover your flight and accommodations if you'd be available to come out early next week. Let me know by the end of the week if you're interested—we could fly you out Saturday morning, get you settled, and meet bright and early Monday morning.

Best,
Ben

My heart pounds as I read the email, and my mind races with a mixture of excitement and uncertainty. They want to fly me to New York. This isn't just a local meeting—it's an invitation into a world I've only dreamed of. I can practically see the skyline already, feel the buzz of the city, the energy that would be pulsing all around me. The thought is exhilarating—and terrifying.

New York City. The Big Apple. It's the place to be where you want to pursue your big dreams, your ambitions, your goals. It's all about the hustle and bustle, engaging with strangers that fuel your inspiration. I imagine myself sitting in a cute café and bookshop where Times Square glistens through the big windows, screaming that this is where you need to be. It's a city vibrating with opportunity around every corner and those who strive to make their dreams a reality.

I remember I visited New York very briefly with my parents on the way home from a wedding in Boston when I was younger. We walked through Times Square. I remember there being lots of people on the sidewalks and streets, and taxis swerving and honking through the non-stop bustling intersections. It felt like stepping into a whirlwind—alive and chaotic. It was amazing and, to be honest, a little hectic and scary. But I was just passing through, a tourist for a day, not an up-and-coming writer being invited there to interview at a national literary magazine. And now... now I might actually go there with a purpose.

My fingers drum lightly on the laptop as I stare at Ben's email. Could I really do this? Jump on a plane and head to New York like one of those cool, spontaneous people who don't check their email sixteen times before hitting send? A nervous thrill shivers down my spine all the what-ifs. What if I'm a total imposter? What if I show up and Ben realizes I'm not "literary magazine material?" What if I mess this up? What if I go to New York and forget how to string a sentence together, or I say something cringe in the interview and they regret ever featuring me? It's not just that I'm scared I don't belong—it's that I'm scared I finally do, and I could ruin it.

What if I'm the girl who finally got her shot... and blew it?

But as soon as that self-doubt creeps in, a small voice interrupts. This is an opportunity—a real opportunity. I've spent years perusing over every line, editing every paragraph, and learning this craft because I believe in stories. My story included. And *Poets & Writers* sees that in me enough to ask me to meet them in New York. They want to meet me. Not to tear me apart (hopefully), but to talk about my work. This has to mean something.

I glance back down at my laptop and hover my fingers over the keys, slowly grazing them as my heart sputters at a higher speed. I shouldn't rush into this. I need to take a step back and give myself some time before launching into this. It's a wonderful opportunity, yes, and probably once-in-a-lifetime for me. When would I get another chance like this? Should I just say yes and call it a day? Give in to the mystery that will unfold before me? I sigh and close my eyes for a moment.

I've worked very hard for what I have so far, I admit that. I put myself through college, and didn't listen to anyone else telling me to pursue another degree. Because to be honest, this is what I enjoy. This is what I want to do with my life. And I need to realize that the only thing stopping me... is me.

♡

I shut my laptop and set it back on my desk. I then grab my new notebook and form a pros and cons list of this opportunity meeting with *Poets & Writers*. For starters, it's fucking New York City. I write that on the pros side. My mind wanders to the uncertainty of them not liking me, and I scribble that under the cons.

But, honestly, if they didn't already like me, they wouldn't have reached out to meet and discuss my story, right? I nod to myself and remember that it's an all-expenses paid trip. I jot it down under the pros.

"Free trip? Yes, please," I mutter as I write. "Chance to impress Ben and his boss? Also yes." I pause. "Chance to blow it and end up lost in New York City?" Another con, and I scribble it quickly.

After a few more back-and-forths on paper, I close the notebook and run my fingers over the cover. I've managed to balance my pros and cons list like I'm some seasoned life coach, but I can still feel the nerves jumping inside. I wish I could fast-forward just a little, just to peek and see if everything turns out okay. But then, where's the fun in that?

I set my notebook and pen on my desk and head to the kitchen. My stomach rumbles with hunger as I open the freezer and pop a couple of waffles into the toaster. I pour myself a mug of coffee and lean against the counter. I notice a scrap of paper near the coffee maker and realize it's from Tish. She had to leave for work early this morning and won't be back until later this evening. Apparently she has a lot of catching up to do at the bar.

My waffles pop up from the toaster and I eat them with the homemade syrup Tish and I found at a craft show a few months ago. It's thick and rich and oh so good. I devour them and take a seat on the lounger near the fireplace, already turned on and warming the room. Ollie yet again lounges in front of it, his belly exposed and absorbing the heat.

For now, I think I will call my mom and ask for her input on New York. She's always the one to go to for advice. And the one to go to for the best homemade brownies, which make my mouth water just thinking about them. She really needs to make them for me soon.

As I settle into the soft embrace of the lounger, the weight of the world feels just a little lighter. My fingers drum rhythmically against the mug. When she answers, her voice flows like honey, sweet and soothing. "Well good morning, Zo. What's up, sweetie?"

I curl my legs up beneath me, tucking them snugly into the blanket, feeling the heat from the fireplace. "Hey, Mom. So, you know that short story that my professor submitted to that literary magazine? Well, I got an email from them, from *Poets & Writers*, and..." I take a deep breath, the excitement bubbling in my chest like the frothy coffee in my mug. "They want to fly me to New York. To meet with the head editor and interview me. *In person*."

There's a brief pause on the other end, and I imagine Mom's eyes widening as she processes the news, possibly spilling her morning coffee in her excitement. And then, she bursts with joy. "Oh, honey, this is huge! Congratulations, baby. Ever since you were little you've always been a reader. You get that wonderful trait from your dad."

Her enthusiasm washes over me, buoying me up like a wave on a summer day. But a storm of butterflies flutters in my stomach, battling the surge of excitement. "Thanks, Mom. I couldn't have gotten this far without you and dad. I mean, it's just that..." I chew my lip, pulling the throw blanket a little tighter around me as if it could shield me from my own doubts. "What if I show up, and they think I'm not good enough? Like, what if they realize I'm not 'New York-ready' and send me packing?"

Her laughter rings out, a comforting sound that dances through the phone, easing my worries. It's that indulgent laugh, the one that says, *"I'm your mom, and I know you better than you know yourself."*

"Sweetheart, if they didn't think you had something special, they wouldn't be investing in this. But, honey, you've worked so hard for this opportunity. And who knows? This could lead to something even bigger. Maybe a column, or even a book deal. Wouldn't that be something."

My heart skips at the thought, and I can't help but smile, gripping my mug a little tighter. "Let's not jinx it, Mom." But in my mind, images flash like snapshots: me in a quaint café, sunlight filtering through dusty windows, scribbling notes in a tattered notebook, editors nodding thoughtfully over a manuscript, and maybe, just maybe—my name embossed on the cover of a book, glimmering on many shelves in bookstores across New York.

Mom's voice softens, tinged with nostalgia. "And don't you worry about New York. Just find yourself a cozy little spot if you're feeling overwhelmed. You've always felt at home in places like that. You've always had New York on the brain, ever since we drove through the city way back when on the way to your second cousin Jesse's wedding in Boston. I remember you were utterly mesmerized by the city."

I close my eyes, letting her words wash over me, conjuring an image of a hidden café with worn bookshelves, the air thick with the scent of fresh coffee and pastries. I can almost hear the soft clinking of plates and silverware, the murmur of conversations blending with the gentle rustle of pages being turned. A little haven amid the whirlwind of the city—a perfect escape where I could breathe and dream.

She continues. "You know, Zoe, I've always thought you'd end up in New York someday. You have that dreamer's heart. Just... go for it. If nothing else, it'll be an adventure."

Her words wrap around me like the coziest blanket, extinguishing any flickers of doubt. "Thanks, Mom. You're right. Toaster waffles and coffee are great, but I think I can branch out a bit."

We share a laugh, and as I hang up, a surge of confidence settles over me like the warm sun breaking through the clouds. I set my phone aside and glance down at Ollie, who has finally emerged from his fiery nap to jump on my lap. His fluffy tuxedo fur is a delightful mess, tousled and soft like a cloud, and his big green eyes gaze up at me, shimmering with sleepy affection.

I scratch his head gently, feeling his warmth radiate against my lap. "Looks like you're rooting for me too, huh, Ollie?"

He lets out a luxurious yawn, stretching his plump paws across my thighs, making biscuits. His contentment is contagious, and I smile down at him, my heart swelling. Despite my swirling thoughts and the jitters of impending change, I feel anchored by the love of my mom and Tish and this sleepy, fat cat. I'm reminded that I'm not alone in this adventure—there's a whole world waiting, and I'm pretty sure I'm ready to leap into it.

Chapter 18

Later that evening, Tish and I arrive at the best pizza joint near the university. The restaurant thrives with college students, and there's crowds of families and friends gathering in front of the restaurant. The air is thick with the mouthwatering aroma of melting cheese and fresh tomato sauce, and my stomach rumbles in anticipation.

The neon sign flickers above the entrance, bathing the sidewalk in a warm glow. The inviting clamor of laughter and clinking cutlery drifts out as we push open the door, and I'm greeted by the sight of a bustling interior. Checkered red and white tablecloths adorn the small wooden tables, and the walls are plastered with photos of happy customers devouring slices almost as large as their heads. A bar extends out and string lights hover above it, and dozens upon dozens of bottles of wine and liquor stand like soldiers behind it. A chorus of laughter and animated conversations fills the space, creating a cozy, welcoming ambiance.

"Remember, this is *my* treat, so get whatever you're craving. We're going all out tonight, girl! A celebratory dinner for my best friend who is going to take New York by storm!" Tish says, excitement coating her voice.

I smile and yank my arm through hers. "Aw, thank you, Tish. I'm so excited to try this place. To imagine we haven't stepped foot in this place since we moved here two years ago."

She laughs and glances around the restaurant, the hostess nowhere in sight. It's definitely a busy night to kick off the weekend. As we stand in the entrance, the vibrant atmosphere wraps around us like a warm, cheesy hug. I take a deep breath, letting the mingling scents of basil, oregano, and something delightfully garlicky fill my lungs. It's a feast for the senses, and my stomach rumbles again, echoing my enthusiasm.

"If they don't serve pizza with a side of happiness, I'm demanding a refund," Tish quips, and I burst into laughter.

We finally spot the hostess, who is hustling to seat a family of six. Her hair is a chaotic bun that seems to have a mind of its own, much like Ollie when he's had too much catnip. "It must be a wild night if even the hostess is breaking a sweat," I whisper to Tish, and she stifles a giggle, nodding in agreement.

After what feels like an eternity of waiting, we're seated at a snug table near the back, the soft glow of a hanging Tiffany light fixture casting a golden hue over our spot. Tish leans forward, her eyes sparkling with mischief.

"All right, what's on the menu for our epic feast? I say we each order a whole pizza and just pretend we're training for an eating contest."

I nearly spit out my water and wipe my mouth with a napkin. "I am famished but don't think I can eat a whole pizza. But I'm strongly considering a specialty pizza just for me. The kind smothered in extra cheese and peppers, oh, and mushrooms!"

She smirks and nods in agreement. "That sounds fan-fuckingtastic. I think I'll get the same. Oh, and we must get cheesy bread!"

Once the waitress takes our orders, Tish asks for a bottle of white wine and glasses. And as if the waitress knew we were celebrating something, she appeared moments later with the whole shebang. Tish pours our glasses and raises hers for a toast (she really likes toasts).

"Here's to New York. Yet another dreamer coming to your lively abode. And may she succeed and perhaps have another chance at love!"

I feel my face reddening at Tish's words, but smile and clink my glass with hers. "Oh, stop it. You know that is not the reason why I'm going. It's for my career, to talk about my story with the magazine, with Ben and his boss."

Tish takes a sip of her wine and purses her lips. "All right, all right, I know. But come on, wouldn't it be wonderful? If you fell in love in the big city every girl dreams of? Admit it, it sounds pretty great, don't ya think?"

"Okay, fine, maybe it does sound pretty great," I concede, rolling my eyes dramatically. "But let's not go jinxing my potential career as a famous author with romantic fantasies just yet."

"Hey, the world needs more compelling, emotionally-charged stories!" she counters, grinning widely. "Besides, it's New York. You can't tell me you're not envisioning an epic love story already."

I take a sip of my wine, swirling it as I ponder her words. Maybe I *do* have a tendency to daydream about love stories, but right now, my focus should be on the story I'm about to have published. But then again, a little escapism isn't the worst thing in the world, right? I find myself wondering how many writers have found inspiration in a chance encounter, a surprise meeting with someone from their past. Wasn't that how so many great romances began?

♡

Our order finally arrives half an hour later. The melted cheese stretches like that scene in *A Goofy Movie*, and I can hardly contain my glee as I take my first bite. The flavors burst in my mouth, an explosion of deliciousness that makes my entire soul happy.

"Oh my god, this is the best pizza I've ever had," I say, the cheese stretching from my mouth as steam rises from the slice.

Tish nods in agreement. "It's definitely super good. I am so glad we came here."

I find myself observing the restaurant. Who knows, maybe I'll feel inspired to write another short story after this evening. Maybe even one set in New York, given my upcoming adventure. College students smother the restaurant and bar, laughter and smiles filling the air as funky Italian music blasts from the speakers.

My gaze suddenly lands on a familiar figure near the front entrance, half-hidden behind a crowd of college kids. My heart skips a beat.

It's James.

I stiffen slightly, unsure whether to look away or maybe just disappear under the table. But before I can decide, Tish follows my gaze and lets out a tiny gasp of recognition.

"Zoe, isn't that James?" Her eyes sparkle with mischief, and I already know what she's about to say.

"No," I whisper, trying to steer her focus back to our pizza. "And yes. But maybe he didn't see us?" I'm half-tempted to dive into the nearest plant for cover, but Tish just rolls her eyes.

"Oh, babe. You just saw him at the laundromat and met up with him at the café, so I'm confused as to why you're feeling spooked."

I ponder her statement for a moment. Maybe she's right. Maybe I am freaking out just a little. I mean, after meeting up, things did feel more comfortable. *Maybe* we reached closure. *Maybe.* So Tish might be right. Why am I freaking out? It's James. Yes, it's a bit odd he's here of all places, but it's just a restaurant. People gotta eat, right?

I take a deep breath, and my pulse gradually returns to normal as I remind myself: I am not about to turn into a rom-com protagonist who dramatically dives under tables at the sight of an ex. I lean back, slice in hand, and let out a sigh, allowing the stretchy, melted cheese to drape from the slice with a certain elegant sloppiness. If I'm going to survive tonight, it'll be with a lot of pizza and maybe another glass of wine. Or two.

"Besides," I whisper to Tish, who is trying to stifle her laughter as I delicately bite into the oozing masterpiece, "I have enough gone on without adding *another* run-in with James to the list."

Tish raises an eyebrow, the glimmer of a grin still dancing on her lips. "Maybe he'll just be an extra bit of inspiration?" she teases. "You're a writer, after all. Don't stories just come crawling out of awkward encounters?"

I take a deep breath, feeling Tish's encouraging gaze on me as I place my glass down and decide to approach James. My legs feel wobbly for a moment, and my heart knocks at my rib cage, but I remind myself that he's just James—a guy I used to know well, maybe a bit too well. And if I'm going to New York in a few days, I might as well practice braving these small moments. What's the worst that could happen? Maybe a bit of awkwardness, maybe a little forced laughter, but nothing I can't handle. I wipe my hands on a napkin, then stand up and head toward him. Tish winks and sways her hands in encouragement.

My knees begin to shake as I walk toward him. I take in the details I once knew so well. He's leaning against the bar, one hand resting casually in the pocket of his dark jeans, the other wrapped around a pint glass. His hair, thick and dark, is slightly tousled—probably from running his hand through it, a habit he apparently hasn't kicked. Under the warm lights of the restaurant, his light olive skin has a soft glow, his jawline shadowed by a hint of stubble he didn't have just a few days prior. His cheekbones covered with an array of freckles are still as defined as I remember, giving his face a certain intensity that makes it hard to look away.

As I get closer, he notices me, his deep blue eyes widening with a glimmer of recognition. Those eyes—they're the kind that always shift in color depending on the light, flickers of deep blue and gold catching in the low-lit restaurant. Tonight they have a cool hue, a mixture of surprise and curiosity that deepens when he smiles. It's a slow, lopsided grin that pulls up one side of his mouth more than the other, the kind of smile that, once upon a time, had a way of making me forget what I was about to say.

"Zoe," he says, his voice deep and even, a hint of surprise underlying the warmth. "Well, hello there again. And to think the other day was going to be the last we'd see each other."

I give him a playful smirk, crossing my arms. "The universe is funny like that. And I figured I'd come over and say hi," I say, trying to keep my tone casual. Trying to hide my thumping heartbeat wanting to rip out of my chest. Trying to not think about the kiss.

He chuckles, his eyes lighting up with amusement. He lowers his face closer to mine just a fraction, his smile widening, that dimple on his left cheek making a surprise appearance. "But seriously, it's good to see you." Clearing his throat, he continues. "Look, I'm sorry about the other night. When I kissed your cheek. That was crossing the line, so I'm sorry."

I blink a few times and try to register his words. He's sorry? He crossed a line? I rub my palms now coated with sweat on my jeans, attempting to hide whatever look I have on my face. I lick my lips and slowly nod.

"I appreciate that, thanks."

I have to change the subject. I really don't feel like talking about that right now or... ever. "So, what's new? I mean, since we last saw each other?" I can feel my subconscious rolling her eyes at me. "Besides the stubble, which I assume is the result of a new-found literary persona?" I give him a teasing once-over, pretending to examine him like he's trying to impress.

He laughs, rubbing his jaw as if realizing the stubble is, in fact, noticeable. "Oh, this? Pure laziness, I swear," he says, though I catch a hint of a self-satisfied grin. "But hey, it kind of works, right? Makes me look a little more... mysterious?"

"Oh, sure," I say, raising an eyebrow. "The mysterious brooding author. You just need a well-placed fedora and maybe a trench coat, and you're ready for the book signing."

He grimaces, pretending to be horrified. "Oh, please, no. I'm awkward enough on my own. I don't need props to make it worse."

"Wait—so this is an actual book signing?" I ask, feigning surprise but not hiding my curiosity. "James, that's huge. I thought book signings were, like, sacred rites for authors, complete with sharpies, semi-gloss photos, and maybe a fan or two who asks for a selfie."

He chuckles, looking down as if embarrassed. "Yeah, something like that. It's my first one, so I'm kind of half-excited, half-terrified. Mostly terrified, actually," he admits, rubbing the back of his head. "That's why I was here this past week, to get that all put together with my agent. But I must say, I have this recurring nightmare where no one shows up and I'm just sitting at the table alone, staring at a pile of my own books."

"Oh, stop," I say, giving his arm a playful nudge. "People are definitely going to show up. I mean, I'd show up just to hear what kind of author voice you'd use while signing my book. Do you, like, try to sound serious and brooding? Or do you say something quirky and cute?"

He snorts, rolling his eyes. "I haven't exactly practiced my 'author voice.' I think I'm just supposed to nod and look wise, maybe mumble a quote from Hemingway or something."

"'Write drunk, edit sober?'" I tease, earning a laugh from him.

"Exactly. But hey, Hemingway probably never had to worry about getting ink stains on his fingers from signing, what, fifty copies? At least, that's the number my mom promised she'd get her book club to buy."

The thought of his mom rallying her book club to support his work makes me smile. "So, you're already out here gathering groupies, huh?"

"I wouldn't say groupies," he says, looking a little embarrassed, his cheeks flushing faintly under the restaurant's dim lights. "More like... loyal supporters. The kind who will hype up their son's mediocre plot twists like they're winning Pulitzer Prizes."

I laugh, loving this glimpse into the more down-to-earth side of him. He always had a self-deprecating charm that kept him grounded, even if his writing ambitions were sky-high. I take a sip from the drink I'm still holding, savoring the warmth of the wine and the buzz of our shared laughter.

And to think I stressed myself out over meeting him at the coffee shop the other day. Yes, I feel like my feelings were valid, given our history. But maybe there was nothing to truly be afraid of? And here we are again, talking as if time hasn't passed since we dated. Thinking back, though, perhaps it was meant to work out that day. Maybe a friendship of some sorts (if you can even call it that?) is just the thing we need from now on. Rooting for one another from a distance and giving each other supportive smiles and nudges along the way. And somehow, I still feel just a smidgen of a spark. What is it?

I leave it be for now and gaze up at him, wondering out loud. "Do you remember when we used to talk about stuff like this?" I ask, leaning back on the bar and letting my gaze drift, memories flickering up like scenes from a reel. "How you'd be the next big novelist, and I'd be the supportive girlfriend, proudly sitting in the front row at all your book signings?"

He grins, looking almost boyish as he glances down, rubbing the back of his neck. A hint of blush rises to his cheeks. "Yeah, we had big dreams. We were pretty great, weren't we?"

"For a while there, totally unstoppable," I say. "But hey, who says you can't have your first signing be a huge success? I mean, imagine you're there, signing book after book, maybe even autographing a hand or two because your fans are that desperate."

"So now I'm autographing body parts?" he asks, eyebrows raised in mock alarm. "I'm not exactly rock-star material, Zo."

"Hey, give it time," I tease. "One successful signing, and you'll be swatting away adoring fans with, like, your limited-edition, leather-bound pen."

He chuckles, shaking his head. "It's always a pleasure seeing you again."

I smile softly, nodding in response. "Yeah. Yeah, you too."

As I turn to walk back to my table, I feel lighter. There's no lingering what-ifs, no bitterness—just the strange, unexpected ease of two people who once meant everything to each other, standing on different paths and being happy to be there. I glance back once, catching him waving goodbye with a smile, and I can't help but wave back.

But why do I suddenly feel the weight of an elephant on my chest? Why are butterflies floating around my stomach?

Chapter 14

When I return to the table, Tish raises her eyebrows, giving me a mischievous smile. "So? How'd it go?"

"It went surprisingly well," I say, picking up my slice of pizza, unable to hide my smile. "Just two grown-ups, reminiscing about book signings and literary dreams."

Tish laughs, clinking her glass against mine. "Well, here's to moving on—with style. I mean, look at us, we're looking better than ever!"

I smirk and nod in agreement. Our glasses clink and I feel a sense of warmth throughout my body, and not just from the wine. I settle back into my chair, wrapping my hands around the base of my wine glass as I let Tish's words hang in the air. *Moving on—with style.* A smile tugs at my lips as I glance down at the table, tracing the condensation on my glass with my thumb. There's a finality to it, the way things ended with James. I know it. But still, there's a flicker of something I can't quite name, like a soft itch under my skin that I can't ignore.

"Was it weird?" Tish asks, nudging my leg under the table. Her eyes sparkle as she leans forward, hair falling around her shoulders. "Seeing him again... *again*, I mean."

I take a slow sip, savoring the tang of wine on my tongue as I search for the right words. Was it weird? Yes. And no.

"A little of both," I admit, feeling my cheeks flush. "He apologized for the cheek kiss, and we went on to talk about the past a bit. But it didn't feel heavy. Just two people who used to know each other well, you know?"

Tish grins knowingly. "Wow, so maybe he really has changed, huh. But, come on, babe. That look on your face says it wasn't *just* nice."

I laugh, rolling my eyes. "I don't know, maybe I did feel a *tiny* spark. But it's not the same anymore. We're... He's part of a different chapter. Like I told him, we're both different people now."

"Uh-huh," she teases, dragging out the syllables as she wiggles her eyebrows.

I swat her arm, laughing. "Stop it. I'll say it again, I have to leave the past in the past." But her words linger in my mind. There was a small... something. It was, I don't know, soft and bittersweet. It was more nostalgia than anything. I think back to how easy it was to talk to him, how the years fell away as we shared memories and inside jokes. It felt almost as if time hadn't passed. Though we had already had our possible closure moment just a few days ago, it was like he was someone else, someone I was meeting for the first time.

Maybe it's me who is different. Right now I feel steady, like my feet are perhaps firmly planted, my heart safe in my own hands. I've moved on. I know I have. Yet there's that flutter, faint but insistent, as if the remnants of our old life together haven't quite settled.

I glance out the window, where the rain has slowed to a gentle drizzle, casting the street in a soft, shimmering glow. The small city lights reflect off the wet pavement, creating ripples of yellow and orange that stretch into the night. A chill runs through me as I think of what's ahead.

New York. My story. The literary magazine. It's the life I've wanted for so long, and now that it's here, it feels unreal, almost too good to be true. But maybe that's what makes it worth it.

Tish is watching me, her head tilted, waiting for me to say something. I look back at her, my thoughts heavy but my smile light.

"I mean it. The past is the past and that's exactly where James is staying," I say, pushing my glass toward her for yet another toast. "Maybe it is time to let go of the what-ifs."

She clinks her glass against mine with a triumphant grin. "To letting the asshole stay in the past, for good. And to new what-ifs, like New York!"

We sip our wine, letting the warmth spread through us as we sit cocooned in the gentle buzz of the restaurant. The noise fades, leaving only the soft hum of rain outside and the quiet space between us. I let myself imagine, just for a moment, what it will be like. My story in print. My words in a magazine, reaching people I've never met. It's exhilarating and terrifying all at once, and yet I feel ready.

Tish's voice pulls me back to the present. "Do you have a plan for New York? When do you leave?"

"Saturday morning," I say, my voice barely more than a whisper. The reality of it settles around me, heavy and thrilling. "I'm meeting with them on Monday. It's surreal, Tish."

Her eyes soften, and she reaches across the table to squeeze my hand. "I've said it probably a dozen times now, but you deserve it, Zoe."

I nod, feeling a lump form in my throat. There were so many nights I spent pouring over words, revising drafts until my fingers were numb, wondering if any of it would ever amount to anything. But here I am, on the brink of everything I've dreamed about. I glance at Tish, and I know she sees the emotion on my face, the tangled mess of pride and fear and anticipation.

"I'm proud of you," she says softly. "And I hope this is just the beginning."

"Thank you, Tish." I grip her hand, letting her warmth seep into me. "You've been here through all of it. I couldn't have done it without you."

She waves her hand as if to brush off the sentiment, but her eyes are misty. "Oh, please. I'm just here for the free book signings and the fame by association."

We both burst into laughter, and the tension eases, replaced by a lightness that feels like a breath of fresh air. As I look at her, I know that no matter where life takes me, this friendship, this grounding force, will always be here.

The server comes by to check on us, and I glance down at the nearly empty plates. The remnants of our dinner, the scattered crumbs and wine-stained napkins, are like little markers of the night—a celebration, a closure, and a beginning all rolled into one.

Tish settles the bill with a flourish, refusing to let me pay. We gather our things and step outside into the cool night air. The rain has stopped, leaving the streets quiet and glistening under the glow of the streetlamps. I pull my coat tight around me, feeling the chill seep through but somehow savoring the way it wakes me up and brings me back to the present.

She wraps her arm around my shoulders, pulling me close. "Ugh. I can't believe you leave in just a few days. Promise me you'll call every day," she says, her voice soft.

I laugh, nudging her gently. "You know I will."

As we walk in silence, I feel the weight of it all—the change, the goodbye, the unknown. It may only be for a few days, but it feels so daunting. But it's also so wonderful. It's the first step toward a life I've been chasing for so long, and I think I'm ready to take it.

Chapter 18

I settle under the covers as I lie in bed later that night, feeling scatterbrained to say the least. New York. I made a pros and cons list, and talked to my mom and Tish about it. And yet my thoughts are still so jumbled I can't think straight. My mom was right—I'm a chronic overthinker at heart.

I flip onto my back and stare at the glowing stick-on stars on my ceiling as if they were in the sky. They bring a small comfort that keeps the room from feeling so empty. But in this silence, something within me buzzes with nervous energy. My heart can't quite settle. For some reason, I am still nervous and anxious. It's only for a few days, so it's not like I'm moving there. It's simply in honor of my writing and the story that is getting published. Why am I not feeling more excited? I shouldn't keep going back and forth with this, I already said yes to Ben. It's New York City, for crying out loud. Why am I so scared?

And then it hits me. It will be my first time traveling alone. *Alone* alone.

A trip to New York by myself. Part of me feels exhilarated at the thought of stepping out on my own, of being in a city where everything seems possible. But another part of me feels raw, exposed, as if just setting foot there could strip away all my protective layers. It's as though New York itself will see through me, past the writer who can edit words with ease but can barely speak her own thoughts sometimes, past the ambitious dreamer who's still secretly terrified of failing.

The sound of purrs slowly grow louder as Ollie makes his way toward me, rubbing his head on my chin. I kiss his head as he settles next to me. Sometimes I feel like he senses my anxiety and just wants to comfort me. And for that, I am forever grateful for his round and chunky self.

I sigh and sit up, Ollie moving to the end of my bed and settling his head down as he closes his eyes for his beauty sleep. I glance at my desk and remember a work deadline is coming up just before I have to leave. It's a small project, a few short personal essays I have to edit by tomorrow evening. But since I'm wide awake by the constant thoughts of New York, I may as well finish it now.

I shuffle over to my small desk, flipping open my laptop and adjusting the lamp's dim glow. The soft hum of the computer loading is oddly comforting as I pull up the second essay. It's rough, but I like the premise, and there's potential buried under the clunky sentences and typo minefields. My fingers hover over the keyboard, and I get lost in the rhythm of the words, rewriting awkward passages, inserting comments, restructuring sentences. It's funny how diving into someone else's world, someone else's story, can ease my own anxieties.

I pause to take a sip of my now cold tea I'd forgotten on my desk hours ago, wincing at the bitterness, but I let it fuel me. I peek at the clock on the bottom of the screen: 3:47 AM. The realization makes me laugh softly to myself. Well, so much for a good night's rest.

Yet I feel lighter somehow, as if the weight of my fears has eased just a smidge. Maybe it's because I see a reflection of myself in this story—a character trying to navigate unknown territories, stumbling and doubting but moving forward anyway. And maybe that's what I have to do too. New York won't wait for me to be ready; it's there, bright and loud and unapologetic, and all I can do is show up as I am, messy nerves and all.

I save the document filled with my edits and email it to my client. The glow of my desk lamp vibrates off the walls, and I leave it on for a moment longer, just enjoying the stillness. I turn it off and settle back into bed shortly after, curling up with Ollie by my side, his warmth, a small comfort against the uncertainty that still hums beneath my skin.

As I close my eyes, sleep comes slowly. But my thoughts are gentler, like waves receding quietly at the shore. And just before I drift off, I hold onto one last thought: New York is waiting, and maybe—just maybe—I think I'm ready to meet it.

♡

The smell of fresh coffee looms in the air as I stretch my arms and shimmy out of bed. The clock on my desk reads a quarter past eight. I leave for New York in just two days.

It's really happening.

I smile at Ollie, who rolls onto his side at the end of the bed, purring against my touch as I pet his soft fur. He love bites me and I boop his nose. It's our love language; he gets it.

I slip on my cow slippers and throw on a black turtleneck, a white and black checkered sweater vest, black mom jeans, and my favorite pair of white high-top Converse. I brush out my hair and put it up halfway with a small bun and throw on my usual pearl earrings. I'm feeling more confident than normal this morning and lather on a blush lipstick. Taking a step back and looking in the mirror, I smile at myself and do a little dance.

New York is in two days!

I shove my laptop in my tote bag, grab my water bottle, and head out of my bedroom. Citrus and strawberry attack my nose as I notice a few candles lit around the living room and kitchen. The TV has one of those cozy autumnal ambiance videos playing as Tish bounces out of the bathroom.

"Oh, good morning, sleepyhead. I hope I didn't wake—" She stops mid-sentence and does a double take. Her eyes examine me up and down. She looks like she's just seen a ghost. "Well, well, well. Someone is dressed a little fancy this morning, aren't they? Where are you going? You look cute, babe!"

I smirk and fill my water bottle with water and ice from the fridge. "I decided last night I am not going to be scared of New York anymore, Tish. I am going to embrace this opportunity and run after it with open arms. I'm heading out to The Bean to do some writing last-minute freelance work. I'm feeling inspired by all of this New York talk."

Tish tilts her head and laughs. "Okay, where is my best friend Zoe and what have you done with her? I'm loving this new confidence on you, sweetie. Adds a glowy look to you."

I twist my water bottle shut and lean against the counter. "I appreciate that. I guess I'm just over my anxiety attacking my chance to be happy, you know? I want to go to New York and take it by storm! This is an opportunity of a lifetime. My mom said even if it doesn't work out, treat it as an adventure nonetheless. And that's what I plan on doing."

Tish smiles as she tosses her purse over her shoulder and grabs her thermos filled with steaming coffee. "Well, I like this confident Zoe. I hope to see a lot of her from now on. But I'm heading out to work now for some overtime. I'll be back hopefully around six and I can help you pack, sound good?"

I nod and give her a hug. "Sounds good. I'll see you later tonight." I notice the candles still burning on the countertop and living room table. "But let's do that after I blow out the candles *somebody* decided to light this morning. We don't want a fire happening while we're out, am I right?"

Tish rolls her eyes and laughs. "I don't know about you, but I mean, it's a good excuse for meeting handsome firefighters."

I can't help but laugh as I open the door and we walk out to start our days.

♡

The chilly morning air greets me, and I take a deep breath, letting it fill my lungs with a clarity that feels refreshing, like a wake-up call straight from the universe. The street is quiet at this hour, with only a few neighbors passing by on their way to work or morning routines, heads down, bundled up against the crispness of fall. The mailman jogs up and down driveways as he passes out the morning papers and mail.

The Bean isn't too far. When I enter, the rich scent of roasted coffee and baked goods wraps around me, instantly warming me up from the inside out. I make my way to the counter, order my usual, and claim my cozy table by the window. It's a cozy nook with a view of the bustling street outside, ideal for people-watching and the occasional inspiration spark.

Settling in, I pull out my laptop, set up my new notebook, and spread out my pens like an arsenal of creativity. I feel a surge of excitement. There's something thrilling about being here, ready to work, and feeling in control of my day. The barista calls my name, and I grab my latte, savoring the sweet scent of white chocolate as I take my first sip. Perfect. I set the cup down, open a fresh document, and begin typing, each tap of the keys building momentum.

The words come easily today, perhaps fueled by the knowledge that in just two days, I'll be in New York, surrounded by skyscrapers and possibilities. My mind flickers back to my conversation with Tish this morning, her amused smile at my sudden burst of confidence. I picture myself in the city, navigating the subway, strolling through Central Park, maybe even finding a quiet bookstore nook that holds a little New York magic. The thought makes me grin ear to ear.

As I settle into the flow, crafting sentences, adding notes, and losing myself in my work, I almost don't notice the time passing. It's like I've found a secret pocket of focus where everything outside my writing fades away. I only come back to reality when the café door jingles and I glance up to see an older man sitting down across from a little girl, her hair in two bouncy pigtails. She's clutching a hot chocolate with both hands, her eyes wide with excitement as she talks animatedly about something—I can only guess the latest cartoon or school story. Her enthusiasm is contagious, and I smile, thinking about how pure it is to be so effortlessly excited. Maybe I can take a cue from her.

Eventually, I stretch, saving my work with a satisfied sigh. I'm all set with my freelance work just in time before New York. The sky outside has shifted to a warmer hue, signaling that it's later than I thought. I pack up my things, feeling that productive buzz, and toss my bag over my shoulder. I might've spent all day here, but it feels like I've tackled a mountain of work—and somehow, I'm even more excited for what's ahead. For tonight, I start tackling the exciting task of packing for this weekend.

♡

The sun has dipped lower in the sky now, casting a deep warm yellow glow across the street as pinks and oranges fill the sky. I feel the excitement beginning to hum through me, a quiet buzz under my skin as I walk home. I pass the florist again, the scent of fresh blooms hanging in the air like a promise of new beginnings, and my steps quicken. There's something about this time of year, with its fleeting moments of golden light and crisp air, that always makes me feel like everything is about to change. Like the world itself is holding its breath.

When I arrive at the apartment, Tish is sprawled out on the couch, her legs thrown over the armrest, and her eyes glued to her phone screen. She looks up when I walk in, the corners of her mouth curling up in a lazy grin.

"Well, look who's back," she says, her voice playful, as she props herself up on one elbow. "Did you solve the meaning of life in that tiny coffee shop of yours?"

I roll my eyes, tossing my bag onto the counter and heading straight for the kitchen. "I solved a new short story, finished my freelance work, and made a packing list. Not quite life, but close enough."

She sits up fully now, tilting her head as she watches me. "So, what's the verdict? Are you still feeling ready for New York, or is your excitement dwindling in the 'mild panic' stage? Or are you still holding on to the new-found confidence of this morning?"

I laugh, sinking onto the couch beside her. "It's a little bit of both. But honestly, I'd say I'm definitely more excited. I feel like I have so much to do before I leave. The packing, the itinerary, making sure I don't forget anything important… like my toothbrush."

She chuckles. "It's the little things that always get you. But I'm pretty sure you're gonna be fine. You're practically *made* for New York."

I roll my eyes again, though her words make me warm. "'Made for New York?' That's a stretch. I'm just a small-town girl who drinks too many iced coffees and talks to imaginary people in her head."

She gives me an exaggerated look of disbelief. "Don't sell yourself short, babe. You got your short story in a national magazine. You've got the chops, girl."

Her confidence in me always has this magical effect, like a shot of caffeine straight to my soul. I smile at her, feeling lighter. "I appreciate you more than anything."

"Anytime." She winks, then immediately turns her attention back to her phone. "All right, enough pep talk. Now go pack so you can stop stressing about it."

I stand up, feeling more grounded than before, and head toward my room. The task ahead is daunting, but as I grab my suitcase from the top shelf of my closet and set it on my bed, I realize it's not about the clothes or the accessories—it's about what this trip represents. This is my moment. A few days in a city that holds the promise of so much more. New York is where my story will be discussed, where the next chapter of my life will begin. And no matter how much I worry, or how many things I forget to pack, that's the part that matters.

I unzip and stretch it open. I start pulling some clothes out of my dresser drawers and closet and begin folding them, crossing items off my list—comfortable shoes for all the walking I'll inevitably do, a couple of dressy outfits in case I need to look professional (but still me), and, of course, my new notebook and pens. The essentials.

Tish pops her head in the doorway, leaning against the frame. "Do you need help packing? I can be your personal stylist. Or, I don't know, throw some clothes at you?"

I chuckle, shaking my head. "I think I've got it, but thanks. You're better at the spontaneous, 'throw-it-together' look."

She grins as her eyes scan the room like she's preparing for a mission. "Fair enough. But if you need me, I'll be out in the living room, silently judging your wardrobe choices."

I roll my eyes again but feel a sense of comfort in knowing that even when the stakes are higher, even when life feels a little less predictable, Tish is still here to keep things light.

As I finish packing, the reality of the upcoming days begins to settle in. But it's not fear that fills me. It's excitement. Yeah, sure, I'm nervous—but that's just a sign that

I'm heading in the right direction.

I zip up my suitcase, take a deep breath, and smile. I've got this.

Chapter 16

It's 5:15 on Saturday morning and Tish is driving me to the airport. The world outside feels like it's barely waking up, still caught in the haze of pre-dawn. The air is cool and brisk, a welcome reminder that autumn is truly here. The sun is just beginning to creep over the horizon, casting a soft orange glow that feels like the first warm breath of the day.

Today is the day.

I'm buckled into the passenger seat of Tish's car watching the sleepy town pass by, the streetlights flickering out one by one as we head toward the airport. Tish taps her fingers on the steering wheel to a beat only she can hear, her messy blonde bun bobbing with every turn of the wheel. The car smells like the cheap lavender air freshener that she adores, and the radio hums a Gracie Abrams song quietly in the background, but it's mostly the sound of our breathing in sync with the quiet anticipation of the morning.

I glance over at her, trying to keep my nerves from getting the best of me. "I can't believe it's finally happening," I say, watching the houses blur past. "I'm really going to New York."

Tish offers a sleepy grin and grabs my hand as she turns the wheel with the other, rolling the car just as the stoplight turns yellow. "This is *your* moment, babe. New York is ready for you, and I know you're just as ready."

I squeeze her hand and smile. She's been my best friend since the seventh grade. We've practically been inseparable ever since graduating high school, going to college together, then moving into this cozy little apartment together. She's been by my side through it all and I am forever grateful for her.

I look at her through misty eyes, feeling tears well up. I can't help it. She's my rock, just as I am hers. All the support she's given me; it's been too much and yet... just enough.

She peeks at me and sighs. "Oh, sweetie. Now you're gonna make me cry and we're not even at the airport yet."

"I c-can't help it. I-I'm so grateful for you, Tish. T-thank you for being h-here for me and for being m-my best f-friend."

Tish bites her lip, inhaling and slowly exhaling as her eyes glisten. "Anything you for, Zo. You know I love you, babe." She then releases her hand from mine and puts her hands at ten and two as we swerve into the airport lane, making our way slowly toward the arrivals entrance.

The large green, blue, and white airport sign welcomes us, glowing like a beacon above the brake lights and tired goodbyes unraveling at the curb. A line of cars are stopped in front of us, most of them with their hazards on. The airport is bustling with families saying their goodbyes and friends hugging one another as they take selfies in front of the entrance.

The car pulls to a stop behind a red minivan with a pile of children exiting the vehicle, laughing and smiling, jumping up and down in excitement as they wear "Family's First Trip to Disney

World 2024" t-shirts. I smile and giggle at them.

We get out of the car and Tish pulls my luggage out from the backseat, wheeling it toward me. I nuzzle my coat closer and adjust my pink beanie. I can feel my nose going numb as the cool air whips against my face. I grab my luggage and walk toward the entrance, and Tish follows.

Tish smiles at me and falters for a second, and I can see the tiniest flicker of concern in her eyes. She reaches out, pulling me into a hug that's warm and solid like she's anchoring me in the moment.

"I've said this a billion times now, but I am so proud of you, Zoe. You've got this. Just promise me you'll text me every day, 'kay? Or even just send a 'Hey, I'm alive' text. I'll take whatever I can get."

I squeeze her back, a lump forming in my throat. "I promise. I'll text you every day. Even if it's just to tell you how many coffees I've had that day."

She laughs, pulling away. "Perfect. I'll be counting the lattes. Love you!"

I kiss her cheek and walk closer to the entrance as the doors open automatically. "I love you too! See you soon."

She waves, her goofy grin still on her face, and I watch as she fades into the distance, the streetlights turning everything golden behind her.

♡

The airport is a world unto itself, its early morning stillness broken only by the constant shuffle of footsteps and the soft murmur of conversations. The fluorescent lights above hum steady and sterile, giving everything a glow that feels both comforting and impersonal. The space feels vast, stretching out in every direction, the walls lined with bright signs that point toward gates, baggage claim, and security. I tug the strap of my bag higher on my shoulder and follow the signs toward security, trying not to feel like I'm on autopilot.

I pass a few scattered travelers who look just as bleary-eyed as I feel—some clutching cups of coffee as they shuffle toward their gates, others scrolling through their phones with a detached focus. A family rushes by, their kids bouncing on the balls of their feet, excitement and energy crackling in the air around them. I can't help but smile, feeling just a little bit of their energy rub off on me. But then the line for security appears ahead, and the warmth of the moment dissipates.

My least favorite part of traveling.

That's when I feel a buzz in my pocket. I pull out my phone and there's a text from an unknown sender. Oh no, here we go again. This better not be one of James's friends trying to pull something on me. I don't have it in me right now.

I open the message and it's from Ben. *Good morning, Zoe. It's Ben. Apologies if I'm overstepping with a text, but I wanted to wish you safe travels to NY. :)*

He texted me at the crack of dawn just to tell me safe travels. I can't help but grin. It's just a text, we all send them. *Don't overcomplicate it, Zoe.* Still, the thoughtfulness settles me in a way I didn't expect.

My fingers immediately race across the screen. *Thanks, Ben. That's really thoughtful. Ngl, I'm still a ball of nerves!*

The text bubbles appear instantly, like our own little code. Just us. I feel my chest warm at the thought knowing he's a text away, aiding in calming my nerves. It's strange how quickly he's managed to make me feel less alone in this whole whirlwind.

His text pings through. *Totally normal, Zoe. I have no doubt in my mind you'll be great. And if not... well, you can put the blame on me.*

I let out a small laugh. The security line keeps calling for me, and here I am texting my editor. I send back a quick text. *Haha, I appreciate that. I'm at the airport now. See you soon! :)*

I tuck my phone back into my pocket, smiling despite the nerves twisting in my stomach. Just knowing he's there, checking in, makes New York feel a little less overwhelming. I take a deep breath, letting it out slowly, and make my way toward security.

I'm in line behind a couple who are arguing about whether they need to take off their shoes. It's an oddly mundane argument, and one that makes me wish I could just skip ahead and avoid the whole process altogether. The line is moving at a snail's pace, but I find my mind drifting back to Tish's pep talk, to the thought of New York, and to everything that's waiting for me there. *Focus on the next step,* I remind myself, forcing my attention to settle back in the present.

When it's finally my turn, I take a deep breath and move forward. The security officer gives me the usual instructions—shoes off, bag in the bin, arms raised for the scanner. I quickly slip off my shoes, tuck my phone and wallet in the plastic tray, and shuffle through the scanner, trying not to think too hard about how many strangers have probably walked through this same checkpoint before me. A small wave of discomfort passes over me as I stand there waiting for the green light, but it's soon gone, replaced by the rhythmic beep of the scanner and the small nod from the officer that signals I'm good to go.

On the other side, I grab my things with a sense of relief, pulling my shoes back on and stuffing my phone into my bag. There's a small amount of chaos as people rush to put their things back together, but it's a chaos that feels safe and predictable, almost comforting. The overhead announcements blur together, but I don't pay attention, instead keeping my eyes on the gate sign that's directing me toward my next step.

As I make my way through the terminal, I pass rows of shops, restaurants, and cafés, their windows glowing with advertisements for the things I'll never need, like an $8 bottled water. I catch the faint hint of vanilla perfume from a passing traveler, the soft sound of a child giggling as they chase after their parent, and the murmur of a couple deep in conversation. Everything feels like a dance of moments, little snippets of lives clashing in this shared space.

I walk with my head slightly down, focusing on my steps and avoiding eye contact. Not because I'm nervous, but because I don't want to be pulled out of my own head. I find my gate easily enough, the blue signs above pointing the way. There's a small crowd already gathered there—some reading, others scrolling through their phones, even one woman half-heartedly knitting a purple scarf.

I find an empty row of seats and claim a spot by the wall of windows, watching as planes taxi down the runway, their engines roaring with the kind of power that always seems to make my heart race just a little bit faster. I settle in and pull my coat off, placing it over my chair. I whip out my phone and check the time again. An hour. Just an hour before I'll be boarding the plane that will take me to the city of my dreams.

My stomach rumbles. Tish and I left in a hurry this morning. We overslept just a little and didn't have time to eat. I eye the stores and restaurants around me and spot a Dunkin' Donuts (or, as I call it, *Dunkie*) near my gate. The bright orange and pink sign gleams in the corner of my vision like a beacon of comfort. The thought of iced coffee pulls me toward it, my body moving before I even consciously decide to go. I wind through the crowd, the bustle of the terminal starting to fade as I get closer to the line, and the smell of freshly brewed coffee and sugar-heavy pastries fills the air.

I notice the long line darting out in front of the counter and roll my eyes. Just what I need this early in the morning. But within seconds I get an overwhelming sense of familiarity surrounding me. And that's when I see him, in all places, in this very fucking airport.

James.

Chapter 17

It's as if time stands still as my eyes land on him. His brown curls are suffocating under his black beanie. He's wearing a dark green sweater and a gray puff vest as jeans hug his muscular legs. He glances up at the menu and tilts his head around the guy in front of him, anxiety running through his veins as he waits to get coffee.

My stomach drops, but I can't tear my eyes away. He doesn't seem to notice me yet, his focus on the menu yet again, squinting like he's trying to decide whether he wants a donut too. It's surreal, the way he fits in this moment, as if he's always been a part of the background noise of my life. And here he is again, unannounced, like an unwelcome guest at my own party.

A party I desperately want to leave.

He then looks around the airport and his piercing blue eyes catch mine. I can't help but feel my knees shake and my hands ooze with sweat.

I wipe them on my jeans and walk toward him. Now is not the time to feel nervous. *You've been nervous all week and now it's time to slap it away. You were fine at the pizza shop, and were capable of making small talk with him. Now it's time to be fierce, to be that confident Zoe you were yesterday.*

A smile forms at his lips. My heart flutters a beat and I yell at it to knock it off.

"Zoe?" He looks back at the line in front of him and exhales with a sigh, making his way out of it and toward me. "Hey, fancy seeing you here."

I force a smile and shrug. "James, hi. Yeah, what are the odds? Why are you at the airport this time of day?"

He smirks. "I can ask the same thing about you. Remember the book signing I mentioned the other day? Well, it's in New York at a Barnes and Noble. The biggest one, apparently."

I nod and bite my lip. "Wow, Barnes and Noble. It's every booktoker's literary dream and then some. But really, good for you."

He bites his bottom lip, and my nostrils flare a little, trying not to absorb all his attractiveness at once and melt into a Zoe puddle in the middle of the airport. I mentally shake myself out of it. His voice creeps through my thoughts.

"So now we've cleared my agenda, what brings *you* here?"

I feel my cheeks warm, and I shrug. "Oh, I'm actually on the way to New York as well. I have that interview with *Poets & Writers* on Monday." I mentally slap myself.

He smiles and nods, absorbing what I just said. "That's right. Good for you. I'm happy for you, Zo."

I shuffle in place and adjust my beanie. "Thanks. I gotta admit, it's a big step for me. Traveling to New York alone, a big new city to explore all by myself. It feels scary, but I know I'm ready, you know?"

James smirks, pulling out his phone, probably checking the

time. "You've always been ready for New York, Zoe. It's always called for you and here you are..." His voice trails and he glances back at the Dunkin' line. "But how 'bout we head back in line and I'll buy you a coffee. Call it an IOU for all the weirdness the universe keeps shoving in our way."

I'm not used to this generous side of James. He used to be a bit selfish, like it was always him first and never *us* first. This feels unfamiliar. Maybe I need to accept it. Perhaps James is changing. Perhaps this is a new James that I need to get used to. The universe has been putting us together at random occurrences, but it almost feels intentional. And maybe that isn't a bad thing.

Smiling, I nod and walk with him, making it just in time as the line cleared. Standing in front of the counter, James orders a large hot French vanilla with extra vanilla and whipped cream, and I order my usual. I remember him having a huge sweet tooth back in the day. I thought it was adorable. Maybe it still is.

As I stand beside James in line, I can't help but notice how much he's changed. The old James—the one who would steal the last bite of pizza without a second thought or get lost in his own ego—feels like a distant memory. This James, the one offering to buy me coffee with no strings attached, is someone I'm not sure I recognize. Yet there's something about him that feels familiar and safe, like slipping into an old sweater that still fits just right.

"So," I say, trying to hide the fact that my heart has started doing little somersaults in my chest. "French vanilla? Extra vanilla and whipped cream, really?"

He grins, a playful twinkle in his eye. "You remember that, huh? It's still my go-to. I mean, what can I say? I like my coffee sweet, just like my personality." He winks, clearly enjoying himself.

I roll my eyes, though I can't suppress the smile tugging at my lips. "Yeah, you were always the sugar-and-spice type," I tease, leaning casually against the counter. "You know, it's a little ridiculous how much of your order I remember. Are you sure I didn't spend years of my life cataloging every little detail about you?" I raise an eyebrow, pretending to be shocked.

"Hey, I'm unforgettable," he says with a mock-serious tone, holding up his hand as if it's a matter of fact. "I'm like the perfect iced coffee: smooth, complex, and a little addictive."

I snort, trying to mask my amusement with a cough. "Yeah, sure, James. We'll go with that."

The barista calls his name, and as we grab our drinks I feel the awkward tension of old habits creeping in. *What is this?* I wonder. *Is this us? Is this the new normal for us now?*

We walk back toward the seating area, my mind still running through the bizarre coincidence of everything. Here we are, two exes, two people who had drifted apart like leaves on a windy day, yet somehow brought back together by fate... or maybe it's just the fact that New York has a way of making everything feel interconnected in some magical way, and yet everyone is so different.

I keep glancing at James as we walk, feeling his presence beside me like a magnetic pull. He's still *him*, but... softer, somehow. Different in ways that are impossible to ignore. I notice the way he pauses every so often, like he's double-checking if I'm still with him, making sure I'm comfortable. *He's supposed to be the jerk who ripped your heart out and crumbled it into pieces. Now is not the time to fall back in love with him.*

Ew.

We reach the seating area by the gate, and I notice him walking toward a seat across from me, his bag plopping next to him like he's settling in for the long haul. My pulse picks up. *Wait, hold up. Does that mean...*

"No way," I murmur to myself.

James sits down, flashing me a grin over his coffee cup. "What? You thought we were just gonna part ways after this?"

I blink at him, my heart leaping into my throat. "Are we... on the same flight?" I ask, half-laughing, half-shocked.

He raises an eyebrow, clearly amused by my disbelief. "I mean, it looks like it, doesn't it?"

I sit down across from him, my mind racing a little. How is this even happening? I thought I'd escaped the possibility of *any* interaction with James once I boarded my flight. Once we had our talk at the café last week. And then we met again at the pizza shop earlier this week. And yet, here we are, once again thrown together by some bizarre twist of fate.

"Well," he says after a beat, stirring his coffee with a little too much concentration, "I guess this is one of those things we just have to accept, huh?"

I glance down at my iced coffee, then back at him. His eyes are flickering with something I can't quite place. Maybe it's the nerves about the trip. Maybe it's the strange comfort of seeing a familiar face, even if that face was once a source of pain. I take a deep breath and shrug.

"Yeah, I suppose so. The universe is being a little, I don't know, ridiculous right now."

He laughs, and the sound is warm, soothing. "It's definitely not boring, that's for sure."

We fall into a comfortable silence, and I find myself stealing glances at him—those longing blue eyes, the dark curls peeking out from under his beanie, the way he seems to have grown more relaxed over time. And suddenly, I feel the pull of something—something deep in my chest I can't quite shake.

"You know," James says, breaking the silence, his tone suddenly quieter, "I'm glad we're both doing this. Going after what we want. New York. *Poets & Writers*. Book signings. I mean, it kinda feels… right, doesn't it?"

I smile, that same warm feeling from earlier making a return. "We might have different meanings of 'feels right,' but I guess it does."

I let myself sink into the quiet of the airport, the low hum of people rushing by, the soft tap of his coffee cup against the table next to him. In a weird way it feels oddly peaceful, the two of us sharing this space in this strange, serendipitous moment.

And as much as I want to pretend that everything between us is still buried deep in the past, the truth is, I can't help but wonder. *What if this is how things were always meant to be?*

The woman behind the podium at the gate entrance calls everyone to start getting in line. The plane starts to board in groups, and I feel my pulse quicken, not because of the flight, but because of the realization that James and I are now officially on this plane *together*.

As we inch closer to the gate, my thoughts race. I try to mentally prepare myself, reminding myself this is just a flight—three hours, max—and it doesn't have to be weird. Except that it's James. And for reasons I can't quite articulate, this feels like a much bigger deal than just the flight itself.

I can't help but feel my hands oozing sweat and that damn lump forming in my throat again. I can do this. It's going to be fine. I gather my belongings and stand up just as James stands. I look at his face and it's like I've just stepped onto some rom-com set. Of course he looks effortlessly perfect in an airport, his brown curls poking out, making him look like he's just come out of a model brochure for "Winter Chic." It's annoying how easy it is for him to make anything look this good.

A smile tugs at his lips. "Well, ready or not?"

I suddenly feel a bit dizzy thinking about the next few hours, and my heart knocks at my chest a million miles a minute. It feels as if my legs don't want to function properly. I close my eyes for a second, feeling myself swaying back and forth. I take a moment to inhale a deep breath and hopefully exhale all my anxieties. I don't need this to be the part where I faint in front of my ex and cause a scene in the airport.

He tilts his head down in front me, nearly catching me off guard as I wobble in place. His muscular hand holds my back, balancing me. My heart does a somersault in my chest, and it needs to knock it off.

He takes a step closer, his breath warm against my neck, his voice lower now, teasing. "If I didn't know better, I'd think you were having a mild panic attack right now."

I half laugh, half groan. "I'm fine. Just trying to enjoy the 'magic' of flying."

James smirks, clearly amused by my inability to keep it cool. "Sure, Zo. Enjoy the magic. Meanwhile, I'll just be over here… floating like a pro."

We approach the boarding gate, my mind still running through the hundred different ways this flight could go. As our group is called, we shuffle up to the podium, hands gripping our boarding passes like they're passports to a new life. I look at James, who is scanning his own ticket with no sign of the nerves I'm feeling.

"Here we go," I mutter under my breath.

"Here we go," James agrees, his tone low but steady.

I step through the agent's line, scanning my boarding pass, but then I stop. For a brief second, I almost forget to breathe. I'm just standing there, waiting to board the plane with James. I'm not used to this. But as we walk down the jet bridge, my heart starts to race in a way that has nothing to do with flight safety. It's because of him. Again.

Focus, I tell myself. *Focus on anything but the fact that you're with your ex on the same flight.*

Once inside the plane, the aisles are crowded and I suddenly lose James. I can feel the heat of the crowded space, the sounds of passengers shuffling to their seats, luggage being stowed overhead, and the occasional burst of laughter or muttered complaints. I look around, trying to spot my seat number on the overhead bin. When I finally do, I stop dead in my tracks.

Because there, sitting in the aisle seat of my row, is James. He's already buckled in, his headphones hanging loosely around his neck. He looks up as I approach, a small grin spreading across his face. The moment our eyes meet, my stomach does that little flip it always does when I see him.

"Wait," I say, blinking. "This is our row?"

He looks back at me, trying to hide the amusement in his expression. "What, you thought we wouldn't end up next to each other? I thought it was pretty obvious from the universe's track record, Zo."

I'm still processing the realization that we're not just on the same flight—we're sharing a seat row. Just the two of us. Of course, this would happen. Because why wouldn't it? James and I are so good at "coincidences."

I shake my head in mock disbelief. "Well, this is unexpected."

James's blue eyes sparkle as he pulls his headphones off, tucking them in his bag. "That's one way to put it. You know, I'm starting to believe in destiny with all these run-ins we keep having."

"Destiny?" I say with a laugh. "Are we sure we're not

just a prank show?"

He leans back in his seat with an exaggerated sigh. "No prank show would be this elaborate. We're not that lucky." His grin widens, making my pulse skip.

And without skipping a beat, he stands and lifts my luggage above our seats. His sweater tugs up slightly above his jeans, showing just enough skin to make my cheeks flush. His tanned skin pokes out from under his shirt and I want to graze my fingers over his stomach. His jeans loosely fit around his waist as his powerful muscular body moves with easy grace as he pushes my luggage into the cubby. Dammit, Zoe, get a *grip*.

I sit down in my window seat, buckling my seatbelt, still in shock that this is my reality right now. *Okay, just breathe.* It's not like this is a date or anything, just two former lovers awkwardly sitting next to each other on a plane. Just two people trying to make their way to New York for two very different reasons, trying to pretend like nothing happened between them. I can do this. I'm fine. I hope.

Before I can lose myself to my thoughts, I pull out my phone and quickly text Tish.

Boarding the plane now! Can't believe this is happening. Wish me luck! I'll text you when I land! Love you!

A text instantly buzzes back. *You got this babe!! Be safe! Lots of love!!!*

I pause for a moment, almost second-guessing my choice of words. I don't know if I'm ready to fill her in on this particular detail just yet. The whole thing is just so... bizarre. But I hit send, mentally bracing myself for whatever bombshell I'll have to drop next.

I put my phone on airplane mode and turn to James, who's looking at me with a sly grin.

"So, are we gonna talk about how we keep running into each other, or is this just gonna be one of those 'sudden-death' situations?" he asks, clearly amused by the awkwardness in the air.

I roll my eyes, feeling my cheeks flush. "What is this, a rom-com? I'm not ready for the montage of 'We Keep Running Into Each Other' music to play right now."

James laughs out loud, and I can't help but smile at how easy it is to slip back into the rhythm of teasing him. Maybe it's not so bad that we're sitting next to each other after all.

"All right. Well," James begins, looking out the window as the plane begins to taxi down the runway. "Tell me about this interview you're going to. It sounds like a pretty big deal."

My nostrils flare. I'm suddenly feeling self-conscious again. "Yeah, it is. I'm getting a feature published on my short story." I try to keep the excitement from my voice, but I can't help the way it bubbles up. "New York is huge. I've never been there alone before."

James nods, a small smile tugging at the corners of his lips. "I get it. But you're gonna nail it, Zo. You've always had that in you, even when you didn't think you did. And you're not in this alone."

I glance up at him, those blue eyes staring into my soul. "What do you mean?"

He smirks and leans back in his seat. "I mean that I'll be there too. Sure, we're going to be in New York for different things, but that doesn't mean I won't be supporting you from afar. And who knows, even though New York is a big city, that doesn't mean we won't run into one another, even if you are there for just a few days.”

I feel my heart flutter, the sincerity in his voice catching me off guard. “That’s very nice of you to say, James. Thank you.”

He shrugs, his gaze flickering between the window and me. “Just speaking the truth.” His eyes dart at the ceiling and then the floor, and now back at me. His face fully devours me as if he’s reading a story. James is just so... magnetic. It’s like he’s some kind of literary heartthrob straight out of a rom-com. That forest-green sweater fits him just right, hugging his shoulders and chest in a way that’s almost distracting. And don’t even get me started on those piercing blue eyes that seem to miss nothing. They’re the kind of eyes that have always seen right through me.

He clears his throat and takes out his phone. “And if you want... we can exchange numbers. If you’re feeling anxious, call me. Or text, whatever feels comfortable to you. Call this straightforward, but I mean it, if you ever feel lost or lonely, or whatever it may be, you can reach out to me, Zo. You can, I don’t know, treat me as a safety contact, emergency contact, whatever you wanna call it.”

He pauses, biting his bottom lip, his eyes appearing ever so serious. “I promise that no matter where I am or what I am doing, I’ll answer you. You can rely on me, Zo.”

I pause for a moment, trying to swallow the wave of warmth that rushes through me at his words. I grab his phone and input my number, naming my contact Zo, and I hand it back to him.

A smile creeps up his lips and his blue eyes crinkle at the sides, twinkling the slightest specks of gold.

“There. I labeled myself as ‘Zo,’ so you’ll know immediately who it is. But James, thank you...” My voice trails as I let my eyes stare into his. “I appreciate the gesture. And who knows. Maybe you'll be the one I'll reach out to find the best bagels at midnight."

He chuckles, leaning back in his seat with an exaggerated sigh, clearly enjoying himself. "You already know I'm all about bagels. If you text me at midnight looking for a bagel shop, not only will I answer, I might just join you."

I smirk and nod in agreement. Then realize he has his book signing. "But won't you be busy with that book signing of yours? I wouldn't want to take your time away from all that…"

"I mean, yeah, I'll have that going on," he says with a shrug, and there's that familiar ease in his voice. It's funny how we used to talk about our futures, him with his books and me… well, I wasn't sure what my path would be then. Yet here we are.

"I'll have some free time between events. And if you're around, maybe I could take you to lunch or show you a couple of spots," he adds, his eyes gleaming with that playful spark I know so well.

The flight attendants start making their rounds, reminding everyone to buckle up, and I glance out the window, trying to focus on anything other than whatever feeling this is rumbling inside me. And for a second, everything outside the window blurs into one surreal scene. We're really doing this—heading to New York, our worlds crashing together all over again in a way I never would have expected.

My heart stumbles at his words. He makes it all sound so easy—getting lunch and exploring the city together. First he asked to meet up for coffee, and now he's already requesting meeting up a second time. Offering himself as my own personal tour guide. And it somehow feels like he's trying to make up for the past. I can't help but feel a blush rising to my cheeks.

"Is that so?" I reply, and I barely manage to keep my voice steady. The idea of him showing me around—a city so vibrant, intimidating, and full of life—has my heart skipping for reasons I'd rather not admit. "I think I'd manage," I say, pretending not to notice his gaze on me. But then, feeling a rare bout of bravery, I add, "Maybe I'd let you show me a thing or two."

He leans back in his seat, looking pleased, his fingers tapping a quiet rhythm on the armrest between us. "There she is. That's all I'm asking, Zo."

Just as the plane gathers speed down the runway, our hands brush when we both reach for the armrest at the same time. The touch sends a spark up my arm, a jolt I'm not quite ready for, and I pull my hand back, laughing awkwardly as if that could somehow dilute the tension. He chuckles too, and for a moment, we just look at each other, sharing an unspoken understanding of all the things left unsaid between us—our shared memories, the way we can still read each other in these small, silent moments.

I tear my gaze away, trying to focus on the clouds outside the window. But it's no use; my thoughts have already wandered to him. To us.

Because what is this feeling? This weird, slightly wonderful, maddening sense that I'm back at square one, just as infatuated and curious and eager to know what he's thinking. To know why his words carry this double-edged gentleness, like he's remembering us the way I am—how we used to be inseparable, how he made me laugh until I was breathless, how he knew just how to bring out the best in me in ways that felt like fate. And now he's here, on this very plane, offering to show me around New York, to be there for me, in a way that's so…James. And yet, my mind wanders to the old him.

I remember the countless nights I stayed up waiting, convincing myself he'd be home soon, only for him to come through the door hours late with flimsy excuses and that same damn charming smile. The nights I'd bend and stretch, making myself smaller just to accommodate him—his career, his whims, his time, his everything. It was always James first, his schedule, his needs. If there was ever a conflict, I was the one who had to make room.

And then, of course, there was the night I found out—the quiet confession, the "slip-up" that broke every unspoken promise. The other girl that stole his heart. The stupid Jessica Simpson look-a-like. Suddenly, every late night and half-truth flooded back with a new, bitter clarity. I'd put so much of myself into supporting him, into believing in him, that I'd left none for myself.

He's talking to me now about safety contacts, showing me his sweeter side, and it's… confusing. There's part of me that wants to roll my eyes, to dismiss all of this as another performance. After all, James has always been good at putting on a show.

I glance sideways at him, at the way he's casually resting against the seat, and he catches my gaze with a small smile, his eyes warm and attentive. A tiny flutter rises in my stomach, but this time it's mixed with the bitterness of all those memories, the undeniable ache that never fully faded.

He seems quieter now, even more grounded than the James I used to know. But I can't just ignore the parts of him that once left me shattered.

Maybe he's changed, but can I trust that?

With a sigh, I close my eyes for a moment and take a deep

breath. I rub my palms against my jeans and roll them into small fists, exhaling slowly and opening my eyes once more. I notice he's watching me, an almost tender expression on his face, like he's as deep in thought as I am, caught up in this messy, tangled web of what we were and whatever it is we might be now. And before I can catch myself, I'm smiling too, a small, reluctant smile that says more than words ever could.

There's something about the way his blue eyes soften, just for me, as he quietly observes. And now, watching him looking so effortlessly handsome, I remember every single reason why I once thought he was everything I wanted. His curls are a little longer than I remember, sneaking out from under his beanie, giving him that bookish look that makes him look like he's walked right out of a paperback romance. Those splattered freckles painted on his warm skin. And those eyes... they're exactly the same. They miss nothing, not even the quick flicker of nervousness that crosses my face.

He clears his throat, licking his lips and biting the corner, his gaze earnest as he looks me in the eye. "I don't mean to be a broken record or anything, but I mean it, Zo. If you feel lost or lonely or whatever... reach out. No matter where I am or what I'm doing, I'll answer you. Promise."

For a second, I just stare, feeling a warmth rush through me that's hard to ignore. He doesn't have to say these things, doesn't have to offer himself like this. But he does. And I can feel it—perhaps he means it. This is the James I fell for. The one who looked out for me when I was too stubborn to admit I needed help, who saw the best in me even when I couldn't. And he's here now, offering me that same safety net.

I swallow, nodding. "All right," I say softly, meeting his gaze, letting the words settle between us like an unspoken vow.

He smiles and takes off his beanie, lowering it over his eyes, and closes them. I take it as a cue he's going to nap during this flight, and I don't blame him. The hum of the plane surrounds us, and the world outside is only clouds and sky. I also take off my beanie and set it on my lap, brushing through my hair, hoping it isn't a mess.

I notice in my peripheral vision that James is looking at me. I can't help but feel warmth devouring my cheeks and entire face. He makes me nervous and, at the same time, at ease. With James beside me, I feel like I've stumbled into something uncharted, something thrilling and comforting all at once. It's weird, this feeling. It's the kind of place I thought I'd left behind but can't seem to escape.

Chapter 19

The plane continues its steady course weaving through the endless blue sky as we glide through the cotton balls of clouds, with the gold sun glimmering in the distance. I shift my vision to the window and suddenly feel my brain cluttering with thoughts. I'm literally on a plane on the way to New York with my ex-boyfriend sitting next to me.

It still feels surreal. I glance over at him. He's already fast asleep, his head leaning against the seat, his mouth slightly open, his breathing soft and steady. He is still very attractive, I can admit, but this can't be real. First the text, then the laundromat, the pizza shop, and now... this. It's as if he's stalking me, literally.

But then again, it felt like James truly meant what he was saying. He was, *is*, supportive of my ambitions and accomplishments. He's being sweet and nice, like paying for my iced coffee. He even let me have the window seat. It's like he hasn't forgotten about me... about us... about the little things. He confessed that he hasn't stopped thinking about me. But should I take it as a good thing?

I still wonder if he's truly changed. It just feels too... weird? For a lack of a better word. Maybe I'm just not used to seeing this side of him. We did have a nice conversation at the café, and I honestly feel like things got settled. And then the universe decided that wasn't enough and just kept pushing him my way.

I'll admit there is a part of this that feels comforting. Maybe it's because of our history? He's not a stranger per se, but part of me still feels like something is missing. I just can't figure out what.

It's silly, really. I'm not on the way to New York to try to solve this puzzle. I'm on a plane to New York—my dream come true—for an interview on my published short story, a chance to step into the literary world I've always admired, a world where I know I belong. I need to focus on that and not on James.

But I can't help my eyes wandering to him. A few brown curls hang just over his face but don't cover it completely. His long eyelashes drape down as his mouth twitches, probably from dreaming. His chest rises and falls in a slow, steady rhythm, his breathing soft. He's so calm, so peaceful. There's just something about the way he looks in this moment—his slightly crooked nose, the shadow of stubble along his jawline, the little crease between his brows as he dreams or simply drifts through a restful sleep—that makes something inside me stir. Why does he have to be cute? Why am I even thinking about him like this?

I shouldn't be. He's not the same person I fell in love with, and even if he's changed, it's not my responsibility to figure out if he's worth it. But the longer I sit next to him, the more I can't help but feel like he's... different. The way he talked at the café, his apology, the way he *listened* to me, really listened, for the first time in forever. It wasn't just a quick exchange of words. It was meaningful, like he actually wanted to know what was going on in my life, what had changed, what hadn't. He genuinely seemed interested in my work, and he is still showing interest.

And even now I catch myself remembering how kind he was, how sweet it was when he offered to show me around New York, how he insisted on paying for my coffee just because he remembered I like it iced with extra whipped cream.

I mean, we did exchange numbers just in case, which, I had to admit, was really nice of him. I unlock my phone and immediately open his contact. I kept his contact name as "James" to keep it simple. A smile creeps to my lips. I can't help it. I appreciate his gesture; it gives me a feeling of security.

The clock on my phone reads 8:45, which means we have about forty-five minutes left on the flight. And it feels like it's dragging as James is asleep next to me. I then remember he purchased a wi-fi plan for the duration of the flight, and I immediately open my laptop and connect to it. While he's fast asleep, I guess I could start one a new freelance gig in the meantime. Maybe it'll help with making time move faster.

And before I know it, my fingers race across my keyboard as I begin to write and edit a few pieces.

♡

In the middle of a paragraph, I feel it. That soft, almost imperceptible shift in the air between us. James stirs, his body stretching a little, his arm brushing mine. I freeze, an electric jolt running through me at the contact. It's such a small thing, but my skin reacts as if it's something much bigger, much more significant. My heart speeds up for no reason at all, and for a second, I almost forget where I am. Forget everything.

After all this time, my heart still sputters from his touch. Why?

We've been apart for so long. It shouldn't be this easy for him to make my pulse race, to make me forget everything else.

Before I can lose myself in this thought again, I hear his voice, soft but clear. "Hey," he says, and I jump, startled out of my inner turmoil.

I turn to him, finding him blinking at me with that sleepy, half-amused expression I remember all too well.

"What's up?" His voice is still thick with sleep, but there's a warmth in it, an undercurrent of familiarity that makes my stomach flip.

"Nothing. Just, uh… working." I glance at my laptop, feeling embarrassed that he caught me staring into space.

"Mm-hmm." He's grinning now, fully awake, his eyes more focused. "You know, you're really good at pretending like I'm not here."

I laugh, a little louder than I meant to. "I'm not pretending! I'm just… really good at zoning out. And you were sleeping anyway, so whatever."

He chuckles, stretching his legs out in front of him. The movement is so casual, so easy, like this is completely normal. But it isn't normal, is it? This is weird. I mean, we're exes. On a plane. To New York. *Together.*

My overthinking is getting the better of me… yet again.

"Fair enough," he says, smiling. There's a twinkle in his eye—something playful, something *familiar* that I can't quite ignore. "But if you keep ignoring me like this, I'm going to get suspicious. What's really going on in that head of yours?"

I try to suppress a smile. "Oh, nothing. Just wondering how you managed to fall asleep so quickly. I wish I had that ability."

He raises an eyebrow, his gaze shifting to the window. "Hmm, oh-kay. Well, I was kind of hoping you'd be able to distract me with your continuous typing, but clearly that's not happening." He's teasing me, and I can't help but laugh.

I look away, suddenly feeling shy. "It's just work. Nothing exciting."

He leans back in his seat, his expression softening. "I'm just glad you're doing what you love. You've always had that spark, Zo. I missed that."

His words catch me off guard, and for a brief moment, my chest tightens. There's something about the way he says it, so genuine, so *real*, that I feel our old connection flicker to life. I swallow, trying to keep my composure. "Mm, thanks."

He nods and continues to stare at me. "So besides the curiosity of my ability to sleep ever so quickly, what is *really* going on in that head of yours?" He pokes my temple with his warm fingers.

I save my work and close my laptop. I know he senses my uncertainty about him. He's always been good at these kinds of things. Sensing things, I mean. I inhale and exhale a deep breath, then position myself toward him and look into his gold-flaked blue eyes.

"Fine," I start, my voice coming out a little more hesitant than I intended. "Why are you being so nice to me, James? You've been, like, ridiculously sweet since we met up again. I don't... I don't get it. After everything...."

He tilts his head slightly, his eyes narrowing in thought. The way he looks at me, with genuine curiosity, makes me question my own uncertainty. He doesn't seem defensive, doesn't flinch at the question. Instead, he's just listening, waiting for me to continue.

"Like, I appreciate it. I do. But it's... *weird.* I never expected this... version of you. After everything that happened." I glance at him quickly, then look back at my hands in my lap. "I mean, we didn't exactly leave on the best of terms back then, right? And now, here you are, acting like nothing ever happened."

James takes a moment before responding, his eyes softening. He shifts in his seat, folding his arms over his chest. "Look, Zo, I'm not doing this because I expect anything in return, I swear. I just... I wanted to show you that I'm not that person anymore. I've made mistakes. I can't take them back, and I wouldn't expect you to forgive me for everything overnight. But I want you to see that I'm trying. I've been trying for a while now." He pauses, pressing his lips together in a thin line as if hesitating. Then he looks directly in my eyes. He's always been good at eye contact, unlike me. "The apology the other day, I truly meant it. They're just words, sure." He places his hand over his heart, "I'm sorry for what I did to you. I don't want to ever make you feel that way again."

His voice is steady, but there's a vulnerability to it that catches me off guard. James has always had that knack for saying the right thing, for being able to make you feel like the most important person in the room. It's one of the reasons I fell for him so hard. But now? Now I'm just not sure if he's still the same person underneath all the right words.

"I don't know," I say softly, still feeling the weight of my doubts. "It's just hard for me to believe in all of this, you know? It's not just the past with us, James. It's... everything. How do I know this is real? How do I know you're not just... playing a part?"

He looks down for a second, nodding as though he's processing. There's a slight frown on his face. He seems to genuinely understand my skepticism. When he looks back up at me, his expression is open, no longer guarded.

"You're right," he says, his tone more serious now. "I can't expect you to just trust me again. Not after what I did. But I'm not pretending, Zoe. This is who I am now. And I guess that's the hard part for me, too. I have to *show* you I'm different, that I've learned, that I've changed. I'm not the same selfish, angry person I used to be. But I can't do that if you're not willing to see it."

I feel his words sink in, and I realize how much this might really matter to him. He's not just apologizing for the past. He's not asking for anything, either—he's just showing up. Trying to prove something, even when the odds are against him.

But my heart, my mind, are still hesitant. "But how do I know? I'm still not sure, James. You've always been good with words, always good at making everything sound perfect, like you *mean* it. And maybe you do mean it, but how can I know for sure that this isn't just... a moment? A brief feeling? I need more than that."

He leans forward slightly, his gaze intensifying. And all of a sudden, my hands are wrapped in his. His warmth sizzles around them and I feel myself softly gasp at his sudden movement. "I get it. And honestly? I don't have an easy answer for you. I'm not asking for your trust just because I said some nice things or because I'm being all sweet or whatever. That's not what matters. What matters is the *action* behind it, the way I show up every day, even when it's hard. And I'm okay with that. I'm okay with waiting for you to see that I'm different, to see that I'm not that guy anymore."

There's a sincerity in his voice that hits me deeper than I expected. I want to believe him. I want to trust that the person sitting next to me on this plane isn't the same person who broke my heart all those months ago. But part of me, the part that's been burned before, still holds on to the question. *What if he hasn't really changed?*

My eyes flick to his face again, his expression soft but unwavering. "But I don't want you to think I'm being difficult," I say, my voice quieter now. "And I don't mean to keep bringing this up, James. I just need time to process. I need time to really... see it. See you. Because I don't know if I can just forget everything that happened."

He doesn't flinch at my words, doesn't pull back. Instead, he nods, like he understands, and I believe him. "I don't expect you to forget, Zo. But I hope one day you'll see that I'm not the same guy who hurt you. I don't want to be that person anymore."

For a second, the words hang between us, suspended in the air like a breath neither of us is quite ready to take.

The plane lurches slightly as we start to make our final descent into New York. The city below us stretches wide, glittering with lights like a vast ocean of possibility.

I turn and glance out the window, then back at James, his eyes still on me, watching me carefully. I lick my lower lip and take a breath, formulating the words that I know exist in me. I just need to let it out. Be honest with him.

"I don't know what this is yet, James," I say softly, my gaze flicking back to his. "But I think... I think I need time. Time to figure it out. Time to see if you really have changed."

"I can give you all the time you need," he says, his voice sincere.

"I'll be here, Zo. However long it takes." He smiles and continues. "Like I said before, I'm up for a late night two-in-the-morning bagel with you."

I softly laugh at his comment and nod, feeling the weight of his words inside me. "I'll hold you to that. And James?"

"Yeah?"

"Thank you for the apology. Second apology, technically."

He smiles. "Of course, Zo."

I can't deny it. There's still something here. I'm just not sure what it is yet.

Chapter 20

I press my forehead against the cool window, squinting as the skyline of New York City begins to emerge through the thinning clouds. It's breathtaking, like a painting brushed with soft strokes of silver and gold. The buildings, tall and proud, stretch toward the heavens as if daring the sun to rise higher. Each tower glints with a warm, amber light as the first rays of morning cascade down their glassy surfaces, giving the entire city an ethereal glow.

The Empire State Building stands tall among its companions, unmistakable even from this distance, and the sprawling urban landscape stretches out in every direction. The bridges below look like delicate threads gracefully connecting the boroughs, weaving the city together into one vibrant, living tapestry. Below, the rooftops are flecked with patches of green and yellows and reds, and I can just make out the shimmering ribbon of the Hudson River as it winds its way through the city, reflecting the early morning light like a strip of glittering silk.

As we draw closer, more details come into view—the tiny yellow specks of taxis zipping along, the tree-lined avenues, and Central Park nestled like a green gem amid the steel and concrete.

The sight fills me with a strange mix of awe and anticipation, a sense that I'm about to enter a place pulsing with stories, ambitions, and secrets, each one waiting to be uncovered.

I press my hand to the glass, as if I can feel the city's heartbeat, its energy sparking under my fingertips. This is the city I've read about in novels, the city where countless writers and dreamers have come to prove themselves. And now, here I am, on the brink of my own story, about to add my voice to its endless symphony.

James's face appears next to mine and I can feel his breath against my cheek, the warmth sending my heart into outer space.

"Welcome to New York, Zo," he murmurs with a slight grin, his eyes reflecting the city below.

I give him a soft smile, caught in this surreal moment. There's something undeniably electric about sharing this view with him, even though part of me feels a twinge of hesitation, a reminder of why we parted in the first place. "Guess this is it—the big city."

He smiles and sits back. "You're going to be just fine. Just re-member that you have my number. Any time of day for anything, I'll be there, okay?"

I nod and feel my cheeks warm. "I know. I promise to bombard you with calls and texts so that you grow tired of me."

He laughs and shakes his head. "I could never grow tired of you, silly."

I roll my eyes and shrug. "All right, if you say so."

The plane jolts onto the pavement and nearly throws me out of my seat. I feel that familiar flutter in my stomach, both from the drop in altitude and from the realization that this is it. I'm really here. A wave of giddiness swells up inside me, and I pull up my phone to turn off airplane mode and shoot Tish a quick message: *Just landed safe and sound! New York is... wow.*

Not a moment passes by before she replies. *OMG!! Text me a selfie with your first bagel. And don't go running off with random writers or poets. Unless they're super cute.*

I laugh and notice James smirking too. "Already informing everyone we know, aren't we?"

"Oh, whatever. I'm texting Tish and Ben, the acquisitions editor."

He nods, his smile fading. What is that? It can't be that James is... jealous? Ben is merely a work acquaintance. I barely know the guy and have no clue what he looks like. Not that looks are the only important aspect. But still. And yet I find it cute. James possibly being all jealous.

I then text Ben as well. *Landed! NYC, here I am.*

Like Tish, he replies immediately. *Great! You should get your hotel confirmation email shortly, and I set up an Uber for you. A black Cadillac Escalade will be waiting outside. Welcome to the city, Zoe. Looking forward to our meeting.*

I can't help but smile. I'm here. My literary journey begins here. This is what I've worked so hard for. I can't help but feel giddy. New York, my story, my chance—here I am.

♡

We grab our bags from the cubbies above and begin to exit the plane. We make our way through the terminal side by side, both of us weaving through the crowd like two people who've done this before. I'm clutching the handle of my carry-on so tightly my knuckles turn white, but it gives me something to focus on, something steady in the whirlwind of emotions spinning around me.

James walks close, close enough that our shoulders brush every now and then. Each time it happens, a warm thrill trickles through me. He's here, with me, even if only for these last few minutes. The terminal around us is alive, buzzing with voices, snippets of laughter, and the muffled announcements echoing overhead. People shuffle around us in a blur of colors and movement, but in this moment, it feels like it's just the two of us, caught in a soft, invisible bubble.

The polished floors glisten under the fluorescent lights, reflecting the hurried strides of travelers, and the scent of freshly brewed coffee wafts from a café just ahead. I catch myself glancing at James every few steps, taking in the curve of his jaw, the way he tucks his hand into his pocket, looking both comfortable and slightly out of place. It's strange, seeing him here with me, in this new chapter that feels like it belongs only to me. But somehow he's a part of it. The thought makes my heart flutter, but I push it aside.

When we finally reach the end of the concourse, he stops, his expression shifting from playful to something more serious, more thoughtful. He studies me, his gaze softening like he's trying to hold onto this moment as much as I am.

"You have my number, right?"

I blink in surprise. Of course I do. He saw me put it in my phone. "Yeah, I do."

He looks at me, his expression unreadable for a moment, before his face softens. "Good. Because I mean it—I'm just a call away." He reaches out, hesitating for a second before he gently pulls me into a hug. His arms wrap around me, warm and steady, grounding me as everything else fades away. For a moment, the airport noise dims, and all I can feel is him—his heartbeat close to mine, his hand resting lightly on my back, like he's reluctant to let go.

I nod and close my eyes, leaning into him, and breathe in that familiar scent of cedar and something a little sweet, something that's uniquely James. It stirs memories of late-night talks, of easy laughter, of moments when I thought he was my forever. There's a softness to his embrace, a kind of gentle warmth that feels both comforting and bittersweet. This is just another one of our stolen moments. I can feel the warmth of his breath against my hair, the way his arms tighten slightly, like he's holding onto something he knows he can't keep.

As he pulls back, his hand lingers on my arm, his thumb tracing soft circles that send shivers up my spine. I look up at him, and our eyes meet. There's a vulnerability in his gaze that I haven't seen in a long time. It makes my heart ache. His face is close, so close that I can see the flecks of gold in his twinkling blue eyes, the faint shadow of stubble on his jawline, and for a heartbeat, I think he might lean down and kiss me.

My pulse quickens, and a million thoughts swirl in my mind, but I just stand there, caught in this moment that feels like it's teetering on the edge of something.

He gives me a small, almost wistful smile, breaking the spell. "You're going to be amazing here, Zo. I know it." His voice is barely above a whisper, but there's a sincerity in it that makes my chest tighten.

I swallow, forcing a smile and nodding again. "Thanks. You too.

Your book signing is going to be so great."

He smiles and wraps his hands around his suitcase. "I'll look forward to your calls or texts. I'll see you, Zo."

"Yeah, see you, James." My voice trembles ever so slightly. I swallow and take a breath, exhaling everything out. He turns and walks away, his figure fading into the crowd, and I watch him go until he disappears around a corner.

I grab my luggage and head toward the pickup area, my heart thumping with each step. Outside, the air is brisk, carrying the faint scent of roasted nuts from a nearby vendor and the tang of car exhaust. I locate the Cadillac and climb in, settling into the back seat as we pull away from the airport and merge into the pulsing flow of city traffic.

The driver weaves through the streets, each turn revealing a new layer of the city. People dart across crosswalks, taxis honk and maneuver like they're in a dance only they understand, and neon signs blink and buzz against the buildings. I stare out the window as we pass street after street, my eyes widening at each iconic landmark. There's Times Square, already blazing with vibrant neon signs even in the early morning light, and a hint of Central Park's trees swaying gently beyond the traffic.

The city feels alive, like it's welcoming me, wrapping me up in its dizzying hum. I'm mesmerized, barely able to tear my eyes away from the view. It's loud and chaotic and beautiful.

The driver must catch my wide-eyed expression in the rear-view mirror, because he chuckles. "First time in the city?"

I nod, grinning. "Is it that obvious?"

He just smiles. "You'll get used to it. Give it a few days, and you'll be jaywalking with the best of 'em."

Chapter 21

I lug my suitcase and tote bag out of the SUV and thank the driver as I step out in front of the hotel. The sidewalk fills with laughter and conversation as I soak everything in, simply embracing the fact that I am finally in New York. The place where dreamers live their dreams, making them realities.

This is an opportunity to put myself on display this time. I'm always overthinking and second-guessing my intuition, when truthfully, I need to just relax and embrace the journey. I've worked hard to get here, and frankly, New York is going to be quite the journey. At least, that is what my gut is telling me.

The wheels of my suitcase follow me as I walk toward the hotel entrance. Large clear windows absorb the bright sun, and pink, red, and purple flowers hang above the doorway. The hotel has to be at least fifty stories high, which makes my stomach turn a little. The lobby fills with people of all colors and sizes and shapes, all smiling, laughing, or giving the stern frown of disapproval at their bill.

My sneakers tap against the gleaming tile as I make my way toward the front desk, a woman in a blue pantsuit waving me over with her dazzling white smile. "Hello there, welcome to the War-wick Hotel. Are you checking in?"

I can't help but smile in response. "Yes, I am. I have a reserva-tion under..." My voice trails when I suddenly have to grab my phone and check the email Ben sent me. "I'm sorry, it's under Cartwright. It wasn't made by me, but the acquisition editor, whose boss is interviewing me for a short story I wrote, and flew me all the way to New York from Cleveland, Ohio. It's such an op-portunity, you know?"

The woman blinks at me in confusion but nods, smiling as she taps away on her keyboard. I mentally slap myself in the face for rambling. *Note to self: learn not to ramble in New York.*

"I believe I see you right here. You're Zoe, I presume? May I see your ID?"

I nod and shake my wallet out of my tote bag, handing it to her. Her French manicure glistens, not like my dull nail beds. I bite my lip and look around the lobby, suddenly feeling self-con-scious. The whole place is glistening with guests walking around in high-end attire while I'm shoved in Converse and jeans. Way to make a statement, Zoe.

I still cannot believe this is my reality. I made it to New York and this is my life now. I take a small breath in, and exhale as I lean my elbows on top of the counter until the receptionist's voice interrupts my thoughts.

"You're all set, Ms. Donovan. Your room is on the twenty-eighth floor, room 28-06, right next to the stairway. I hope you enjoy your stay with us."

She hands me back my ID and I feel the sides of my mouth twitch in delight. "Thank you so much."

My fingers clasp around my luggage's handle and I make my way toward the elevator as the illuminated gold numbers count up to a capital L. I follow behind the small crowd into the elevator and make my way to the only corner left. I close my eyes for a moment and feel my heartbeat slowing down.

That's when I feel my nostrils flare as my phone pings, my eyes opening to the sound. I lift it out from my tote bag pocket and the screen lights up. A text from James pops up and my brows crinkle in curiosity.

Hey, you. Are you free for lunch? I'm sure that coffee didn't fill you up. Let me know soon. I know a good spot for a newbie in New York.

I smirk at his text and shove my phone back in my tote bag. Not even twenty minutes in New York and I already have a date. Is this a date? No, it's certainly not a date. We're just meeting up for lunch, that's it.

The elevator dings, pulling me out of my thoughts, and I step onto my floor, dragging my suitcase behind. The hallway stretches out before me, carpeted in a rich burgundy with gold accents that swirl like vines. The walls are lined with modern golden light fixtures, each casting a soft, warm glow. My shoes make a muffled *tap-tap* against the carpet as I roll my suitcase forward, glancing at the room numbers. Twenty-eight-oh-two... twenty-eight-oh-four. There it is. Twenty-eight-oh-six.

I pause for a moment, staring at the door as if it holds the secrets to my New York journey behind it. Well, probably not all of its secrets, but I'll take what the room is willing to share. With a deep breath, I slide the key card through the lock. A green light flashes, and a satisfying *click* grants me entry.

The room is stunning. Large windows dominate one side, offering a breathtaking view of the city below. Skyscrapers glint in the sunlight, their windows catching the golden rays like a thousand tiny mirrors. The bed is massive, draped in crisp white linens with a plush gray throw folded neatly at the foot. A small seating area with a velvet armchair and a sleek glass desk sits in front of the window. The room on the other side appears to hold a couch alongside a flatscreen television, coffee table, mini fridge, and a kitchenette area perfect for some writing and reading.

I roll my luggage next to the mirror right as I enter, and drop my tote bag onto the bed. I collapse beside it, arms spread wide as I stare at the ceiling. "Okay, Zoe," I mutter to myself. "You're in New York. You're here for an interview, not to worry about James. Even if he somehow showed up what seems like every day back home out of the blue and followed you to New York."

Why did he have to text me so soon? I'm sure he has a life of his own to live, being a famous writer and everything. And why did my stomach just *have* to flip when I read it? It's just lunch. With my ex. In a city that practically screams romance at every street corner.

I groan and cover my face with a pillow. "Focus!" I say, my voice muffled. "You can't let your brain turn into a rom-com just because *he* happens to be here." Maybe more like followed, or stalked, but whatever.

I sit up and glance at my phone again. The message from James still sits there unopened, taunting me.

I tap my foot against the carpet, debating. Ben and his boss aren't expecting me until Monday morning, and my stomach is growling louder than a subway train. What's the worst that could happen? It's just food.

I type out a reply before I can overthink it.

Sure! Where and when?

The response pings almost immediately.

Does 1 p.m. work? We can meet at Ellen's Stardust Diner. You'll love it. Trust me.

I glance at the alarm clock on the nightstand. It's 11:45 a.m. That gives me just enough time to unpack a little, freshen up, and maybe take a cat nap. I take off my shoes and shimmy my coat off to hang in the closet. I place the *Do Not Disturb* sign on my door.

Unraveling the comforter, I snuggle underneath the sheets, feeling the softness of the pillow conform against my head. And before I know it, my brain immediately shuts off and no more thoughts on James tumble about.

♡

My eyes flutter open as the warm glow of the sun gleams against the sheer curtains while dust dances through the rooms. I turn off my phone alarm and sit up and stretch, feeling a crack of my back.

It's just about 12:30, so I should have enough time given the diner is super close. I grab my make-up bag and walk toward the bathroom. The lights flicker on and I immediately splash cool water on my face, setting my hands against the marbled countertop.

I stare at my reflection and shake my hair down from my bun. I scrunch my orange hair to loosen the curls around my face, brushing them out. My orange bob floats along my shoulders and my curtain bangs flutter around my eyebrows and temples. I lightly coat mascara over my lashes and dab on a bit of lip gloss.

I am in severe need of a change of clothes since I've been in them since the airport, so I pull out all of my outfits that were neatly vacuum-sealed and lay them all side-by-side on the bed. I study them for a moment and opt for a pair of black wide-leg mom jeans, a cozy white sweater tucked into them, my pair of red Mary Jane flats, and my go-to silver hoops with a few silver rings on my fingers.

A girl always needs accessories.

I pull on my coat and red scarf, grab my tote bag and hotel key, and head out.

♡

By the time I step out of the hotel, the city is alive with energy. Yellow cabs honk impatiently, and the scent of roasted nuts tickle the air from a nearby cart. I clutch my phone like a lifeline, following the Google map as it guides me to the diner.

Not even ten minutes later, Ellen's Stardust Diner is impossible to miss. Its retro neon sign glows brightly, promising a slice of New York nostalgia. I step inside, greeted by the sound of a server belting out a Broadway tune while expertly balancing a tray of milkshakes.

The diner is brighter than I expected, its chrome fixtures gleaming under the glow of glitzy neon lights. Inside it smells like syrup, sizzling bacon, and a hint of coffee—comforting, yet intoxicatingly alive with the energy of the city. A server croons *New York, New York* into a retro microphone. Her voice carries effortlessly over the clinking of plates and the low hum of conversation.

And then his face emerges behind a couple carrying a bag of food.

James sits near the window, his silhouette outlined by the

street's chaotic vibrance. His navy sweater fits him too well, and his elbows rest casually on the table. He's scrolling through his phone, his brows slightly furrowed in concentration.

I pause for a moment, my heart doing an uninvited somersault. Why does he always look so effortlessly put together, like he just stepped out of a magazine? I tug at my coat nervously, suddenly hyper-aware of my slightly windblown hair.

As if sensing me, he glances up, and his face breaks into a grin—slow, warm, and maddeningly familiar. He stands, waving me over.

"Zo," he says, his voice soft but carrying just enough weight to make my knees wobble. "You made it."

"I did," I reply, trying to sound breezy and not like I spent the past five minutes outside debating whether to walk in. "This place is... wow. Very New York."

He chuckles. Suddenly, the sound of crinkling intrigues my ears and I notice he lifts a bouquet of yellow and pink tulips, handing them to me. "These are for you. I'm sorry they're not bigger. I just know they are—were—your favorite."

I can feel my nostrils flare and I swallow the last bit of saliva in me. I grasp my hands around them and lift them to my nose, inhaling the sweet aroma of the flowers, feeling a sense of nostalgia for our first date way back when. James got me the same flowers when he picked me up, knowing they were my favorite. They still are.

I smile and place them next to me. "They're lovely, James. Thanks. Buying me flowers, coffee. You're just full of surprises I suppose." I grab the menu and glance at him over it. "And yes, they're still my favorite."

He shrugs and chuckles. "I'm not trying to do anything, Zo. I saw them on my way here and had to grab them."

I roll my eyes and bite my lip, feeling his foot tap mine. His golden blue eyes quickly look back down at his menu, and he takes a long sip of his drink. "But hey, this place is bit of a spectacle, but the food is worth it. Plus, I thought you'd appreciate the theatrics."

"Oh, sure. Who doesn't want pancakes with a side of jazz hands?"

His laugh—low and genuine—makes my chest hiccup. *Get it together, Zoe,* I scold myself.

A server appears, dressed in a vintage uniform with a beaming smile. We place our orders—pancakes for me, a burger for him, and coffee all around.

"So," James says, leaning back in his seat. "How's New York treating you so far? I mean, you've been here what, an hour?"

I smirk, shrugging my shoulders. "About that," I reply, tracing the edge of the menu with my finger. "I've already managed to embarrass myself at the hotel desk by overexplaining my reservation. I think I'm off to a strong start."

He grins. "Let me guess. You gave them your entire life story?"

"Just the highlights," I say, rolling my eyes. "You know, Cleveland origins, mid-tier nail beds, aspiring writer who can't seem to stop rambling."

"That's so you," he says, his grin widening. "New York won't know what hit it."

Our coffees arrive, and I take a cautious sip, letting the warmth settle me. "Enough about me. How's the glamorous life of a best-selling author? I imagine it involves a lot of leather-bound notebooks and wistful gazes out of windows."

He chuckles, shaking his head. "Not quite. It's mostly emails, deadlines, and trying not to panic when the words aren't coming. Though I do own a leather notebook. Haven't written in it, but I must admit it looks pretty damn good on my desk."

I snort into my coffee. "So the myth is shattered. Good to know."

His gaze softens, and for a moment, the playful banter fades. "Seriously, though. I'm glad you're here. Getting your story published—it's amazing."

I glance down at my coffee, suddenly shy under his steady gaze. "Thanks. It still doesn't feel real, you know? I'm waiting for someone to jump out and tell me it was all a mistake."

He leans forward, resting his forearms on the table and his hand over mine. A warm familiarity rushes through me, as if embracing and accepting the touch. "It's not a mistake. You're talented. Always have been. I mean, damn, look at you. New York, interviews, fancy hotel reservations. You're living it."

I laugh despite myself, the tension in my chest easing just a little. "Yeah, it's pretty exciting."

The food arrives, and as we eat, he starts telling me about his first apartment in the city—a sixth-floor walk-up with ceilings so low he had to duck in the shower.

"I'm serious," he says, gesturing with his fork. "I had to shampoo in a squat like some kind of urban goblin."

I nearly choke on my drink. "That sounds deeply tragic. And very on-brand for New York."

"Oh, it gets better. The stove sparked if you looked at it wrong, and I had exactly one window—which faced a brick wall."

"Ah yes," I say, grinning. "The classic scenic alleyway view."

"Where pigeons went to die and dreams went to nap."

I laugh, resting my chin on my hand. "And yet, I bet you kind of loved it."

He shrugs, a nostalgic smile playing at the edge of his mouth. "I did. It was terrible. But it was mine."

The laughter settles into a comfortable warmth as we finish our meals. A server bursts into a rendition of *Don't Stop Believin'*, and James taps his fingers to the beat, mouthing the words.

"You're really leaning into the theme here," I tease.

"Hey, it's all part of the experience," he says, grinning.

When the check comes, he waves me off as I reach for my wallet. "My treat," he insists.

"James—"

"Consider it a welcome-to-New-York gesture," he says, his tone leaving no room for argument. "I bought you coffee and lunch, now you can buy us dinner and dessert, right?"

Outside, the city feels sharper, brighter, the air crisp against my cheeks. We linger on the sidewalk, the buzz of the diner fading into the background.

"Well," I say, crossing my arms to ward off the chill. "Thanks for lunch. And the laugh. I needed that."

He smiles, his hands tucked into his pockets. "Anytime. But, hey, I was wondering, if your day isn't jam-packed with literary world business, I'd love to show you around some of the city."

I hesitate, the weight of his words settling between us. Is this nostalgia talking? Or something more?

"I'm actually not busy at all today. My interview isn't until Monday, so I am free till then," I say.

"Got yourself some free time, that's great. Now, what shall

I show you first…" His voice trails momentarily until those bright blue and gold orbs stare back into mine. He then turns around and waves his hands around his head. "Times Square!"

I tilt my head, considering. My gut tells me this could be a terrible idea. But my heart? Well, it's always been a hopeless romantic.

"Okay, okay. Show me all of what Times Square has to offer, besides the best pancakes."

A smile beams across his face as his fingers wrap around mine, making my heart do a somersault in my chest. Why am I doing this? It feels different… in a good way. Should my heart be smiling with joy? Is this okay to feel? My mother told me to give him a second chance, as she gave my father a second chance, and, well, the rest is history with that one.

I tighten my grip as he gently pulls me next to him, his hand on the small of my back, his coat brushing against mine. Without missing a beat, we continue toward the crowds that emerge under the brilliant lights and sounds of the street ahead.

Chapter 22

The lights glimmer above as James and I walk through the crowds of Times Square, immersed in the hecticness that surrounds us. Everyone around us is to themselves and yet in a hurry as boots and sneakers and heels clop against the sidewalks. Always in a hurry to get somewhere. But hey, this is New York.

He brushes his thumb against my hand, allowing a warm sensation to shiver up my spine and insides. I try to redirect my focus around the city, the Apple store glowing as we walk down Fifth Avenue, the famous Plaza Hotel in all its glory.

The yellow and orange tones from the sun warm the sky. It gets darker earlier these days. The crowds don't seem to lighten up, they're just as bustling as ever it seems. We'd been walking for hours, weaving through Central Park and past glittering storefronts, but I'm not tired.

My mind can't seem to allow me to focus on all of that. It's James that crams my thoughts and wipes every other thought that tries to transpire.

"So," he says. "You gotta be excited about the interview, right?"

I nod and glance at the bouquet of flowers in my other hand, smiling as a breeze lightly ruffles them. "Absolutely. I don't want to ruin it. Mess it up. You know? Oh, and I'm thinking we could just drop these flowers off at my hotel if you'd like? Unless you want to show me around some more as the city expert."

He chuckles. "Well, no need to worry. If they didn't already like you, you wouldn't be here, now would you? But yeah, we can drop off that lovely bouquet at your hotel. I picked out some nice flowers, didn't I?"

A laugh emerges from me and I shake my head. "They're lovely. How about we head back? The hotel isn't too far from here anyway, maybe twenty minutes if you're up for a walk. Think you can handle it, city boy?"

"I'm pretty sure I can handle it. C'mon, I know a shortcut." And he whisks me toward him, lightly brushing against him. My cheeks and neck warm as James squeezes my hand once more.

♡

We dropped off the flowers at my hotel, where the concierge kindly offered to find a vase for them. As we stand in the lobby, James's phone buzzes with a notification.

"I should probably let you get ready," he says, tucking his phone back into his pocket. "Dinner tonight, right?"

"Right," I say, suddenly acutely aware of how little time I have to prepare.

He nods in agreement and winks a deep blue eye at me as he disappears into the crowd piling up on the sidewalk.

Back in my room, I sink into the plush bed and pull out my phone to FaceTime Tish. She answers on the second ring, her face lighting up the screen.

"There's my favorite New Yorker!" she exclaims. "How's the Big Apple treating you?"

"It's... a lot," I admit, propping the phone against a stack of pillows. "But also amazing. And you know, *complicated*."

Tish raised an eyebrow. "Ugh, still? C'mon, babe, spill."

I hesitate, then launch into the story of my day with James. By the time I finish, Tish is practically vibrating with excitement.

"Zoe, you're still into him," she declares. "Don't even try to deny it."

"It's not that simple," I say, fiddling with the hem of my shirt. "He hurt me, Tish. And I don't know if I'm just nostalgic or lonely or..."

"Or still in love with him?" she finishes for me, her tone softer.

I sigh. "Maybe. I don't know. It's been years, and yet he's still... James. It's like no time has passed."

Tish leans closer to the screen. "Look, sweetie, you deserve happiness. If there's even a chance that James could give you that, then maybe it's worth exploring. I mean, look at your mom and dad. She gave him a second chance and they're more in love now than ever, am I right? You're smart, babe. Just make sure to protect that big, mushy heart of yours."

I smile, grateful for her unwavering support. "You always know what to say."

"Now, let's see what you'll be wearing," she demands, clapping her hands.

Laughing, I stand and retrieve the sleek champagne-colored dress from the closet. It's simple yet stunning, with a daringly low back and a subtle shimmer that catches the light. Just a little something extra I tossed in while packing, that's all. It's

New York City after all.

"Holy hell, Zo," says Tish, fanning herself dramatically. "Sorry not sorry if this is too much, but if James doesn't propose on the spot, I will."

Blushing, I slip into the dress and twirl for the camera. "Oh, geez. You think it's too much?"

"Not even close. You're going to knock him dead," she says with a wink.

We end the call and I rush to the bathroom, emptying my make-up bag on the counter. A bright crimson lipstick tumbles out. Tish. I'd never wear red lipstick, but something about it excites me, so I roll it on and dab my lips with a tissue. I brush my hair just a tad and opt for a thick gold pair of hoops.

"Okay, Zo. You look simply gorgeous, just don't chicken out last minute. This is just dinner, nothing more." I do another looksie in the mirror, grab the vintage clutch my Granny gave me, and lock the door. It's just dinner. What's the worst that could happen?

♡

James decided on Buvette, a charming bistro in the West Village. As we step inside, the scent of fresh baguettes and roasted garlic smother my senses.

The restaurant is cozy, with tiny tables close enough to encourage whispered conversations. Warm light from antique sconces bathes the room in a golden glow, and the buzz of quiet chatter creates a bubble of serenity in the bustling city. James pulls out a chair for me—a gesture that feels surprisingly natural despite the years apart. A white collared button-down hides underneath a golden sweater that hugs his lean torso, while a pair of grayish slacks and brown shoes cover his feet. He does look yummy, I have to admit.

"You look... stunning," he says as I settle into my seat, his voice carrying a sincerity that makes my cheeks flush. He then kisses my cheek softly, making me blush redder than my lipstick.

"Thank you," I reply, tucking a loose strand of hair behind my ear. "You clean up pretty well yourself."

The flickering candlelight reflects in James's eyes, making them impossibly warmer. The wine flows, loosening our words and peeling back the layers of each other's lives that had crept in over the years.

By the time we leave the restaurant, the crisp night air is a refreshing contrast to the cozy warmth inside. We stroll back toward my hotel, our steps slow and meandering as if neither of us wants the night to end. My thoughts are a little jumbled, and my balance a little off. I feel tipsy but not drunk. Maybe I needed this. I feel a little more relaxed around James. And I don't think that is a bad thing.

James slips his arm around my shoulders, pulling me closer. I pull my translucent shawl around me. The city's noise fades into the background, replaced by the steady thrum of my heartbeat. When we reach the hotel, he hesitates, his hand lingering on my arm. A touch I'm getting more used to by the minute.

"Zoe," he says, his voice low and unsteady. I can tell he's a little tipsy too, and it makes me giggle as he slightly slurs my name. But it's cute.

His deep blue eyes then all of a sudden have me in a chokehold. They glisten against the golden streetlights above. He clears his throat and the seconds ticking by have me on my toes.

"I still love you. I truly don't think I ever stopped. You're... the good one that got away, Zo."

The words hang in the air between us, heavy and electric. My breath catches, and before I can overthink it, I simply reach for his hand and pull him inside the hotel. The elevator ride is a blur of stolen glances and unspoken words, the tension crackling like a live wire. Maybe it's the wine, maybe it's all the crashing into each other that's catching up with me, and the universe really pushing us together again. Whatever it is, I allow it to take control.

The moment the room door closes, the sound of our breath fills the silence. It's heavy and uneven, a rhythm that matches the pounding of my heart. James's hands trail down my sides, his touch like fire against my bare skin. His lips follow, exploring the curve of my neck and the hollow of my collarbone, each kiss deliberate, lingering, like he wants to memorize every inch of me.

You shouldn't be doing this, my brain yells at me. I bury it.

I gasp as his hands slip lower, his fingers brushing the sensitive skin under my thighs, throbbing for him to continue. He pauses, his eyes meeting mine, dark and full of hunger, but also something tender, like he's asking for permission. I nod, my breath hitching, and his lips curve into a smile that sends a wave of heat through me.

It's feels like he's trying to find the version of me who used to belong to him, but she's not here. He's searching like we're still us.

But we're not.

His fingers seem to know my body as if a day hasn't gone by. They grow deeper inside me, toying with me, allowing me to curve into him. I bite his shoulder as my hips shudder against his touch, begging for more.

His shirt is already sliding off him, and I push the rest off his shoulders, my hands greedy for the warmth of his skin. The scent of his cologne is intoxicating, mingling with the faint trace of wine on his breath. I trace the contours of his chest, the muscles taut under my fingertips, reveling in the way his breath hitches at my touch.

"Zoe," he murmurs, his voice low and hoarse, like he is barely holding himself together.

"James," I whisper back, my voice trembling with need. "Don't stop."

He doesn't. His lips find mine again, the kiss deep and consuming, his hands memorizing every curve of my body. He shifts us, lying me down against the bed, his weight pressing me into the mattress in a way that feels both grounding and electrifying. His lips trail lower, leaving a path of heat down my torso, his hands following, sliding over my hips and thighs.

I feel his pressure touch me, solid as a rock. I moan out and lean my hips into him. The anticipation is almost too much, a delicious ache building inside me. My hands thread through his brown locks, tugging gently, and he groans, the sound vibrating against my skin. He pulls at my lower lip and lifts me, allowing me to wrap my legs around him. He tears himself away and glances at the nightstand.

"Do you need me to..."

Shit. Condoms.

He nods as if understanding my thoughts. He hops off the bed in a quick and swift motion and yanks a condom out of his wallet. He tugs the condom over himself, and I bite my lip at the sight. I should say something, anything. I should stop this.

But I don't.

He pulls me toward him, embracing me and hovering over me as he lays me down gently. He brushes my hair behind my ears and kisses my temple and my forehead, and trails them down my neck. I wrap my hands around his neck and pull him toward me, our lips colliding. It's messier now, though. It's a sensation of what was, of what he was, what I was.

Like we're simply shoving why we broke under the covers.

James cups his hands on my face, nuzzles his nose against mine, and rests his lips on my forehead, mumbling against it. "I love you, Zoe. You're the real deal. You're the one."

I swallow and absorb his every word. The one. I'm the *one*. He loves me. It doesn't seem real, and here we are, here's James telling me I'm the one. I feel my breath quicken, like the words are there and I just need to say them.

But I don't respond.

He then moves his pressure deep inside me, meeting mine, and I moan, arching my back in response. He continues to thrust against me, and I reach across his back and pull him against me. He pulls back and pushes with a deliberate slowness, like he wants to savor every moment, every reaction. His hands slide under me, lifting me closer as if he can't get enough.

He whispers my name against my skin, his voice thick with emotion, and it sends a shiver down my spine. Every sensation heightens, every touch electric, building in intensity as we found a rhythm that felt as natural as breathing. I cling to him, my fingers digging into his back.

When we finally collapse into each other, our bodies spent and tangled, sweat gliding down our skin and mixing together, the sheets beneath us are damp, cold and warm all at once.

James holds me close, his breath warm against my temple, his arms wrapped around me like he never wants to let go. So I let him.

The stillness in the room devours me, whispering something I already know but don't want to face. Its hushed words creep into my mind, screaming at me, yelling at me that this moment isn't it.

This isn't love. It isn't closure, either.

It's grief wearing the costume of desire. And I should have never invited him up.

The silver moon just outside the window, brushing itself through the curtains, wakes me up around 2:45 in the morning. I drag myself off the bed and cover myself with James's sizeable sweater off of the floor, and crumble on the couch in the other room. A pitcher of water and a couple of glasses still sit on the coffee table, condensation glowing against the moonlight. Room temperature by now, no doubt.

My mind races with back-to-back thoughts on the previous evening. Our warm skin brushing against each other, moaning and kissing, and... I drag my fingers down my face and huff back into the couch, crossing my legs. The lukewarm water streams down my throat.

After a night of sex, I really shouldn't be complaining, nor overthinking. I should be happy, ecstatic. A gorgeous man wanted to sleep with me. Or maybe it was *me* who wanted to sleep with him. But why? Was it from all the wine we had at dinner? Did it make me want to do things I wouldn't otherwise do?

It was me though. *I* took his hand, *I* dragged him up to my hotel room, *I* started making out with him. Was it companionship I longed for? It had been quite some time since I'd slept with some-one. And yet, why him? My ex-boyfriend, scratch that, *cheating* ex-boyfriend, of all people.

I take another long sip of water. I really don't have the time for drama. Is it drama though? A click from the door cuts through my racing thoughts and James emerges wearing only his boxers.

"Hey… what're you doing up so early?" He grabs a blanket from one of the chairs and wraps it around me, and sits next to me.

I nuzzle under it, letting out a sigh. "I guess I couldn't sleep. Tomorrow is officially the interview. You know, nerves and such."

He nods and pulls my legs over his thighs, caressing them slowly. "Understandable. I thought you were upset about… what happened."

I look up at him, his deep blue eyes sinking into mine, express-ing sincerity I've only seen in them once or twice. And yet it seems different now. I place my hand over his and squeeze it softly. "Last night was something I hadn't felt in a long time. It was familiar, but it was something else…"

He smiles and lightly kisses my temple, pulling my head against his chest as he leans us back. "I just hope you know that I meant what I said, after dinner. I'm falling in love with you all over again. The sappy, mushy, lame love in all those cheesy Hallmark movies. I see you in ways I was too blind to notice before, and it terrifies me because I know I don't deserve to feel this way about you again. It's like way back when, I didn't realize how much I needed you until I saw the way you've rebuilt yourself, and now I'm falling for the strength I once took for granted."

The drumming of my heart fills my ears, drowning out every

other sound from outside. The room feels both too warm and too quiet, the muffled hum of the city outside doing little to fill the silence. His words hang in the air, brushing against me like the softest touch, and I can't tell if they soothe or wound. My chest tightens, but not with anger. It's something far more complicated, like a tangle of memories, longing, and the sharp edge of doubt.

I stare at the glass in my hand, his hand brushing my leg up and down. "James... look, for some reason, deep, *deep* down, I want to believe you." I set the glass down and caress his face with my hands, his cool skin soothing against my warm hands, the scruff of the beginning of a coarse beard.

"It's just a little scary, with our history and the future, especially my future, here in New York. It's all new and fresh and exciting, and why worry about that right now?"

He tilts his head against my hand, takes it in his, and places gently pecks down my arm. Goosebumps form as his lips tickle my skin, but it feels so nice. "I'm not asking to settle anything right now. I felt the need to say that because I mean it with my entire soul. It's always been you. And, you know, I wish I could undo the pain I caused, but all I can do is admit every part of me still belongs to you. I can't help this feeling, Zoe."

I nod in response and scoot toward him, wrapping the blanket around him, feeling the warmth of his chest slowly moving up and down. "You're too much, you know? All these cheesy, sappy love lines. You may be a writer, but I sincerely hope these lines are from *you*."

He chuckles and brushes my hair away from my forehead, caressing my head softly. "I meant every word, you silly goose. But in all seriousness, I'll wait for you. I don't plan on ever leaving New

York; it's home to me. As for you and your future, sure, that might be up in the air now, but if you choose to stay here, just know you always have a place to stay… with me."

I smile and slowly shift away as I unwrap the blanket. He gives me the puppy dog eyes and droopy lips in response.

"I appreciate this, James. Even all the mushy sweet nothings. Like I said before, it's going to take some time. But I'll admit… I feel like my heart still beats for yours too. Just a little." I stand up and hold my hand out. "Now, let's get some more shut eye, and tomorrow, uh, *today*, is a new day to explore the city some more with an expert tour guide on New York."

He rolls his eyes and cracks a smile, taking my hand in his and giving it a squeeze. He stretches, raking a hand through his hair, looking effortlessly… James. The boyish smirk, the way his eyes soften when they meet mine—it's maddening.

"Thanks for giving me… *us*… a chance," he says, his voice dipping into something quieter, something vulnerable. It's that side of him that still catches me off guard.

Maybe my heart really does still twist and ache for his. Maybe it's the familiarity and the universe pushing us together. But is this me giving him another chance? I'm not sure. I want to think I'm not. For now, I just need to smother and diminish all of the overthinking thoughts and nerves of the past to remain hopeful for the present, *and* the future.

Chapter 24

"Good morning, sleepy butt."

A husky voice wakes me from my sleep. Soft lips graze my temple and tease down my neck to my collarbone with fleeting bites. It feels so electrifying it has me craving more. "I had room service deliver breakfast this morning. Everything's on the coffee table in the other room, including a sweet surprise."

I moan softly and arch my back as I sit up, smoothing my hair out of my face. I suddenly feel flakey drool on the side of my lips and quickly wipe it away. "Oh, leaving so soon?" And without a second thought, I pull him at his jacket and taste his lips against mine. Call it a seduction call for him to stay, but my brain is telling me *what the hell? Run!*

I can tell he's caught off guard because it takes him a moment to settle on the bed. His large hands cup the back of my neck and pull me closer to him, my lips sculpting against his in a rough yet vanilla manner. I melt into the kiss, the rest of the world fading like a forgotten dream. His lips are soft but certain, moving against mine with a tenderness that sets my heart fluttering. My hands find their way to the lapels of his jacket, holding him as if he is the only thing keeping me grounded in this moment.

When he finally pulls back, he doesn't go far. His forehead rests lightly against mine, his breath warm and steady, mingling with my own. "You have no idea how hard you're making it to leave," he murmurs, his voice soft and low.

I smile, my fingers tracing the line of his jaw, feeling the stubble that always makes him look a little more rugged than he realizes. "That's the point," I whisper back, my voice soft but teasing. "Did you think you could kiss me like that and expect me to let you go?"

He smirks and kisses my nose. "I have to meet with my editor this morning to prepare for my book signing later this afternoon. Shall I expect to see you there?"

I nod and shift my legs over the bed, his oversized sweatshirt still covering me. "I'll definitely stop by, Mr. Famous Writer. And thanks for breakfast, and for... last night."

He beams and strides toward the door, grabbing his coffee from the entry table on the way out. "It was my pleasure, sleeping beauty. I'll catch you later."

The door closes behind him and I can't help but feel my heart kicking at my ribcage. Last night was something else. And he's been so sincere, so sweet, so... wonderful. Perhaps I owe it to Mom and Tish. Maybe people really can change.

I shimmy out of the sweater and undies and turn on the shower, letting it heat up a moment as the steam smothers my vision. I walk into the other room and notice enormous plates with silver covers over them. I lift them and under them is a stack of pancakes, scrambled eggs, sausage patties, and hashbrowns. Orange juice and a large coffee sit beside them. The coffee is my usual.

What the hell are you doing to me, James?

I lick the straw and take a sip. It's chocolatey goodness coating my throat, sending happy sparks all over my body. It has to be the best thing around. I head back to the bathroom and hop in the shower, settling in the warmth as the water glides down me as if washing away all of my worries and thoughts and insecurities.

I wish, but a girl can dream.

The closet is lined with all of the outfits I packed. I wrap my hair and peruse through my selection. I glance out the window and notice the sunshine in all its glory with not a cloud in sight. It's still chilly so I opt for an oversized gray sweatshirt, my favorite black wide-leg ankle pants, and my favorite red Mary Jane flats. I pull out my jewelry bag and pick out a pair of silver ball studs and a few silver rings.

As I blow dry my hair, my phone pings. It's a text, but I can't tell who it's from. I pick it up and see it's from Ben. I totally forgot he has my number. And yet something about his name popping up on my phone makes my stomach do a weird little flip.

His text is unexpected and casual. I stare at the screen, half-expecting some kind of logistical question about books or the interview tomorrow, but no. My inner monologue is immediately at war.

Good morning, Zoe. Hope you slept well. Are you free for brunch today? Thought it'd be nice to meet before tomorrow. Café Cluny? My treat.

Brunch is harmless, right? I laugh to myself. Harmless like yesterday's harmless dinner? Nothing was harmless about dragging my ex up to my hotel room and sleeping with him. Harmless is just the opposite.

I bite my lip as I read his text again, a smile creeping up without permission. Brunch in the West Village? With Ben, the editor from P&W whom I barely know, yet who makes me oddly curious?

I text back before I overthink it some more, my best trait.

Brunch sounds wonderful. What time?

The dots appear almost immediately.

11? It's a little tucked away but worth it. You'll love it.

Will I, Ben? Or is this your subtle way of testing my sense of direction? I glance at the clock. It's just past ten, and I have just enough time to finish getting ready without descending into full chaos mode.

As I tug on my red flats and stretch on my black beanie, I replay his text in my mind. He manages to sound professional while still being quietly charming. It's merely a work brunch—nothing more, nothing less. Of course he wouldn't be interested.

♡

By 10:30, I hop down to the nearest subway entrance and scan my Metro card, courteous of Ben. About twenty-five minutes later, I'm walking down the cobblestone streets of the West Village, the chilly air making my cheeks flush.

The neighborhood is impossibly charming, as if it's trying to win me over with its quaint brownstones and leafy streets. Everyone and their mother appears to own a little brown curly dog and decided to dress them in sweaters, and suddenly I don't feel dressed enough. I spot the awning of Café Cluny, a green striped pattern that's unapologetically cute.

My eyes scour the crowd standing outside. I instantly notice a sleekly dressed man checking his watch, his eyes darting the street. His wavy dark blond hair is partially combed over and partially scuffed up, in a good way. His eyes are hazel drizzled with flakes of gold and gray like cinnamon sugar. And the five o'clock shadow that hugs his chiseled jawline makes my lips twitch. A pink dress shirt with a purple polka-dot tie wraps around his torso and a dark navy blazer and pants to match hang down his long legs. He has to be at least six two, maybe six three. And I suddenly felt like an ant as I walk toward him.

He looks up as I approach, his face breaking into a warm, easy smile. Now closer, he looks like he just stepped out of a spring catalog. He's absolutely gorgeous.

"Zoe?" he asks, tucking his phone away.

I smile and nod. "Yes? Are you... Ben?"

He grins. "That's me. You're right on time. I like that."

"I aim to please," I quip, looking up at him and trying not to sound too breathless from my speed-walk here from the subway.

He holds the door open for me, and we step into what can only be described as brunch heaven. The place is cozy yet elegant, with small tables adorned with fresh flowers and a warm hum of conversation.

"You weren't kidding," I say as we're led to a table by the window. "This place is adorable."

"I have a knack for finding good spots," he says, shrugging modestly. "And for guessing what people might like."

"Oh, so you're a brunch psychic I see," I tease as we sit at a table in the back corner near the kitchen.

He chuckles, and it's almost disarming. "I prefer 'intuitive.'"

The server comes by as if he's been waiting for us, and we order—him, some kind of fancy farmhouse omelet and coffee; me, French toast and a mimosa because it's brunch and I have priorities.

"So," Ben says after the server leaves, leaning slightly forward. "Tell me about Zoe. What's the story behind the writer?"

My cheeks heat up, and I'm suddenly very aware of how much syrup I might drench my French toast in later.

"Well," I say, dragging the word out, "I love stories—reading them, writing them, living them. When I was little, my dad and I would scour garage sales and book sales for all kinds of books. He has a warm spot for books too, so I guess you could say I get my love for writing from him. He wrote a few stories, even a novel. But never had it published..." I let my words trail and take a sip of my mimosa, letting the citrusy fizz dance on my tongue.

"And I guess that's what brought me here. My endless love for books. Er, perhaps it was my professor, but technicalities. What about you? What's the story behind Ben, acquisitions editor?"

He smirks. "That's a dangerous question. I could bore you for hours about my editorial background and how I ended up as a literary matchmaker of sorts."

"Literary matchmaker?" I raise an eyebrow.

"Pairing writers with editors, I suppose." He traces the rim of his coffee mug with his thumb, and his cinnamon sugar eyes meet mine. "It's an art, if you will."

I can't help but laugh, feeling a little more at ease. This guy might just be trouble in the best way. Brunch with my editor. Extremely cute editor, no less. He makes it so easy to talk. It's like the nerves from my three a.m. freak out are erased.

He takes a sip of coffee and leans closer to the table. I can almost smell his cologne—a mix of vanilla and butterscotch with a hint of musk. It smells delicious and I catch myself before *I* lean even closer to *him*.

"I've been writing ever since I was little. I always enjoyed English class the most. Having to read and write all day? The best. My dad was a writer at the New York Times. We moved to New York from Georgia when I was, I want to say ten? Ever since, the city has been a place to call home."

I smile softly at his words, tilting my head as I listen. I can listen to him talk all day.

"I remember the first time I set foot in P&W. I was freshly out of college with a degree in English Literature and I was interviewing for so many jobs then, just hoping the next one was the one. I started out in the mailroom and kept pushing myself until I got to the editorial department. And then I met Margaret, my boss. She practically took me under her wing. We got to talking one day when I was passing out mail and I told her I was interested in editorial work—proofreading, copy editing, that sort of thing. I guess you can say she pulled a few strings, and here I am."

It's like he's living my dream, and I feel proud of him. Feels like I already know him.

He clears his throat, a pink tone brushing his cheeks. A warm chuckle dances off his lips. "I'm sorry, I'm rambling. I'm sure you don't want to hear my life story, from the life of a mailroom boy to editor extraordinaire."

A laugh escapes my lips, and I can't help myself. My hand

reaches for his arm and wraps around it gently as my body debates the move. The cool fabric of his blazer softens against my palm. I let my eyes slowly match his, shaking my head. "Don't be sorry. I enjoyed hearing a little more about you. What you did takes a lot of work, and you didn't give up. I think it's fascinating, truly, that your dad actually worked at the New York Times. I'm a little jealous, not going to lie."

His head bobs in response, and I can see his lips form a smile. His eyes crinkle at the sides, his golden waves illuminated under the lights. I can tell that he appreciates it. It makes my heart skip.

I notice his eyes trickle down as he glances at my hand. And yet, he doesn't move it. He simply places his hand over mine. His touch is warm, but goosebumps smother my arms underneath my sweater.

He slowly rubs my hand, a small smile tugging at his lips. Moments pass in silence, but it's the kind of silence I don't mind. It's like he's glad I'm here. Glad I came to brunch with him. Glad I'm listening to his story. A handsome acquisition editor has quite the past, and I wouldn't mind hearing more about it.

And as if on schedule, my thoughts run back to James. From last night, the kind of sex you feel in your bones the next morning, to the way he woke up to check on me with that conversation that peeled back the layers. Who else would do that with me, besides Tish? He woke up because he was worried about me. I told him back on the plane that I need to see action, and well, there has been a lot of action since that plane landing. Possibly the best action I've seen in a long time, and from him of all people.

It meant a lot to me, and deep down... maybe I still do love

James. Not just from last night, but even through all of our history—it's him. He's been there for me and has shown me, little by little, that he has changed, that he wants to be a better person. All within a span of twenty-four hours.

Not to be too impulsive with my thoughts and actions, but it just feels right. He makes me feel safe, like his words have meaning behind them, and that's all I can ask for. But... is this all too good to be true? He's still the guy who pushed me around, lied to me, showed me he didn't care about me.

Tish is right, I really do have to get out of my head.

Chapter 25

"Well," Ben quips, smiling. "This was nice. I appreciate you not laughing at me for rambling, Zoe. I guess you can say you made a wonderful first impression."

I press my lips together to try and prevent myself from blushing. How can someone be so nice?

We're standing just outside the restaurant as the line to get in gets longer by the second. The cool air brushes against my face, but it feels nice. The two-hour conversation with Ben makes me feel more at ease, more like I belong here, like I finally feel why everyone says this is a big deal. Not that it wasn't before, it just finally clicked, per se. Like my story means something to more people than I could imagine.

I shake his hand, his warm grip lingering just a moment longer than necessary, and I offer him a smile that I hope hides the butterflies swarming around in my stomach. "No, no," I chuckle. "No need to apologize. I guess you can say getting a peek of Ben behind-the-scenes made it more comfortable. So, thank you. I enjoyed brunch very much, Ben."

A smile curls at his lips. "Then you're welcome, Zoe. I'll see—" He glances down at his phone as it buzzes in his hand. "I apologize. It's my boss. Nonetheless, Zoe, it's been a treat. Take care, all right? If you need anything, you have my number."

I bite my lip and nod. "No worries. Thanks, Ben."

He winks and turns away, catching a cab just as it slows in front of the restaurant. I feel my heartbeat rising at a faster pace than before. My mind is juggling a million and one thoughts and questions. Ben is actually seriously attractive. Like really attractive. And to ask me to meet him for brunch in the West Village? What a guy.

I seriously have to call Tish and talk to her about this, about whatever is going on with me. So I happened to have had sex with my ex-boyfriend and might be falling for him all over again, and then suddenly my acquisitions editor just so happens to be insanely cute?

It's like I'm going through the same thing as the universe pushing me and James together all over again.

I palm my forehead and roll my eyes, sighing. Digging out my phone out of my tote bag, I call Tish and listen to the ring in my ear.

"Heeellooo, New Yorker! What's shakin' babe? How's my lucky girl?"

"You know I literally love that you answer on the first ring for me every time. Just know how much I appreciate you."

Tish chuckles. "I got you, babe. Now, I'm pretty sure my spidey senses or best friend senses are tingling. You okay?"

I walk toward a bench just up the sidewalk and take a seat. "James and I slept together. And I think Ben is attractive, like really cute."

Silence rings in my ears far louder than the hustle and bustle before me in the city. I wait a minute, then another.

"Um, hello? Tish?"

Her laugh then bursts my eardrums, that hold-your-stomach-type laugh. She finally exhales. "Are you telling me that you slept with James and now you have a crush on your editor? Did I hear you correctly?"

I close my eyes briefly before giggling at her laughter blasting in my ear. "Tish, it's not funny! And it's not like that... I don't think. I'm being serious here. Help me."

As soon as the words tumble out, I question them immediately. It's definitely a crush, simple. At brunch, it was dangerously easy to talk to him. His gold-swirled hazel eyes meeting my baby blues had me hooked.

She exhales and clears her throat. "Okay, I'm sorry. I'm just a bit confused. When, how did it happen? You've literally been in New York for, like, a day and a half!"

I groan, leaning back against the bench and staring up at the cloudless blue sky. "Last night. After dinner. It just... happened. James and I were talking, reminiscing, and then one thing led to another. You know how it goes."

"Oh, I *know* how it goes," Tish teases, the smirk in her voice practically audible. "But I didn't think *you* did. Miss 'Can't Stand Him' suddenly takes a nostalgia trip to James-ville. What happened to boundaries, Zo? What happened to holding your ground?"

I rub my temples, a slight smile tugging at my lips despite my-self. "Boundaries got lost somewhere between the wine and his stupid, charming grin. And don't even get me started on the way he looked at me. Like, really looked at me, Tish. It was… ugh, I don't even know. It felt so familiar and yet completely new."

"Uh-huh," she says slowly, drawing out the syllables. "And now you're sitting here, post-hookup, drooling over Ben like a lovesick puppy. Zoe, you are *living* for the drama right now, and honestly? I'm here for it."

I let out a laugh, her infectious energy pulling me out of my spiral. "Only you would say that. I'm literally a walking rom-com cliché. James and I were—are—supposed to be over. So *over*, Tish. And now there's Ben. He's just…"

"Hot?" she quips helpfully.

"Extremely," I admit, groaning. "And kind. And smart. But he's a professional, Tish! This is so wrong."

"Okay, hold up," Tish says, her tone suddenly sharp. "Before we get too carried away, let's not forget something important here. Your best friend's been thinking things over, and she's reconsidering giving James a second chance. Hear me out." She takes a breath and continues. "James *cheated* on you, Zo. Remember that? He really hurt you. He lied to you, pushed you around, and fucking slept with another woman. And now he's waltzing back into your life like nothing happened. I'm not trying to scare you, I just want you to be sure if opening that door is really what you want."

I freeze, her words hitting me like a bucket of cold water. "Wow. Maybe I shouldn't have gone on this trip," I admit, my voice small. "But Tish… I know. It felt so real last night, and even back on the plane. It was like the old James I fell in love with was back. But you're right. He hurt me. A lot."

"Exactly," Tish says, her voice softening. "I'm not saying you can't do what you want. It's your life, and I'm not here to judge. But just... don't forget what he put you through. You've come a long way, Zo. You deserve someone who makes you feel whole, not someone who makes you question everything. And you also deserve to put yourself first. Always. Period. Mic drop."

I shake my head and let out a soft laugh. I swear my best friend is something else. But she gives the best advice, hands down. I bite my lip, and I suddenly feel a lump forming in my throat. "Ugh, you know me so well. I hate that you're always right."

She laughs, her tone lightening. "It's a curse, I know. But seriously, babe, you're in New York City! This is your big moment. Let loose, have fun, and maybe—just maybe—stop overthinking everything. Whether it's James, maybe Ben, or neither, enjoy this time. You've earned it."

I let out a shaky breath, nodding even though she can't see me. "Thanks, Tish. I needed that."

"Always," she says warmly. "Now, go find a cute coffee shop, grab a latte, or, hell, be like Carrie and grab a cosmopolitan, and write this all down. Oh, that would make me your Samantha! Anyway, you're living the dream. Might as well embrace it."

I smile, standing up and brushing off my jeans. "You're the best. I appreciate you. Thank you for being the greatest best friend alive."

"Duh," she says with a laugh. "Thanks for thinking of me, boo. Now go! The city isn't going to explore itself."

I hang up, feeling a strange mix of emotions. Tish is right—I need to stop overthinking and just live in the moment. Even if it's not what I've done for nearly twenty years. As I start walking, I look up at the towering buildings around me, the city bustling with life.

Right now everything seems a little chaotic, a little messy. But maybe messy is exactly what I need right now. That, or a cosmopolitan, whatever comes my way first.

Chapter 26

I stroll down Greenwich Avenue toward Washington Square Park using my Google maps app. The beautiful brownstones collide with the greenery that lines the sidewalks, framing this little part of the city. Oh, wouldn't it just be wonderful to live here?

Walking in New York has put a lot of things in perspective. I've lived in Cleveland all of my life, never lived anywhere else. Sure I've taken small trips to Michigan, Indiana, and even Massachusetts, but nothing compares to New York. It sucks you in, swallows you whole, and somehow makes you want to stay forever.

I pause at the curb, waiting for the pedestrian light to change, and let myself imagine what it'd be like to call this place home. Cleveland has its charms, absolutely, but it's familiar—too familiar. New York? It's messy and loud and overwhelming, but it's also full of possibilities. I could be anyone here, do anything. It's like the city whispers *what are you waiting for?*

The thought sends a thrill through me, followed almost immediately by doubt. Could I really do it? Could I leave behind everything I now for this whirlwind of a city? I shake my head. *Focus, Zoe. One thing at a time. You're here for your story, not some life-altering epiphany.*

But even as I think it, I know it's not entirely true. New York feels like more than just a backdrop for this trip. It feels like... well, like a beginning. I've contemplated the thoughts of leaving Ohio, and maybe being here is my chance. Perhaps this will turn into something amazing and wonderful. A little chaotic, but the good kind.

The clock on my phone reads just past 1:30 p.m. I have time to kill before James's book signing at three at the Barnes and Noble in Union Square. I cross the street and stop just before Washington Square Park. The large arch is so much bigger in person that I ever imagined, and it's so beautiful. I snap a few pictures and make my way toward an empty bench nearby.

The glow of the sunshine peeking just behind it glistens through the clouds as laughter and music fill the air. The park is alive, buzzing with the energy of New York City. A group of musicians has gathered near the fountain, their jazz melodies weaving through the chatter of people strolling, tourists snapping pictures, and children chasing bubbles that float lazily in the air. It's like stepping into a scene from one of those romanticized movies about life in the city.

I settle onto the bench, taking a deep breath of crisp autumn air, and let my shoulders relax. My nerves have been on edge all morning knowing I'll see James again.

I pull out my notebook from my bag, flipping to a blank page. I jot down the scene around me: the swirling leaves, the soft hum of life in the park, the faint scent of salted pretzels from a nearby vendor.

But my thoughts drift, as they often do, to the story I've been working on. A shadow over my page prompts me to glance up, expecting to see a curious child wanting to play or a homeless person asking for some food or spare change. Instead, it's a woman with striking auburn hair streaked with silver pulled loosely into a braid. She's holding a cup of coffee and has a canvas tote slung over her shoulder. Her presence feels calm, self-assured, like she belongs here in a way I never could.

"Mind if I sit?" she asks, her voice warm but tinged with a quiet confidence that catches me off guard.

"Sure," I say, tucking my notebook back into my bag.

"Thanks," she says, taking the spot beside me. She sips her coffee, her gaze sweeping over the park with the kind of appreciation that makes me wonder how long she's been soaking in moments like this.

"Lovely day," she comments, more to herself than to me.

"It is," I reply, though my voice sounds small compared to hers.

She turns slightly, her green eyes sharp but kind. "Are you visiting?"

I nod. "Yeah, just here for a few days. You?"

"Oh, sweetheart, I live here," she says with a small smile. "For the past... goodness, fifteen years, I think? Before that, I was bouncing around, trying to figure out where I belonged."

Her words pique my curiosity. "Did you always think you'd end up in New York?"

She lets out a soft laugh, her expression wistful. "Not at all. I thought the city was too much for me—too loud, too fast, too overwhelming. But then I realized it wasn't about fitting into the city.

It was about letting the city shape me. It has a funny way of doing that, you know?"

I nod slowly, unsure if I really understand but feeling like I want to. "What made you stay?"

She tilts her head, considering. "It was one of those moments that sneaks up on you. I was sitting in a café, feeling completely lost, and this older woman—someone I didn't even know—looked at me and said, 'You're exactly where you need to be.' She was sweet. Even bought my coffee. And for some reason, it stuck. I stopped questioning whether I belonged and started deciding that I did."

Her words settle over me like a warm embrace, and I can't help but feel like she's unknowingly speaking to my own uncertainty.

"That's... really beautiful," I say, my voice quieter than I intend.

She studies me for a moment, like she's trying to read between the lines of what I've said.

"What about you? Are you thinking about staying?"

"I don't know," I admit. "I'm a writer, and it feels like this is where writers are supposed to be. But it's overwhelming, and I don't know if I'm ready for all of it."

She leans back, her gaze drifting to the arch as the sunlight filters through it. "You don't have to be ready for all of it. You just have to be ready for the next step. The rest will follow."

Her words hit me like a revelation. She's right. I don't have to figure out my whole life today. I just have to take one step at a time, even if it's as small as showing up for James's book signing or writing a few more pages of the new story I'm working on.

"I think I needed to hear that," I say, glancing at her.

She smiles, a knowing look in her eyes. "We all do, now and then."

We sit in companionable silence for a while, the park buzzing around us. When she stands to leave, she places a hand lightly on my shoulder. "You're exactly where you need to be," she says softly, then walks away, blending into the crowd as if she was never here.

I tilt my head as she walks away when I feel tears forming and gliding down my cheeks. Why am I crying? Shit, maybe I really did need to hear those words. They seemed like words of encouragement from the universe. Though with all that's been happening with James and me, I'm not sure I can trust the universe right now.

I open my tote bag to dab my eyes with a tissue and blow my nose. Ugh, I'm a mess in the most wonderful city in the world. My thoughts escape to the past when I broke up with James. And I think about the other night... how sweet and gentle and kind he was. It's been so great to see this side of him I'd never seen. I don't want that to be a temporary change for him. It needs to be a permanent change, just like how I hope and dream New York might become my permanent change.

I know I tend to bottle things up, so maybe I needed a good cry after everything that's been going on. It felt good to let it out.

I pull my notebook back open and begin writing. Maybe I need to let these things out on paper. I've talked them out to James, Tish, and even my mom. I can't help these thoughts keep chasing after me. They're inside still but I know I need to let them go. Just like Tish said, I need to stop overthinking everything.

These thoughts are not allowing me to grow, they're simply taking control of me. But I'm not going to do that anymore. I'm going to throw them onto paper and let it end here.

Nearly an hour later I've filled roughly seven pages with my thoughts and freed them to the land of paper in my notebook. I toss my notebook into my tote bag and exhale a breath I've been holding longer than I should, feeling like a huge load has been lifted from my entire soul.

I hop off the bench and head toward Union Square, following the map app per usual. I swear, it's so handy. I smile to myself. I'm actually looking forward to seeing James in action with his novel and everyone giddy to get his autograph. I clutch my tote bag close to me, letting the crisp breeze push me toward him.

♡

By the time I reach Barnes and Noble, a line has started to form outside the door, stretching across the sidewalk like someone had let loose a million sticky gum wrappers. I am proud of James for achieving this dream. Ever since high school, he's been into writing like I was. But to actually write and finish a book is insane. I feel goosebumps rising under my sweatshirt, observing the crowd before me.

It's buzzing with excitement and it oozes over the sidewalk. The closer I get the more anxious I am, and I don't know why. Maybe it was what that woman told me earlier at the park. *You're exactly where you need to be.* Maybe at this very moment I'm supposed to be here with James at this book signing, just like we were meant to be together at the laundromat, then the pizza shop, the airport, and the seats on the plane.

I feel my heart beating faster. James was there all of those times, and maybe just to let me... talk. And he listened. He listened during our conversation at the café, soaking in my words and hopefully taking them to heart, apologizing for his ways. He listened to me requesting action, and he gave that to me. He listened to me at three in the morning and pulled me close to him, listening intently and practically inviting me to stay at his place. He listened to me and told me he's never stopped loving me, and he will wait for me.

He's shown me he has changed. And yet, Tish is telling me to be cautious, given what happened to us the first time. The lying, the yelling, the cheating, the betrayal. It was all so much, so hard to consume that I had to let him go.

Right now, though, replaying what that woman told me in the park, I'm taking it as a sign. A sign that New York is going to be my city with all its beautiful mess and chaos. Maybe it's just the mess I don't want to clean up.

I finally reach the entrance and slip away from the line, grabbing a copy of his book and wandering down my go-to aisle. Romance. I skim through the first few chapters, but my mind keeps drifting. It feels strange to read his words—knowing he's now this published author, surrounded by fans.

I flip through a few more pages, and then my eyes land on something that makes my stomach drop. It's not the beginning of the book that catches me off guard—it's the middle, where the story takes a sharp turn. The characters, who seemed so far removed from the people I knew, start resembling us.

The names are different, sure, but the details are undeniable. The argument about a forgotten anniversary, the way the boyfriend yells at his girlfriend for only trying to give him his lunch as he left for work in a hurry—something trivial but somehow so massive when we were living it. The way I used to shut down, stonewalling him when I couldn't handle the pressure anymore, how he'd get frustrated and say things he didn't mean, things that made me feel small.

"I've been seeing someone else," he says, his voice barely a whisper, full of guilt. "I'm sorry. It wasn't supposed to happen, but it did."

My heart slams into my ribs. I can feel the weight of those words, the exact same ones he said to me in our old apartment. *I'm sorry. It wasn't supposed to happen, but it did.*

The day I found out. The day everything shattered.

It's all here in this book, fictionalized, but I know it. I know those moments like they're branded into my skin. He's written it. He's written us, but not as we were. The names are different, but I can see it, feel it all over again.

I keep reading, unable to stop myself, my eyes moving faster, my heart racing. The scene where the two characters have an emotional confrontation, only for one to leave and the other to break down alone... That's us. The rawness of it, the tension, the way we'd tear each other down over things that didn't matter but felt like the world. How could he do this? How could he take our private moments—*our pain*—and twist them into fiction for the world to consume?

I feel my face flush, the heat of embarrassment and anger rushing to my cheeks. The worst part isn't even the way the events are portrayed—it's the fact that he's written it but made it so clear that it's us. He's taken our worst moments and offered them up as entertainment. I slam the book shut, unable to stomach another word.

Tears start falling before I even realize what's happening. My chest tightens, and I can barely breathe. I have to get out of here.

I don't even look back as I turn on my heel and hurry toward the exit. I can feel the weight of the book in my hands, but I don't want to hold it any longer, don't want to carry around the reminder of what I've just read. I drop it back on one of the tables as I stride past it. The doors seem to open in slow motion, and the cool air outside hits me like a slap in the face.

I can hear the voices of the crowd behind me, but all I can focus on is the tears blurring my vision. I wipe my face furiously, trying to hide the redness creeping up my neck, but it's no use. My face is blotchy, my eyes swollen from the emotions I can't contain. I hear James's voice calling out to me, but I can't stop. I can't go back in there.

"Zoe!" he calls, his voice full of confusion, concern. "Wait!"

But I don't stop.

As I hurry down the street, I can feel the eyes of the crowd on me, the whispers already starting, murmuring about what's happening, why I'm running. But I don't care. All I can think about is the book and the way he's turned our relationship into this.

I hear footsteps behind me, James trying to catch up, but I'm not ready to face him. Not after seeing our worst moments laid out for the world to see, like it's just another story.

I keep walking, the tears still streaming down my face, unsure of where I'm going but knowing I need to get away from all of it.

Chapter 27

"He wrote his book about your relationship? Your *past* relationship? Are you fucking *kidding* me?"

Tish's voice echoes through my phone's speaker as I lie on my bed at the hotel, my head hanging off the end and my feet pressed against the pillows. I changed into my pajamas and ran a warm bath, soaking away all of the pain and anger that flowed through me.

"Yup, I'm not joking. It was *us*, Tish. From him yelling at me over spilled coffee, to the way he almost hit me after he forgot his stupid lunch. It's all there, every fucking detail. And I didn't even know it at the time." I close my eyes, the steam from my bath still swirling around the room like the twisted feelings I can't quite unravel.

Tish snorts, the sound so sharp it almost makes me laugh. "What a narcissistic move. He really had to turn your heartbreak into his next bestseller, huh? Damn, Zoe. I can't believe you didn't see this coming. I'm so sorry, sweetie."

I roll my eyes, even though she can't see me. "Yeah. And you know the best part? I didn't see it coming because I was too busy loving him, Tish. I ignored all the warnings my brain was signaling at me. I thought we were... I don't know, falling back in love maybe? For real this time?"

I wince at the word as it leaves my mouth. Real. Funny how we can think something's real and then find out it was just a story he was trying to write before he even knew he was going to end it.

He was real the other night. He expressed his emotions, his intent, his feelings, all of it, at three in the goddamn morning. For what? To show me he's really changed, or just to string me along and give him an ego boost?

I exhale and roll over onto my stomach, picking at the lint on the comforter. "He told me he's still in love with me. The other night after dinner. Before I dragged his ass up to my hotel room and we..." My voice trails and I hear my throat getting caught as the tears trickle down my cheeks.

"Oh, hun. He isn't worth the tears. He lied to you about this book. Telling you he's a big published author now and hauled himself to New York, showing you all his fame and glory to get you into bed. It's a typical asshole move."

I can feel the tears slide down my face, hot against my skin. I wipe them away, but they keep coming. Stupid, stupid tears. How could I have been so gullible? So naive? Tish's voice is still going, her words a sharp contrast to the mess of emotions tangling up inside me.

"Zoe, I'm serious. You're worth so much more than him. He doesn't get to treat you like this. Not for a second time. You deserve someone who sees you for everything you are, not just for the drama he can turn into plot points for his next book. You're a fucking novel all on your own. A bestseller in the making. Don't you ever forget that."

I can hear the fire in her voice, the way she always knows what to say to snap me out of my thoughts and funks. I let her words sink in, pushing back the rising wave of frustration that's been threatening to swallow me whole.

Tish's right, of course. I shouldn't be crying over him. Not anymore. But the thing is, it's hard to get over someone who's suddenly made you feel like the center of their universe, only to turn around and treat you like material for their next big hit. It's like he wrote the story of us... but left out the part where I'm the one who gets to move on.

"I just don't get it," I mumble, the words slipping out before I can stop them. "He's the one who fucked up. He's the one who cheated and then ghosted me for months. And yet, I'm here, apparently *still* trying to figure out how to move on while he's out there... profiting from *our* pain."

Tish's response is immediate. "Because he's a coward. And you're the brave one. You're the one who's going to walk away from this, no matter how much it hurts. You're going to be stronger for it."

I snort softly, the sound wet with tears. "Stronger? Right. I feel like a damn mess."

"You are *allowed* to feel like a mess. You've been through hell. But listen to me—*he's* the one who has to live with what he did. Not you. And when you do walk away, and you will, you're going to be the one with the last laugh. He's going to be the one regretting everything. Being all sweet and nice to you. Who does that? And fakes it? Asshole."

I let out a small laugh, half-hearted but thankful. "I don't know. Right now, it feels like I'm just trying to survive this damn trip.

And to think I have that interview tomorrow bright and early, and today, of all days, my world comes crashing down. I can't even look at my phone without feeling like I'm drowning in his words. Like he's still everywhere, even when he's not."

Tish sighs deeply, and I can almost picture her running a hand through her hair, that dramatic gesture she does when she's about to say something wise but utterly ridiculous. "Maybe you need to get out of that hotel room. Go for a walk. Clear your head. Forget about him for a second. Hey, now here's a damn good reason to get yourself a cosmopolitan. I mean, he's practically Big."

My eyes flicker to the window, the city lights flickering just beyond the glass. New York at night is beautiful, in a chaotic, never-ending way. I should be enjoying it. But instead, I'm stuck here, drowning in memories of someone who doesn't even deserve the air I'm breathing.

"Yeah. Maybe you're right," I say, half to myself, half to her.

"Of course I'm right. I'm always right."

I snicker at that. "True. Have you ever considered being a motivational speaker?"

She chuckles. "Oh, sweetie, I *am* a motivational speaker, just *your* motivational speaker. The only one who truly deserves my words of wisdom. Now go, babe. Get yourself that drink."

I throw my legs over the side of the bed, my feet barely hitting the cool floor. I set the phone down and pull my hoodie over my head, slip on the same jeans I wore today, and lace on my pink Converse. I'm not sure where I'm going yet, but I know I can't stay here, stuck in this room, stewing in my own misery. Maybe the city will offer me something more than the pain of his words. Maybe I'll find something that reminds me of who I really am, not just who he made me believe I was.

"Okay, okay. I'm going. But I'm blaming you if I get lost."

Tish laughs, and I can almost hear her dismissively waving her hand. "Make sure to take some cute pictures of New York for me. You know, for *inspiration*."

I chuckle, rolling my eyes as I hang up the phone. Inspiration. Right.

I pull the hotel door open and lock it with my card. The buzz of the city seeps into my skin as I make my way toward the elevator, nuzzling my hands in my hoodie pocket and watching the illuminated numbers slowly count down.

I step out of the elevator into the lobby and pull my hoodie over my head. I yank my phone out of my pocket and notice twelve missed calls, five voicemails, and eight texts from James. I feel my nostrils flare as I shove it back in my pocket when I suddenly bump into someone.

"Oh, sorry," I exhale.

A large pair of hands hold both of my arms, stopping me from exiting the hotel. "Excuse me, what the hell are you doing? Let me go!"

The hands forcibly yank back my hood. I look up and see James. The last person I want to see.

<h1 style="text-align:center;">Chapter 28</h1>

His deep blue orbs look into mine and his hands slowly release me from his grip. His eyes are red and puffy, like he's been crying. His breath is quick and exhausted, and his curly, brown hair is tousled above his head like he's been running for hours.

I'm sure he'll claim he was.

"James," I say. "I don't want to see you right now. I was about to head out for a walk."

He tilts his head as if questioning my decision. As if I can't do such a thing without permission.

"I have been trying to call you for hours, Zoe. I left voicemails and texts and not a damn one was answered. I'm at my book signing and see you just run off, as if you were being chased by security or saw a ghost. I mean, what am I supposed to think? I was worried, Zo. You scared the shit out of me. Why the hell did you run out like that?"

Some people appear unbothered, while others have looks of concern. I suddenly can't seem to look into his eyes. Tears bubbling up from inside start trickling down my cheeks alongside my nose. My lips feel hot and start trembling. I quickly raise my hands to wipe them away, but James grabs my hands and steers me out of the lobby straight back into the elevator. His grip isn't as hard as moments before, more gentle but firm. He pulls me into him, his hands running down my arms as if soothing me. And I let myself go.

Fuck.

I let the tears fall, and they don't stop. His fingers brush my hair and he kisses my head. He was never this kind before. I clench my fingers into his coat, gripping so hard my fingers tremble.

The elevator dings on my floor and he slowly releases me, pulling me toward my room at the end of the hall. I feel his fingers checking through my pockets until my key card appears in his hand. He swipes it at the door and ushers me inside.

He takes off my glasses and sets them on the nightstand, followed by my hoodie and jeans. My shoes come off next until I'm in just my underwear and tank top. He takes off his coat and shoes, setting them near the entry table. He walks toward me and pulls me against him, placing soft kisses along my arm, up my stomach, nibbling the side of my neck.

And he places both hands on my face, as if he's telling me it's going to be okay. His golden blue eyes stare into mine as his eyebrows crease with concern, maybe even worry.

"I'll start a warm bath for you, okay? But first, I need you to tell me what's wrong, Zo. I can't understand until you speak."

I should be mad at him. I should be yelling at him. I should have fought with him in the lobby, made a scene. I should have told him everything right then and there. But I didn't. I'm not the kind of girl who loses it on people. I'm the kind of girl who bottles shit up and stays quiet. Who constantly overthinks. And my mind boggles with thoughts left and right.

I breathe in and exhale, my breath shaking. I pull away from him and he sits on the bed, looking at me with those big, blue, worried eyes.

"You lied to me. Your book… it's about *us*. Why would you ever think writing about all that shit is okay?"

He sucks in a breath and brushes his fingers through his hair. He looks at the door, the floor, then back at me getting more impatient each millisecond.

"I didn't lie. I guess the subject of my book never came up. But I never lied, Zoe, you know that."

My heart skips a beat when he says that. *I never lied.* I stride across the room and look out the window, clutching my arms close to me. I then realize I'm still half naked and move toward the bed, sitting as far as I can away from him. He turns himself toward me, his full body facing me. He reaches toward me, and my nostrils flare at the sight. I flinch, and he folds his hands in his lap.

"I *know* that? You did fucking lie, James. You lied all those years, you lied and never cared that you did, so you just kept lying to me. I mean, what am I supposed to believe now, huh? Even after the other night…"

He pauses and places his hand on the bed, gripping the comforter. He swallows and sighs, looking down. His expression shows worry, but who am I to say that's real?

James sits there, staring at me like he's trying to solve a puzzle that's missing half its pieces. His lips part, and for a moment, I think he's going to say something—something that will make it all make sense, something that will justify all the lies—but nothing comes out. Just silence. It stretches between us, taut and fragile. The kind of silence that feels like it might shatter with the faintest breath.

I want to scream at him. I want to yell and throw something, anything, just to cut through the suffocating silence. My fingers twitch at my sides, itching for action, but instead I sit frozen, clutching my arms tightly around myself. The chill of the room seeps into my skin, even as my face burns with heat, a dizzying mix of anger and heartbreak.

"You can't just write about us and pretend it doesn't matter, James," I finally say, my voice low but firm. "You don't get to use our past for content and slap it between a cover like it's some made-up story. That was *my* life. My *heartbreak*. Don't you get that?"

He leans forward, his elbows on his knees, hands clasped so tightly his knuckles are white. "*Your* heartbreak? You act like it wasn't mine at all, like I didn't feel shitty after either. And by the way, it wasn't even like that."

His jaw flexes, and I can see the effort it takes for him to stay composed. "It wasn't even like that back then, and you know it," he murmurs, his voice barely audible.

I crinkle my eyebrows together, questioning every word he just said. Did he really just say that?

"Then what was it like?" I snap, my voice cracking halfway through. My words come out fast and sharp, like I'm afraid he'll interrupt me before I can finish. "Explain it to me. Because right now, it feels like every time I trusted you, every time I opened myself up to you, you were just taking notes. Planning how to turn me into a goddamn character for your next book. Was all that talk at the coffee shop and fucking disco diner all lies? You didn't mean a damn word, did you? You reached back out to me to see if you could play your mind games with me like you did all those years ago. Acting like you changed and transformed into a knight in shining armor all to tear me down again, right?"

His head snaps up, and his eyes lock onto mine. Like what I said finally seeped through his veins this time. For the first time since he walked through the door, there's fire in his eyes—a flicker of something raw and unguarded. Anger? Guilt? Regret? I can't tell. Maybe it's all of it.

"Stop it, Zoe," he says, his voice rough, "it wasn't like that. You don't get to say whether I'm a changed man or not. You don't get to say that what I said wasn't real. Look, I didn't write the book to hurt you. I wrote it because it's the only way I knew how to make sense of what happened. Of us. You think it was easy for me? You think I didn't tear myself apart writing those pages?"

I laugh, bitter and hollow, the sound foreign to my ears. "Oh, poor James, suffering for his art," I mock, my words dripping with venom. "How noble of you. Did you cry when you wrote about the night you cheated? Did it break your heart to relive every lie you told me? Or when you got so angry you almost hit me? Or was it just 'good material'?"

He flinches, his jaw tensing like I've physically struck him. Like what I've said sparked something in him to the point of admitting everything was a lie. And for a fleeting second, I feel a twisted sense of satisfaction. But it fades as quickly as it came, leaving behind a hollow ache in my chest that threatens to swallow me whole.

"I didn't put everything in the book," he says quietly.

I narrow my eyes at him, suspicion rising like bile in my throat. "What's that supposed to mean?"

"There were things I couldn't write about," he says, his gaze dropping to the floor. His voice is steady, but there's a tremor beneath it, like he's balancing on the edge of a confession. "Things I didn't want to share with the world. Because they were ours. Because no matter how much I screwed up, there are still pieces of you—of us—that I couldn't let anyone else see."

His words hit me like a wave, crashing against the fragile walls I've built around my heart. My throat tightens, and my chest feels heavy, like the air in the room is pressing down on me. I don't know what to say, so I don't say anything.

James looks up at me again, and his eyes are softer now, pleading. "I know I messed up. I know I hurt you in ways I can't even begin to fix. But I need you to believe me when I say that I never stopped caring about you. Never stopped *loving* you. Not for a second. I mean, damn, how many times does a man have to apologize for his wrongful actions?"

I shut my eyes tight and hope once I open them he'll be gone. I open them, but he's still here. He's still staring at me, his eyes full of concern and hurt. I'm stunned he came up with an explanation for his book. *The only way to make sense of what happened? Wrongful actions?*

Give me a break.

But then my mind wanders to the conversation my mom and I had a couple weeks back about second chances. I feel my heartbeat slowing, my body feeling warm from all the yelling we just did. My face damp from the tears. She gave my dad a second chance, and that chance turned into a happily ever after for her. She's practically living out her fairytale with a wonderful man who treats her how she should be treated.

Just like James treated me all those times when the universe shoved us back together.

The thought makes my stomach churn. My subconscious pounds on my brain, yelling at me to pay attention as a sudden thought comes to the surface: the universe didn't shove us together for love. Not for sappy moonlit walks or whispered promises. It wasn't about fate or some cosmic thread tying us to each other. No, the universe shoved us together for *this*. For his damn book. For his lies. For me to sit here, half-naked in a hotel room, cracking open under the weight of it all.

James is staring at me like I'm the one who's broken him, like I'm the one who's taken everything we were and turned it into fiction. But he doesn't get to do that. He doesn't get to rewrite history and call it art.

He's not an artist, he's a manipulative liar and my eyes are opening wide to finally see it. Clear as fucking day. And it's about damn time.

"I don't believe you," I whisper, my voice trembling. "I don't believe a word you're saying."

His shoulders sag, and he drags a hand through his hair, his frustration bubbling over. "Zo, what do you want me to say? That I'm sorry? Of course I'm fucking sorry. Do I regret it? I do. But I can't change what happened. All I can do is try to make you understand."

"Understand?" I let out a sharp, humorless laugh, shaking my head. "You want me to *understand* why you used me, James? Why you turned my pain into your plot points? No. I don't think I'll ever understand that."

He stands abruptly, pacing the room like a caged animal. "I didn't *use* you. I wrote about us because it *meant* something. Because *you* meant something. You still do."

His words are knives cutting through me with precision. They sound so scripted.

"If I meant something, you wouldn't have cheated on me. You wouldn't have lied. And you sure as hell wouldn't have *published* those lies for everyone to read."

His pacing stops, and he turns to face me, his expression raw and unguarded. "You think I don't hate myself for what I did? You think I don't relive it every single day? I lost you. And I've been trying to figure out how to live with that ever since."

I shake my head, biting back the tears threatening to spill over again. "You didn't just lose me, James. You broke me. No, you broke *us*. And now you're standing here asking me to... what? Forgive you? Forget all of it?"

"No," he says, his voice steady but soft. "I'm asking you to see me. The *real* me. Not the guy in the book, not the guy you've been hating for years. Just me. The man who's still in love with you."

My breath catches, and I stare at him, my heart pounding in my chest. "You don't get to say that," I whisper. "You don't get to *feel* that way after everything you've done."

"It's the truth," he says, his voice breaking.

The truth. The word feels like a cruel joke. James has always been good with words, weaving them into stories that feel too real, too raw. But this? This feels like another manipulation, another chapter in a book I never agreed to be part of.

I stand, folding my arms in front of me. "I need you to leave," I say, my voice barely above a whisper.

His face falls, and for a moment, he looks like he might protest. But then he nods, his shoulders slumping in defeat. "Fine."

He puts on his coat and shoes, lingering at the door for a moment before turning back to me. "Not that it'll matter, but Zoe, I'm still sorry. For all of it."

I don't respond. I can't. I don't even want to think about what I would even say. My throat feels too tight, my chest too heavy. I watch as he steps out of the room, the door clicking softly shut behind him.

Chapter 29

I stand there, frozen, staring at the space where James had been. The room feels impossibly quiet now, his absence amplifying the pounding of my heart. My legs feel weak, unsteady, so I sink onto the edge of the bed, letting the weight of everything crash over me like a tidal wave.

The anger is still there, burning low but persistent, a simmering ember that refuses to be snuffed out. But beneath it, there's something heavier—something fresh and raw and aching that I don't know how to name. It feels like regret, but not for what I said. No, I don't regret standing up for myself, for demanding the answers I deserve. It's the regret of what we once were, the ghost of a love that could've been something extraordinary if only he hadn't shattered it.

I press my hands to my face, trying to will the tears away. But they come anyway, hot and relentless. I don't even know who I'm crying for—the girl I was before James, or the girl I became after him. Maybe both. Maybe neither.

His words replay in my mind, looping like a broken record. *I didn't write it to hurt you. I never stopped caring about you. I'm still in love with you.*

The worst part is, in a way, I believe him. Or at least, I believe that *he* believes it. But love isn't supposed to feel like this. It's not supposed to be a battlefield, as Pat Benatar belted out. It's not where one person holds all the power, rewriting the rules and expecting the other to just accept it. Love is supposed to be honest. Kind. Whole. And whatever James and I had, it was never that.

I get up and pace, the small hotel room suddenly feeling suffocating. My thoughts are a tangled mess, every memory of James clashing against the reality of what he's done. The way he smiled at me that first summer, like I was the only person in the world. The nights we stayed up until dawn, talking about everything and nothing.

And then, the lies. The other fucking woman. The nights I stayed up alone, wondering what I'd done wrong, where he was and why he wouldn't respond to my calls and texts. Why I wasn't enough.

I stop pacing and a sudden shiver springs through my body. Probably from the cold air that James left behind. I pull on my sweatshirt and tug on my pajama bottoms along with my slippers. I lean against the window, staring out at the city lights. They blur and shimmer through the tears clouding my vision, a kaleidoscope of colors that feel as chaotic as my emotions. Somewhere out there, James is probably walking back to his book signing, putting on a smile for his fans. Or maybe meeting up with his editor for a night out in celebration, pretending that everything's fine. That's what he's always been good at—pretending.

But I can't pretend anymore. Not for him. Not even for myself.

I look over at the vase of tulips on the desk. Their leaves are wilting now. I scoop them out and toss them in the small trash bin underneath. It's not like they mean anything anymore. They probably never did anyway.

I reach for my phone on the nightstand, thumb hovering over Tish's name. She'd answer in seconds, her voice full of righteous anger and sharp humor, ready to remind me why I'm better off without him. But tonight, I don't want anger or humor. I want clarity.

My thumb scrolls down my contacts list until it stops on Ben.

Ben, my editor. The man who sat across from me at brunch earlier today, listening intently as I rambled about my writing, about New York, about everything except James. He smiled in that easy, disarming way of his, offering thoughtful advice and the kind of warmth that felt rare and genuine.

Since then, we've exchanged a few brief texts. Mostly about recommendations on what to do in the city, him checking in on me to see how I'm liking it so far, that sort of thing. Though brief, they were enough to keep him in the back of my mind. He's been such a gentleman and so kind. Still acquaintances, he had the courage to open up to me. And I honestly enjoyed listening. Probably silly, but I like to think it's been the highlight of my trip so far.

I don't know what compels me, but I tap his name and hit call.

The line rings once, twice, and then his voice comes through, warm and steady.

"Zoe?"

For a moment, I can't speak. Hearing him—his calm, grounded tone—makes my chest tighten in a way I can't explain. Finally, I manage, "Hi, Ben. I, uh, hope I'm not bothering you."

"Hey, of course you're not," he says immediately, his voice softening. "I'm just finishing up some leftover things from work today." He clears his throat. "Are you all right? You sound upset."

I take a shaky breath, the words tumbling out before I can stop them. "It's my ex, James. He was here. We fought. I just... I don't know what to do anymore."

There's a pause, and when Ben speaks again, his voice is careful but unwavering. "Do you want me to come over?"

His question catches me off guard, my heart skipping a beat. "What? No, I didn't mean..." I trail off, unsure of what I'm even asking for.

"Zoe," he says gently, "Sure, I'm your editor, and I take that professional line seriously. But like I said before, you have my number. If you ever need to talk—about anything—I'm here. Business or not."

His words make my tense shoulders relax against the chair as I sit, and I find myself gripping the phone tighter. "Thank you," I whisper, my voice barely audible.

I end the call and lie back on the bed, starting at the ceiling as my vision blurs, realizing I'm still crying. The tears keep coming, sliding down my cheeks and neck, forming small puddles of water within my collarbone.

What feels like a lifetime, but more like fifteen minutes later, I hear a knock at my door. I quickly wipe my eyes with my sleeve and slide off the bed. My steps are hesitant, my breath shallow, as I move toward the door. I open it and Ben is standing just outside, breathless.

His coat is damp from the evening mist, his hair slightly mussed, and his eyes—those glistening hazel eyes, steady yet thoughtful—are locked on mine. Concern softens his features, but beneath it, there's something else, something I can't quite place.

"You're lucky I was just across the street at Starbucks," Ben says softly. "Hey, Zoe."

He stands tall, his broad shoulders and lean frame dressed in a sleek charcoal-gray button-up followed by black slacks and shoes. His golden wavy hair frames his sharp, intelligent features—a contrast to James's raw and restless energy. His deep hazel eyes, flecked with gold, hold steady, reflecting a quiet confidence that doesn't need words to make an impact.

I quickly wipe my cheeks and eyes, feeling my face and throat warming to the sound of his voice. My throat tightens, the weight of his words pressing against the cracks in my resolve.

And then, from somewhere down the hall, another voice cuts through the silence like a knife.

"Zoe?"

My stomach drops as I turn to see James standing at the end of the hallway, his expression dark and unreadable.

I look back at Ben, then at James, my heart pounding in my chest as the air in the corridor thickens.

Ben's eyes flicker to James, his jaw tightening ever so slightly before his gaze returns to me. "Do you want me to leave?" he asks, his tone calm but his meaning unmistakable.

The words catch in my throat, and I realize, with a jolt of panic, that I have no idea what to say. The hallway feels like it's collapsing around me, the tension between James and Ben radiating like heat. My legs are frozen, my vision slightly blurry, and all I can manage is a breathless, "Sorry, what are you doing here?" directed at Ben.

"I told you," Ben says, his voice quiet but holding a soft firmness to it. "I came because you sounded upset and like you wanted to talk." His gaze shifts briefly to James, not hostile, but firm, before settling back on me. "If I overstepped, just say the word, Zoe."

James takes a deliberate step closer, his presence suddenly overwhelming the narrow space. "Who the hell is this?" His voice is low, almost dangerous—a tone I've only heard once before, the night we shattered everything.

Ben doesn't flinch. His calm remains unshaken, like steel beneath a polished exterior. "I'm her editor," he says simply, his tone even, professional. "And a friend."

James scoffs, running a hand through his hair, his movements erratic. "A *friend*? Showing up at her hotel late at night? Doesn't sound very professional to me."

"James!" My voice cuts through the air, sharper than I intended. "Stop."

He turns to me, his expression a mix of hurt and anger. "Are you seriously defending him right now? After everything we just—" He cuts himself off, shaking his head like he can't even finish the thought.

"I didn't ask him to come," I say, my voice trembling, but I force myself to stand taller. "But I'm glad he's here."

James flinches, the words hitting him like a physical blow. For a moment, his face crumples with something raw and vulnerable, but he quickly masks it with anger.

Ben takes a step back, his hands raised slightly in a gesture of peace. "I don't want to make this worse," he says, his voice steady.

His calmness is almost disarming, a stark contrast to James's volatility. I look between them, my heart pounding so hard it feels like it might burst.

"Stay," I whisper, the word escaping before I can stop it.

James's eyes widen, disbelief flashing across his face. "Are you fucking kidding me?" he says, his voice rising. "You're choosing *him*?"

"No. This isn't about choosing," I snap, the anger bubbling up inside me. "This is about me needing space to think. To breathe. And right now, James, you're making it impossible. Why are you still here, anyway?"

James's expression changes from anger to confusion, like he's baffled by my question. "I... don't know, Zoe. I guess I was debating if I should come back and we could talk some more, to convince you I'm your person and you're mine." His golden blue eyes stare at me, then go to Ben, and back to me. He clenches his jaw so tightly I can see the muscles twitching.

"But maybe I'm just kidding myself. Zoe, you know that I still love you, and care about you more than anything and anyone. I mean that from the bottom of my heart." And without another word, he turns and strides down the hallway, his footsteps echoing long after he's disappeared.

The silence that follows is deafening. My knees feel weak, and I sink back against the doorframe, my hands trembling.

Ben doesn't react immediately, his presence calm and composed, yet commanding. It's as if he knows he's handsome, and I can't help but to keep staring at him, soaking it all in.

I shake my head and bite my lip, trying to comprehend what just happened. Ben steps closer, his presence grounding.

"Zoe," he says gently, his voice pulling me back from the edge. He placed his hand softly on my back, sending a spark through my spine. "Are you okay?"

I nod. I don't trust my voice.

"Do you want to talk about it?" he asks, his tone soft but unwavering. "I'm here for you, whatever you need."

The sincerity in his voice makes my chest tighten, and for the first time in hours, I feel like I can breathe again.

"I don't know," I admit, my voice barely above a whisper. "I don't even know where to start."

Suddenly his hand wavers away from my back and he slowly leans against the wall across from me. He's giving me space, but not retreating entirely.

"Then don't," he says simply. "Start when you're ready. I'm not going anywhere. As a matter of fact, why don't we take a stroll? The New York air might help that sharp brain of yours to relax." He extends his arm, inviting me to grab on and I can only hope to take me away to a magical land far, far away. Maybe further than New York.

I nod and fold my arm through his, his hand covering mine.

"I may not be a therapist by trade, but I'm a damn good listener."

I feel myself smiling. We head toward the elevator, my jumbled thoughts unraveling by the second. I'm actually glad I reached out to Ben. Perhaps he is just the person to help me tame this crazy life of mine.

Chapter 30

We're walking down 6th Avenue and I can't help but feel embarrassed. Over James. Over our stupid "meet cutes" (because there wasn't anything cute about them). Over believing he had changed. Over his constant lying. I can't help but feel entirely over him. I can't stand him. I just want him to go away forever.

I stop walking. And moments later Ben also stops, looking back at me. "You okay?"

I look up at him and feel my nostrils flare. The interview is tomorrow. Fuck.

"Yeah, yeah, no. I just realized it's getting late and the interview is tomorrow. I have barely prepared for it with all of this James drama and feel like I won't be ready."

He turns to me and places both hands on my arms. His hands are warm and steady against them, grounding me in a way I desperately need right now. His gaze holds mine, and for a moment, the chaos of my thoughts quiets. His hazel eyes seem to glow under the soft golden hue of the streetlights, flecks of gold catching the light like embers. A faint hint of his cologne whispers under my nose, making me want to melt in his arms.

I slowly look up and he's staring down at me.

"Zoe, you've got this. Your writing and tone and language were practically screaming off the pages to choose you. You're here because of your talent, and you're going to kick butt tomorrow."

I let out a sigh and nod, his words echoing through me. His eyes hold mine with an intensity that's both sincere and kind, his expression a mixture of encouragement and restraint. He clears his throat softly, and his voice, when he speaks, is measured yet warm.

"You'll be ready," he says, his tone calm and assured, like a mentor coaxing confidence out of a hesitant student. "You've been preparing for this moment longer than you realize. Tomorrow isn't about perfection—it's about sharing your passion for what you've written. Just think of it like telling a story. Don't even call it an 'interview.' I promise, everything is going to be fine."

I blink up at him, torn between the comfort his words bring and the vulnerability of hearing him speak so directly to my insecurities. I try to deflect, attempting to mask my unease. "You're just saying that because it's your job to make writers feel good about themselves," I tease lightly, though my voice falters.

Ben huffs a soft laugh, shaking his head as his hands drop from my arms. Instead, he crosses them loosely, maintaining that professional distance even as his presence continues to steady me.

"No," he says, his voice firm but not harsh. "I'm saying it because it's true. I wouldn't say it if I didn't believe it. You have something that draws people in, Zoe. That's why P&W wanted to publish your story in the first place. You make people feel something."

The way he says it, with such quiet certainty, makes my breath catch. My heart flutters—not just from his words, but from the restrained warmth in his tone, the care he takes to deliver them without crossing any invisible line.

"I don't know if I can do it," I admit, my voice barely above a whisper. I hate how small I sound, but I can't help it. The weight of everything—James, the interview, my own self-doubt—feels like too much.

Ben steps closer, his head tilting as he leans down, his eyes aligning with mine perfectly.

"You can," he says softly. "And you will. And if you stumble, that's okay. You're human. But you're also a damn good writer, and that's what Margaret will see."

His words settle over me and they ease some of the tension in my chest. I manage a small, grateful smile. "Thank you," I murmur.

Ben nods and smiles. "That's what I'm here for," he says, his hands sliding into his coat pockets as he straightens up. "To help you shine—whether it's through your writing or moments like this."

The air between us feels somewhat charged.

He gestures toward the street with a polite nod. "Now, I don't know about you, but I am starving. Up for a late-night snack? It's the best $1.50 slice in the city."

I chuckle and follow him into the pizza shop just a few blocks away. "That sounds amazing. I haven't eaten since this afternoon, and I think my body's starting to remind me of that."

Ben opens the door for me, gesturing me to go ahead. We order a couple of slices and drinks and head back out into the still bustling nightlife New York is known for. I take a bite, and I can't help but moan in happiness. "Oh my god, this pizza is amazing!"

Ben chuckles and sets his drink down between us on a bench just up the street. "I'm telling you, New York pizza is the best, hands down. You can't find a slice better than this anywhere."

I take another bite, allowing the cheese and grease and pepperoni to coat my insides. The cool air whips past us, but it feels nice on my face. I glance at Ben, whose mouth is stuffed with pizza. I can't help but smile as I admire him sitting next to me, eating a slice of pizza. It's so simple and yet, I feel myself biting my lip. He is so attractive and pretty and, well, *hot*.

I shake my head, biting back a sigh as I mentally scold myself. Haven't I learned by now? After everything with James—the heartbreak, the unraveling of who I thought he was—I should know better. I *do* know better. The last thing I need is another man threading his way into my life, especially someone like him.

But I can't help it. I glance up, and there he is—sitting under the glow of the streetlights, the soft gold of his hair catching the light just right, as if the night itself is conspiring to make him look ethereal. Like the city's given him a halo, and I'm the only one lucky enough to see it.

It's stupid. It's reckless. Fantasizing about what it might be like—*really* like—with him. It's a bad idea wrapped in charm and soft laughter. It would be messy. Complicated. He's my acquisitions editor. The man who believed in my story enough to fly me from small-town Ohio to here, who literally got me this close to everything I've ever wanted. His boss is interviewing me tomorrow. And here I am... wondering what his hand might feel like in mine.

I try to ground myself, focus on the greasy paper plate in front of me. But when he looks over, catches my eye with that quiet smile of his, something in my chest stutters. My face grows warm. I look away too quickly, as if that could undo the fluttering inside me. I shove another bite of pizza into my mouth, slurping my drink like it'll drown the blush creeping up my cheeks.

Dammit.

He smirks and tosses his plate in the trash, then scoots closer to me as he picks up his drink. His knee softly grazes mine and I feel that spark again. My heart is getting great at acrobatics because it literally does another flip in my chest.

"So," he says. "You certainly don't have to say anything, but... what happened earlier, with you and James? He's your ex?"

I toss my plate in the trash and shift my body toward his, sitting criss-cross applesauce, feeling safe.

"Yeah, unfortunately he's my ex," I say. "We had a... complicated breakup. He lied, cheated, and I..." I shrug, suddenly feeling small again. "I gave him way too many chances. I thought he'd changed. But clearly, I was wrong."

I swallow, feeling a tightness in my chest. I've been holding this in, pretending that I'm fine, but I'm not. I'm far from it. "I found out today that his latest book—it's about us. About *me*. All of it— the good parts, the bad parts—everything that happened between us." I pause, my heart pounding in my chest. "I didn't even know until I read an excerpt earlier. It's like he wrote our relationship, our entire history, and turned it into a story for everyone else to read. Like it was... nothing."

The words spill out of me faster than I can control them, a mix of frustration and disbelief. "I mean, how do you even *process* that? How could he do that to me?"

Ben listens intently, not interrupting, but I can see the concern in his eyes, the way his jaw tightens as he's hearing me out. I can tell he's not just listening, but really hearing me.

"I'm humiliated," I admit, the words falling out before I can stop them. "I feel so... exposed. Like he just took everything private and turned it into some sort of narrative for the world. It's like he's taking ownership of something that was never his to begin with."

I shake my head, trying to steady my emotions, but they're all over the place. "I didn't even realize how much it hurt until I saw it in black and white."

Ben's gaze softens, and he shifts closer, the heat of his body making me feel like I'm not alone in this. It's strangely comforting. He doesn't say anything at first, just lets the silence stretch, and for a moment it's like the weight of the world has been lifted off my shoulders. I didn't realize how badly I needed to talk about this until now. Sure, I practically threw up all my feelings on Tish earlier, but that was Tish. This feels... different. A good different.

"I'm not proud of it," I continue, my voice quieter now. "I guess I thought... I don't know what I thought. Thought maybe he'd changed, that the things he said about our relationship—about me—were sincere. But this? This is... it feels like deception."

Ben doesn't break eye contact. "Zoe, you don't need to feel embarrassed. You're allowed to be angry. It's not your fault that he did that." His voice is steady, but there's an edge to it now, like he's not just sympathizing—he's protecting me in some way. "He took something that was yours and made it his. That's not fair to you."

I nod, not knowing whether to cry or laugh at how much it all feels like a bad dream. "I don't even know what to do with all of this. I want to be mad at him, but I also just want him to go away. I want to forget about everything he did, about how he…" I trail off, my throat tightening as I remember everything that happened between us. "How he lied. How he *cheated*. And yet part of me wanted to believe he did change. I wanted action, and he did that. He was showing me he was a changed man, a live-action prince charming and all. Part of me, I guess, wanted to believe he could have been the person I hoped for, you know?"

I let out a breath I didn't realize I was holding and fold my hands in my lap. It's not like Ben's offering some magical fix to make everything better. But the way he's listening, the way he's just… here, it's like he's giving me permission to feel what I feel without shame.

Ben's expression softens even more, and before I can stop myself, I continue.

"I guess that's where my parents come in. They're one of the few things that make me believe in second chances, you know? My mom and dad—they separated when I was a teenager, and it was messy. But they ended up finding their way back to each other years later, and now they have this whole 'happy-ever-after' thing going on. They're still crazy in love. And it's like… I saw that, and I thought if it could happen to them, maybe it could happen for me too. With James, I mean."

I laugh bitterly, shaking my head. "Maybe I'm influenced by

this idea that love can come back, that people can change, that second chances can work. But I don't know anymore. Maybe I was just fooling myself."

Ben watches me closely, his hazel eyes never leaving mine. The streetlights cast a warm glow over his face, and for a moment, it feels like it's just the two of us in the world. He reaches over and stops for a moment, like he's thinking. His hand brushes against mine gently, just enough to send goosebumps up my arm. The touch is so easy, but it sends my pulse racing.

"You're not foolish for believing in second chances," Ben says, his voice low, threaded with a softness that makes my heart clench. "Your parents... they found their way back to each other, and that's beautiful. That kind of hope—it's in you, Zoe. I can see it. It clings to your words like ivy. But hope doesn't mean holding on to someone who will hold you back. James..." He exhales, gently shaking his head. "James doesn't deserve that hope. He doesn't deserve *you*."

Something in his tone—so genuine, so full of quiet certainty— makes my chest tighten. His words find their way into the ache I've been trying to ignore for weeks, like they were always meant to land there. His hand lingers just beside mine on the bench, close enough that I feel its warmth, and something deep inside me stirs. I don't even know what to call it, but it feels safe. It feels like being seen for the first time in a long time.

"Thanks, Ben," I whisper, my voice barely hanging on. "I didn't realize how much I needed to say all of that. I'm sorry if I sounded like a broken record."

He reaches for my hand, curling his fingers around mine

with the gentlest squeeze, his thumb tracing the top of my knuck-les like he's trying to soothe something deeper than just nerves. "I'm glad you feel like you can talk to me. I mean, my emotional support rates have gone up dramatically—but for you, I'll let it slide tonight." He winks, and I feel my breath hitch. My nos-trils flare in that telltale, awkward way, and I can only hope he doesn't notice.

He takes a long sip and clears his throat. "And for the record, you're not the only one with a crazy ex. Her name was Melanie."

Chapter 81

Ben's voice is low, as if he doesn't want to share this with anyone else in the world. It's like our little secret. His golden hair curls around his neck, the streetlights shining ever so lightly as tiny droplets of sweat smooths down his neck under his shirt collar.

It's as if he's just as nervous as I am. And I can't help it. It's kind of sweet.

"We were actually high school sweethearts. Looking back, maybe having a high school sweetheart was a sign it wasn't going to end well, huh?" He smirks, and continues. "Anyway, we dated until sophomore year of college. It was long distance. Me at NYU, her at Yale. And I'll admit it was hard. It definitely challenged us in a lot of ways."

He shifts to face me, his gold-flecked hazel eyes now locked with mine. It makes my heart flutter and ache all at once. I take a breath and push it aside. I can't do this right now.

"She got pregnant right before our third year. Turns out it was with a professor. I'm sure you can figure out what happened thereafter. She ended up dropping out and moving with him to his fancy Hampton beach house..."

His voice trails, his fingers fumbling with his cup. "Look, Zoe. I guess what I'm trying to get at with my sappy story is that sometimes life takes a turn you didn't expect. It doesn't mean you're going backwards either. Life sometimes has a funny way of throwing that special someone right in front of you when you least expect it, you know?"

I can't help but feel my face glowing a blush of red. *That special someone.* He's so handsome and sweet. My face probably looks like those dolls with red-painted circles on their cheeks. I gently rub them, hoping he takes it as if I'm just cold.

He's saying all the right things, even when it's about his ex. His voice is traced with charm and it makes my knees weak. And here I am, going through an endless sea as strong waves of James drama crash into me.

He angles himself as his eyes look out at Central Park before us, his eyes glistening with emotion. Now I feel bad about my trauma dumping giving him the need to trauma dump too. Was it to make me feel better? Or simply to know that he understands?

Moments pass, and I softly lace my fingers around his. He looks down, a soft smile forming at his lips.

"Thank you for sharing that. I hope you know that you're such a good person. You invited me to brunch to soften my nerves for the interview. Sorry, 'story.' You immediately made yourself available to come down to my hotel and even share pizza with me, letting me go on about James. And here you are spilling your guts about the ex that cheated on you, all while trying to make me feel better."

I shift closer on the bench, and our shoes nudge one another.

He doesn't move away. "And I'm so sorry for what happened between you two. We both didn't deserve what happened to our past relationships, that's for sure. So, to end my babbling, I'm glad you're the person I called. I'm glad you're here with me. It means a lot to me... more than you know."

Ben lets out a low laugh, nodding in response. It tugs at my chest, just a little bit. "Thanks, Zoe. You have a way with words, I hope you know that."

His eyes—soft brown swirled with gold embers—hold mine in a way that sends my heart tumbling. I swear, in this moment, the whole world blurs. The city noise fades. The streetlights dim. And all I can feel is this strange, beautiful quiet between us.

A slow smirk curls at the corners of my mouth. And then my stomach does a flip. I can't tell if it's the greasy pizza or the way Ben shared a little piece of himself, or maybe the fact that this day—this overwhelming, surreal day—has ended like this, with him. With Ben, who looks at me like I'm something more than a headline or a draft in need of edits.

I hold his gaze, feeling the warmth of his hand still cradling mine. Thoughts swarm my mind, tangled and chaotic, but none of them make it past my lips. There's something so terrifying and comforting about the way he's looking at me—like he sees every messy, complicated piece of me and doesn't flinch. I feel stripped down to my heart, vulnerable in a way that feels... okay.

"I'm not *that* good," I say, my voice soft, tinged with something almost shy. "But I'll take the compliment. And I'm honestly not sure what I would have done today if you hadn't been here."

He tilts his head, a gentle smile tugging at the corners of his mouth. "You'd have figured it out. You're stronger than you think."

His words wash over me like a lullaby, settling into the parts of me still shaken by the past. "Maybe," I say, smiling just a little, "but it's still nice to have someone in my corner."

Ben's smile deepens, and something in his expression softens. I feel the shift before I see it—the quiet recognition between two people who've lived enough to know the difference between convenience and connection.

I fidget with my napkin, twisting it in my lap before looking back at him. "I feel like I can actually talk about my stuff with you without feeling like I'm being too much."

He furrows his brow, shaking his head with a smirk. "Zoe, you're not too much. You're fiery and smart and... cute. And yeah, getting a vibe that maybe you're a little stubborn." He chuckles. "But you're also not 'too much.' At all. I'm honored I get to be part of your writing journey."

His words nestle into me, unexpected and yet exactly what I didn't know I needed. And he called me cute. My cheeks flush.

We sit in easy silence for a while, the buzz of the city softening behind us. It feels like we've created this little bubble here.

I glance over again, and his eyes meet mine—those warm golden hazel eyes that seem to carry stories of their own. Something shifts.

My breath catches. I want to speak, to break the silence, but I don't know what to say. So instead, I smile. And for the first time in what feels like forever, the smile feels genuine.

Then I notice it—Ben leaning in, just slightly. Slowly. His breath brushes my cheek, and his eyes flicker down to my lips. Time seems to stand still.

Every part of me is screaming *wait*, *pause*, *think*. This is complicated. This is too much. I can't do this—not now. Not with everything still so raw.

But then his lips brush mine—featherlight, and almost hesitant.

And I pull back.

My hands press gently against his chest and he immediately coughs, looking away with a nervous chuckle as he sips his drink. The moment cracks.

"Ben, I'm sorry," I say, my voice shaking. "I can't... not after James, and the book, and everything..."

He turns toward me, gently placing a finger over my lips, stopping me mid-ramble.

"No, Zoe, I'm sorry," he says, his voice rough around the edges but steady. "I should be more careful. You just shared so much with me. I should've respected that. I *do* respect that. I'm a professional. And tonight—I didn't act like it."

I let out a shaky laugh, shaking my head. "No, it's okay. I appreciate you saying that. Really. If we can just keep things professional, I think that's best. Even if I did unload a ridiculous amount of James baggage..."

Ben laughs, a low, easy sound. "You're not the only one. But I'm more than glad that you did."

He stands, reaching for my hands, and gently pulls me up. "Come on, Ms. Donovan. Let's get you back to your hotel. We both have a big day tomorrow."

I nod, letting out a long breath as I slip my hand from his, the air cool where his warmth had been. "You got that right."

When we reach the hotel, we stop just outside the entrance. Ben rocks slightly on his heels, his hands shoved into his pockets.

"Well," he says, his voice quiet again, more tentative now. "For what it's worth, Zoe... you've got a bright future ahead. And I'm not just talking about your writing."

His words land gently, not weighty, but sincere enough to make me pause. I feel a blush rise to my cheeks.

I feel a smile pulling at my lips. And for once, I believe the words.

"That means more than you know."

Ben smiles back, hands still in his pockets. "You're welcome. Just... don't forget it, okay?"

There's a quiet understanding between us. No tension, no unspoken promises. Just two people who shared a moment in the middle of a city that never slows down. I nod, grateful for the simplicity of it.

"I won't," I say. "Good night, Mr. Editor."

He smirks. "Good night, Ms. Donovan."

He turns and walks away, blending into the blur of New York's late-night rhythm. I don't watch him for long. There's no need. Whatever was about to happen, whatever we might have turned into, has served its purpose. In a way, he reminded me of who I am. Not through grand gestures or complicated feelings, but by simply listening. And letting go.

Back in my hotel room, I make my way to the window and stare out into the glistening city before me. The city hums just outside, alive and constant. Tomorrow, everything shifts—the interview and maybe the start of something new.

I don't want to pursue another relationship right now. This

isn't one of those small-town-to-big-city cheesy Hallmark movies. I don't need another messy, complicated relationship in my life. I have better things going on for me. Like my short story being published.

Man, Tish would be so proud of me for holding my ground and being a big girl. I can just see her cheering for me and toasting me with a large glass of wine.

Like my mom says, some people aren't meant to stay. They're meant to show up, hold space, and leave you a little stronger than before.

Chapter 82

Once I'm back in my hotel room, I take a seat at the desk, kicking off my shoes and tossing my hoodie onto the dresser. The city skyline stretches out in front of me, the lights twinkling like a thousand tiny promises. I let myself stare at it for a moment, taking a deep breath before heading into the bathroom.

Washing my face feels almost like washing away the evening I just had, and the cool water is a welcome contrast to the lingering heat in my cheeks. I scrub away the remnants of makeup and pat my skin dry, catching a glimpse of my reflection in the mirror.

I can't help myself. I press my fingers softly against my lips, still feeling Ben on them. What was that? I can't get mixed up in anything while I'm here. It's wrong. And yet, I can't help but feel a little something with him. What is it? Sure, he's mega attractive and smart and charming—but it's wrong. I shake my head and my nostrils flare as I look at myself in the mirror.

I can't let anything happen, and I will give my all to not give in to anything. And yet...

After brushing my teeth, I change out of my clothes and put on a fresh set of pajamas—soft cotton and pink with a pattern of tiny bears and red bows scattered across the fabric. My favorite set.

I grab my laptop from my bag and settle onto the edge of the bed, my legs tucked beneath me as I open a document with notes I've been preparing for the interview.

The questions they might ask swirl in my mind: *What inspired you to write? Who are your favorite authors? What do you hope to bring to the literary world?* Each one feels heavier than the last, but I remind myself that I've worked hard to get here. This is my moment.

Still, my thoughts drift back to Ben. To his easy laugh, the warmth in his eyes, the way he made me feel like I was the only person in the world tonight. I shake my head, trying to focus.

I dive into my notes, my fingers flying over the keyboard as I refine my answers and jot down ideas. The hours slip by, and before I know it, the clock on my laptop reads 1:00 a.m. I close it with a sigh, my body heavy with exhaustion but my mind still buzzing with anticipation. I crawl into bed and pull the covers up to my chin, closing my eyes.

But as much as I want to get some shut eye, my mind betrays me, dragging me back to the earlier chaos of the day. I can see it all so vividly—James's book in my hands, the words blurring as tears spilled onto the pages. The knot in my throat that tightened with every chapter, every line that reminded me of what I'd lost, or maybe what I'd never really had. Standing outside the bookstore, my heart was aching in a way that felt sharp and unrelenting, like a wound that refused to heal. And then the argument in this room—his voice raised, my words tumbling out in anger and pain. His eyes that made my skin crawl and had me in a chokehold. The way we talked over each other, neither of us really listening, I'm sure.

I shift in bed, turning toward the window and shoving off the comforter. I flip the pillows to the cool side and stare up at the ceiling. Why did I even argue with him? The question loops in my mind, insistent and unrelenting. Was I hoping he'd finally say something to fix it? To make me feel like I mattered to him? I was upset, mortified, and hurt. But did the argument actually help anything?

No. All it did was confirm what I already knew deep down but had been too stubborn to accept. James isn't going to change. He never has, and he never will.

That's the bitter truth I've been swallowing all day, whether I wanted to or not. I wanted him to fight for me, to prove me wrong. But he stayed exactly the same—charming, selfish, and a manipulative liar—whether he wants to admit or not. And maybe that's the most painful part of all. Realizing that the person you've been holding onto is never going to be the person you need them to be.

I shift to my right side and force my eyes shut. James may never change, but maybe, just maybe, I don't need him to. Maybe I'm ready to let go of the weight of him and all the expectations I tied to him. James is still the past, and I need him to stay there—for good.

Chapter 88

The bathroom fills with steam as I step out of the shower, water dripping from my hair. I wrap my head in a clean towel, feeling like the messiness of yesterday has been washed off. I dry off the rest of my body and cocoon another towel around me as I walk out.

I pick up my phone off the nightstand and notice James has left a few more texts and voicemails this morning. He left them while I was sleeping, around four in the morning.

It's like a ghost refusing to rest in peace.

I shake my head and slide to delete the message thread. I hover my thumb over his contact, debating to block his number. We were messy, chaotic, toxic. I don't want that for myself right now, nor do I want it in my future. I was manipulated in a way that feels so... disarrayed. He stole a part of me and now it feels like I wasted a part of my life when I could have been with someone who loves and supports and cares about me.

My fingers tremble over the block button. James gave me trust issues that honestly, I am still dealing with. Especially finding out about his stupid book revolving around our relationship for the entire world to read. He doesn't deserve that fucking *New York*

Times Bestseller label.

He deserves to feel how I feel. Hurt, conflicted, manipulated, unloved. To think, of all of those moments from the laundromat to the pizza shop to standing in line at Dunkin' to sitting next to each other on the plane. To the other night of that amazing sex.

Oh god, what am I saying? It all meant *nothing*. All of what he said to me was just words, all of it lies to trick me into believing he has changed. I tap the button without a second thought, without overanalyzing it.

I unwrap my towel around my head and exhale deeply. I walk back into the bathroom and blow dry my hair, brushing it out and curling the ends up for a clean yet fun look.

I call Tish without thinking. Maybe she is at work and won't answer. It rings and she picks up on the third ring, sounding out of breath.

"Hey sweetie, how are you?" A woman's voice echoes behind her, letting her know her coffee is ready. "Sorry, I'm picking up coffee on the way to the gym. I really shouldn't be getting this before working out, but fuck it, I need me some caffeine to wake me up."

I chuckle, swaying my legs up and down. "I've been better, I guess. I got some news though..."

"Oh yeah? Spill. Mama needs the details."

I sit back up and grab my brush off the nightstand, brushing out my hair with her on speaker phone. "Ben almost kissed me last night."

Silence fills my ears and I can hear her smiling. "Wow, now *that's* what I call a wake-up call. So what happened then? Did you end up making out, or...?"

I let a soft laugh escape, letting the brush dangle from my hand. "No, I stopped it before it could go anywhere. I really don't need another drama explosion in my life right now, especially with everything going on with James and his stupid book. Which reminds me, he came to my hotel too."

I hear Tish sighing. "Babe, you couldn't start with that first? Why did he show up? He didn't do anything to you, did he? I'll fly myself up there and personally kick his ass."

I chuckle and roll my eyes. "No, no, nothing happened. We just sort of got into an argument. I left the bookstore after finding out about his book and he got all concerned and shit, even blew up my phone." I take a breath and continue.

"Then that's where I called Ben. I don't know why, I just did. Ben came over and then James came over, *again*, and that's when I told James to leave. Ben and I took a walk near the hotel and ate pizza. Which was really good by the way. And that's when Ben nearly kissed me."

Tish lets out a breath, the kind that says she's trying to absorb everything at once. "Damn, where's the wine when I need it. I mean, first Ben almost kisses you and James just *shows up* at your hotel? How are you even functioning right now?"

I sit on the edge of the bed, towel still wrapped around me, the air in the room cool against my skin. The steam from my shower has started to fade from the mirror, leaving behind only a faint, foggy halo. I clutch the phone tighter, grounding myself in her voice. "Barely," I admit. "It's been nonstop since yesterday. Emotionally, mentally—I feel like I've been wrung out and left in the sun to dry."

"I'm serious," she says, her voice edged with concern. "This isn't small stuff. Your ex shows up at your hotel, you find out about a book he basically stole from your life and your guys' relationship, and then Ben—*Ben*—almost kisses you? All in a matter of hours?"

"Yeah," I say softly. "It's like life decided to test me all at once. I'm really starting to form a hatred for the universe."

There's a pause on her end, the background noise of the café replaced by what sounds like the hum of her car starting up. "Start from the beginning. Tell me what really happened with Ben, babe."

I close my eyes for a second and let myself return to that moment—the quiet of the hotel room, the closeness of him beside me, the weight of what wasn't said pressing against the walls like fog.

"We were just sitting there talking. I was overwhelmed, trying to make sense of everything with James, and I guess I needed someone. Ben showed up after I called him—he didn't hesitate, didn't question it. Just came."

"And then?"

I shift the phone to my other ear and reach for the lotion on the nightstand, squeezing a bit into my palm. "We were on a bench," I say. "Just sitting, side by side. And then suddenly there was this moment—quiet, close. I could feel it building between us. But I pulled away before it could happen."

"Because of James?"

I shake my head, even though she can't see me. "No. Well, not just because of James. Because of me. Because I knew if I let it happen, I'd regret it. I'm not ready to open myself up to anyone— not even someone kind and dreamy like Ben. I'm still trying to remember who I am outside of all of this. Outside of heartbreak and betrayal and being the girl who got written into someone else's story without consent."

Tish is quiet for a moment, then says gently, "That makes sense. And honestly? I'm proud of you, babe. You could've let it happen just to feel something good for a moment—but you didn't. That takes strength."

"I told Ben I want to keep things professional," I say, rubbing the lotion into my arms slowly. "That I'm not in a place to give anything beyond that. He respected it. No pushback, no awkwardness. Just... acceptance."

"He really sounds like he's a decent guy."

"He is," I whisper. "Which makes it harder, in a weird way. Because it would be easy to fall into something soft with someone who listens. And the fact that he's super cute and sweet. But... I don't want easy right now. I want something real."

Tish hums thoughtfully. "And James? What are you going to do about him?"

"I already did it," I say. "I deleted all his messages this morning. Erased the voicemails. Blocked his number. It's not just about moving on—it's about no longer giving him space in my head. He chose to tell our story without me. He crossed a line. I can't pretend it doesn't matter."

"Zoe..." she trails off. "I know that wasn't easy. But you're giving off total badass vibes right now and I am loving it."

"It really wasn't," I admit. "But that means a lot, Tish. I feel like one too. I feel... lighter, you know?"

The silence between us is calm now, less charged. I pull on a pair of high-waisted jeans and a soft cream blouse.

"I'm heading to the *Poets & Writers* office in a little bit," I tell her. "Today is the day to tell my story. And Ben's giving me a tour after. He said he wanted to show me the behind-the-scenes side of the magazine."

"Aww, yay!" she exclaims, and I can hear the smile in her voice now. "You're not just closing doors—you're walking through new ones. Ones you opened all by yourself."

I sit in front of the mirror, brushing my hair out in slow strokes. The curls at the ends bounce just the way I like them. For once, my reflection looks like someone who isn't afraid of the day ahead.

"Thank you," I say, voice quiet but certain. "For reminding me of that."

"You don't need reminding," she says. "You just needed space to hear yourself."

I walk toward my closet and throw on an oversized black blazer. I snag some silver rings and braided hoop earrings from the bathroom counter and slip into my red flats.

I am definitely feeling classy for the big city.

"Thanks, Tish," I say once more, smiling at my reflection.

"Anytime, babe," she says, her voice warm. "Now go knock 'em dead! It's simply about your short story, just be yourself and you'll be okay."

"I knew I chose you as my best friend for a reason. I'll talk to you soon, okay? Love you."

I feel the tension in my chest ease just a little. I look at the clock on my phone. It's just after nine. My interview isn't until ten, but better early than late, especially riding the subway. After hanging up, I grab my tote bag, double-check that I have my notebook and pen, and head out toward the elevator.

The brisk New York air hits me as I step outside, and I take a deep breath. It's one of those crisp mornings that smells like opportunity—and maybe a little bit like bagels, which I mentally add to my post-interview to-do list.

The subway ride is crowded but uneventful. I clutch the metal pole, trying not to stumble as the train jerks to a stop. My thoughts flip back to Ben—his warm smile, the way his hand felt against mine, like it belonged there. *Stop it, Zoe. Focus on your story and it'll be all right.*

By the time I reach the building where the literary magazine is housed, my nerves are back. The building is taller and more enormous than my hotel, and suddenly I feel intimidated. I swing the revolving door and push through into the lobby. It's sleek and modern, filled with blues and grays with a variety of gold lighting hanging on the ceiling above me. Greenery fills every corner, while famous book covers decorate the walls from *The Yellow Wallpaper* by Charlotte Perkins Gilman, *Girl* by Jamaica Kincaid, *Désirée's Baby* by Kate Chopin, and *The Tell-Tale Heart* by Edgar Allen Poe, among many others I recall from my college days.

I walk up to the front desk as three receptionists clack away at their keyboards. One brunette waves me over. I tell her I'm here for an interview at *Poets & Writers*. She directs me to the elevator, and as it ascends, I feel like my heart is doing the same thing—rising higher and higher, unsure if it's excitement or sheer panic fueling it. Most likely both at this point.

The elevator glides to a smooth stop on the second floor, the soft chime breaking the silence. As the doors slide open, I step into a sleek, modern lobby where another receptionist desk greets me. Behind it, a man around my age is multitasking, expertly balancing a phone between his shoulder and ear while his fingers fly over a keyboard. He looks up as I approach, his sharp green eyes brightening with recognition.

He gives me a quick wave, his tone polite as he murmurs into the phone. "I'll have to call you back." With a soft click, he hangs up, his attention fully on me. "Good morning! Welcome to *Poets & Writers*. How may I assist you?"

His smile is warm, and I return it, feeling a little of the tension ease from my shoulders. "Good morning! My name is Zoe Donovan, and I'm here to—"

Before I can finish, a large, familiar hand rests lightly on my shoulder, its weight both grounding and electrifying. My breath catches as I glance sideways, already knowing who it is before I see him. The receptionist's gaze shoots up to the man beside me, and a deep blush spreads across his cheeks, his smile turning a little flustered.

"It's okay, Mel," the man says smoothly, his voice calm but unmistakably commanding. "I can assist Ms. Donovan."

I turn fully, my heart doing an entirely unnecessary somersault as my eyes meet his. Ben. He's standing here, tall and effortlessly confident, his golden hazel eyes inviting and just as disarming as last night. The faintest hint of a smirk tugs at his lips, like he's secretly delighted by my surprise.

My nostrils immediately flare and I feel sweat gliding down my neck. I bite my lip and try to hide my surprise, but I'm sure my flared nostrils illustrate just that.

Chapter 34

"Ben?" I manage, my voice barely above a whisper.

"Good morning, Ms. Donovan," he says, his smile widening. "Didn't expect to see you here so early."

Mel clears his throat, his cheeks still bright pink. "I'll, uh... leave you two to it," he says, his voice overly chipper as he ducks his head back toward his screen. The way his eyes flick nervously toward Ben makes me wonder if he's flustered for a completely different reason. And I love that for him.

Ben chuckles softly, the sound low and familiar, pulling my attention back to him. "Come on," he says, gesturing for me to follow. "We can talk in my office."

Ms. Donovan. I can see he didn't forget what I said last night. But part of me wishes he did.

We walk down a short hallway and step into a spacious office flooded with natural light, the windows offering a sweeping view of the city below. The walls are a soft, muted cream, brought to life with pops of color—deep navy shelves stacked with books, a burnt orange armchair in the corner, and framed prints in moss green, gold, and burgundy. Excerpts from famous short stories are mounted in mismatched frames. Behind his sleek glass desk, a few college degrees hang slightly crooked. The desk itself is a whirlwind of notebooks and printed pages covered in what seems like a million red markings and scribbles.

He smiles as he closes his door and gestures me to take a seat. I feel my palms ooze sweat and blame the surprise of seeing Ben nearly an hour before the interview is supposed to commence. He's wearing a dark navy dress shirt rolled up to his elbows and a red tie that hovers over his chest.

His attractiveness seriously needs to tone it down a bit.

I set my tote bag down and sit in one of the chairs across from his desk. He clears his throat as he types something away, the keyboards clacking louder than my pounding heartbeat.

He finishes it up moments later and leans back against his chair, folding one leg over the other.

"So," he says. "since you're here early, I figure we can begin the office tour now? I know I mentioned after the interview, but we have some time to kill. Margaret has another meeting before yours. Are you interested?"

I nod immediately, following him out the door as he locks up. A small whiff of his cologne swirls in the air, making my heart skip a beat. And it smells just like before—utterly delicious.

"Come on," he says again, just a couple of feet ahead of me. His voice is softer this time as he glances over his shoulder with a smile.

Blues and grays drench the walls and smother my vision as I follow him past Mel's desk, who gives me a quick, wide-eyed glance like he's watching a soap opera unfold in real time. I give him a little wave, which he returns a beat too late, almost knocking over his coffee. He fumbles to catch it, and I stifle a laugh as we continue on.

Ben leads me through a narrow hallway lined with framed covers of literary magazines. Some are bold and artsy, others minimalistic and clean, but all of them feel like little windows into someone's dream coming true.

"So," Ben says as we walk, "this is the editorial wing."

The hallway opens into a large common area filled with desks, low chatter, the occasional hum of a printer, and the scent of fresh espresso. I inhale, eyes wide. This... is it. The heartbeat of a publishing house. Editors furiously typing away and hunched over manuscripts, red pens flying, highlighters capping and uncapping like it's a competitive sport.

"There's the break room over there," Ben says, pointing to a glass door where two women are deep in conversation over bright green matcha lattes. "And that corner office belongs to Margaret. When you talk to her shortly, you'll see she's great—stern in a 'loves literary structure more than life itself' kind of way, but nice."

"That's comforting," I say, and Ben lets out a soft laugh.

"Don't worry. She already loves your story."

Something fluttery zips through my chest. I press my hand flat against my heart, like that's going to do a damn thing.

We keep walking, past a wall covered in sticky notes. I slow down when I spot a note written in sparkly purple pen that reads: *"This character makes me want to throw my coffee into the void."* Another says: *"If I have to read one more man who 'runs his hand through his hair,' I will set this draft on fire."*

Ben notices my grin and stops beside me. "Editor wall of drama. Sometimes joy. Mostly caffeine-fueled rage though."

"I love it," I say, genuinely. "This whole place feels alive."

He nods. "That's the goal. We're big believers in keeping things collaborative—and human. Publishing isn't just business. It's story stewardship."

That gets me. Hits me somewhere tender, somewhere that still believes words matter more than anything else.

We turn a corner and pass a small library nook filled with books and a couch that has clearly seen better, more upright days. A fluffy orange cat is curled up on the armrest like he owns the place.

"Oh my god, is that a—"

"Office cat. His name is Fitzgerald. Only answers to 'Sir' and demands tuna every Thursday."

"Of course he does," I whisper, in awe. I can't help myself and lean down to pet him, his purrs filling my ears. I smile. He reminds me of Ollie back home. "He seems like such a sweetie."

Ben shrugs. "Only friendly to people he likes. He once stole Hugh's pen and stared him down while knocking it off the desk. The whole office watched it happen."

I try not to squeal. "I have a fat cat named Ollie back home. I just know they'd get along."

"I don't know," Ben says with mock seriousness. "Fitzgerald's a bit of a diva. Ollie might need references. But it appears he likes you."

We pause near the window at the far end of the floor, the buzz of the office softening behind us. Outside, the city stretches wide and endless, bathed in the soft glow of early morning. Sunlight spills over the rooftops and skyscrapers like molten gold, glinting off glass and steel, painting everything in warm, almost magical light. The buildings seem to hum with energy, a thousand lives unfolding in every direction. I rest my hands gently on the cool windowsill, needing something solid beneath my palms. Something to remind me that this is real.

I'm really here. In New York. At a publishing house. With Ben.

My heart flutters a little—half nerves, half wonder—and I steal a glance at him beside me. He's standing close, but not too close, the kind of distance that feels intentional, like he's giving me space while still choosing to stay near. His presence is steadying somehow, like an anchor in the whirlwind of everything I've been feeling. The quiet between us isn't awkward—it's full. Full of unsaid things and shared understanding.

Ben's voice is low, almost thoughtful. "It's a good place to be, Zoe."

I turn toward him, the light catching in his hazel eyes, soft and flecked with gold. "You mean... this place? Or New York?"

He doesn't answer right away. Instead, he looks out the window with me, like he's seeing the city for the first time. The way his profile catches the light—calm, thoughtful, kind—makes something in my chest pull tight.

Then he turns, and his eyes meet mine fully. There's something sure in the way he looks at me—something that says he's not just offering polite encouragement, but speaking from somewhere deeper. It's like his body is telling me he knows without him actually speaking.

As if he knows, deep down, I want to be here, to make it my home.

His voice then interrupts my thoughts. He casually shrugs as a smile tugs at his lips. "Both."

And somehow, that one word carries weight. I know he's not just talking about a place on a map, or a name on a magazine cover. He's talking about this moment. About me. About how maybe, just maybe, I belong *here.*

I swallow past the sudden lump in my throat, blinking back the emotion rising behind my eyes. I nod slowly, not trusting my voice just yet. Outside the window, the city moves on—cars inching down avenues, tiny people crossing streets, life pulsing with every flicker of light. But in here, in this quiet corner with Ben, everything feels still.

I bite my lip and peruse them with my tongue as I watch the city dance. Ben's voice interrupts my thoughts.

"Come on," he says, nudging my shoulder gently. "Let's swing back to my office. I'll grab your 'story' packet. Margaret should be wrapping up soon."

We walk back in comfortable silence, the buzz of the office around us. When we get back to Ben's office, he unlocks the door and holds it open for me. I step inside and grab my tote bag from the couch. My palms are still sweating, but it's a little less frantic now. Maybe because I've seen the place. Maybe because Ben's made it feel less intimidating.

He hands me a sleek bright yellow folder. "Everything you need is in here—background on the editorial team, some notes about your story, and a general layout of the interview schedule. You're going to do great."

"Thanks," I say, my voice quieter than I mean it to be.

He hesitates for a second, then reaches into his desk and pulls out a granola bar. "Here. In case you skipped breakfast."

I blink at it, then at him. "How did you know I skipped breakfast?"

He grins. "Because you've been wound up about today since last night, with everything going on, too. People like you never remember to eat when they're nervous. Good thing I'm here to remind you."

I purse my lips at his words, immediately blushing. My nostrils flare as if on cue. A lot has been going on, and not for the better. And yet it's like Ben really cares about it, about *me*, and doesn't push me or pry. I mean, last night we talked about what happened, but that was okay. It felt nice to get that off my chest and have someone besides Tish actually listen.

He even let out all his secrets too. He most definitely didn't have to, but he did. Sharing his past with his ex, telling me that it's okay to feel stuck, confused—lost. He spoke from experience all because he wanted to make me feel better. It was sweet, and wonderful.

And I can feel deep down that he's actually one of the good ones.

I sit back down and clutch the granola bar like it's a rare artifact. Inhaling and slowly exhaling. I can do this. Just like Tish, my mom, and Ben said: I'm ready.

Well, almost.

Ben stops typing for a moment, his twinkling brown sugar eyes staring into mine. "By the way, Fitzgerald approves of you."

My eyebrows shoot up. "Really?"

"He didn't hiss when you walked by and he allowed you to pet him. I'd say that's high praise."

I beam, the tension in me unraveling with his words. How does he always know what I need to hear?

Moments later, the door clicks open after a few soft knocks. It's Mel.

"Sorry for interrupting, Mr. Cartwright. Ms. Donovan? Margaret is ready for you, if you'd follow me."

Chapter 88

Margaret is tall, nearly close to Ben's height in heels, making me feel like a munchkin in comparison. Her dark brown pixie cut curls around her ears as large gold hoops cling to her earlobes. She's wearing a purple wrap dress and black cardigan that hugs her long figure. Freckles splatter her skin and her warm smile feels more inviting than intimidating like I imagined.

She reaches out to shake my hand and I grasp it, softly but firm.

"Hello, Zoe. It's so great to finally meet you! All the way from Cleveland, wow. Would you like something to drink? Coffee, water perhaps?"

We both take a seat at her mahogany desk that appears less cluttered than Ben's. I nod and ask for water. I open my notebook to my practice interview questions I reviewed what seemed like a million years ago even though it was just early this morning.

She smiles and Mel reappears moments later with our water, placing a pitcher on her desk. She leans back in her chair and crosses her legs. I can feel my nerves wind back up again, taking a small deep breath and exhaling slowly.

She seems to notice and chuckles. "There's no need to be nervous, Zoe. If we didn't already like you and your story, we wouldn't have flown you to the Big Apple." She expands her notebook and sticky notes on her lap. "So, tell me, what inspired you to write this particular story?"

And with the first question already out in the world, I answer almost immediately. What feels like a few minutes turns into a few hours, from cracking jokes to sharing intimate moments on background of my story and me as a writer. I felt like I could tell Margaret anything, and in a way, I sort of did.

I opened up to her about my past relationship about James, about how he cheated and wrote a book about us. I told her about how I am learning to trust my gut more these days and to not feel like I have to say yes to everything. I am learning to realize that it's okay to say no and do things your way and not what everyone else wants.

This is my time, and I need to do things how I think I should and not by what everyone else thinks. And that's okay. It's hard to do sometimes, but in reality, the right decisions sometimes feel like the wrong ones, but that just means choosing ourselves over others.

♡

My tote bag swings under my arm as I walk out of the elevator. The interview actually went well, as Ben promised.

I can't help but smile to myself, and that's when I hear Margaret's voice behind me. I turn around and there she is, holding a white folder with my name written across it. "Zoe, I'm glad I caught you before you left. I just wanted to say thank you again for coming to meet with us at *Poets & Writers*. You've got talent and energy I haven't seen in a while." She hands me the folder. "This is the final formatted and edited piece of your story and how the layout will look in the magazine. There's a copy of the issue in there as well, thanks to the team. It's not out yet, but don't tell anyone. It's just between you and me."

I smile and can't help myself as I wrap my arms around her, pulling her against me. "Thank you, Margaret. This means a lot to me."

I clutch the folder for dear life against me, feeling an energy flow in me I haven't felt in a long time. I'm a published author, it's for real. My name is out there for all to see and my story is out there for all to read, or will be soon.

She tilts her head and smiles, rubbing my arm in a soft motion. "You're very welcome. I mentioned this already during our meeting, but the editorial team is seeking a new face. Someone bright and witty. Someone, well, like you. We're growing more and more and could really use all the help we can get. I know it's sudden, but I'm looking for another assistant editor, if you're interested?"

I suddenly feel my throat close up, my heart beats faster as her words echo inside me. Assistant Editor. In New York City. At a national literary magazine. Is she for real? Is this really happening?

A few moments pass and she speaks up. "It would be here in New York, and you'd be working two days a week from home." She clears her throat and nods. "Well, just think about it, okay? You know how to reach me, email or text, whatever. I'll look forward to hearing from you, Zoe, okay? Thanks again for meeting with me and safe travels on your way home tomorrow."

We shake hands and I watch her walk back into the elevators, waving as the doors close. I stand there frozen as if my feet are glued to the floor. Assistant Editor? I was literally just offered a job. I could quit my freelancing role and move to the city of my dreams. This is insane. Tish would be so proud of me.

And then my smile slowly fades to a frown as I pull the folder in front of me, opening it up and admiring the magazine with my name written across it in bold, white letters. I trace my fingers over it, and they tremble. If I accept this job, that would mean leaving Ohio. Leaving my family. Leaving all of my roots. Leaving my best friend.

My nostrils flare at the thought. I sigh and slowly walk toward the entrance. A cool gust of air slams into me. I feel the wind knocking out of me, literally. I look around and notice the one person that makes all of my nerves disappear. Ben is sitting on a bench nearby with two coffees in his hand as he strides toward me.

It's like he knows just how to cheer me up.

"Hey there," he says. "So how did it go? I know she loved you, just admit it."

I sip my coffee and nod, the two of us walking back to the bench and taking a seat. I open the folder and show him the magazine. He smiles and nudges my shoulder.

"You can thank me for the magazine, by the way. I was too excited to not show you next month's issue."

I close the folder and place it back in my tote bag. I reach for his hand and hold it tighter than usual. He seems to sense it and leans down, squeezing it and holding it close to his chest. My cheeks feel warm to the touch as I try to rub off the blushing that's happening.

Ben continues, his voice soft and warm like honey. "You can talk to me. I know your brain is going a thousand miles an hour."

"Well, I got a job offer. For assistant editor. Here. In New York. It's like my dream has come true. And yet I feel shitty. I should feel ecstatic, right? I'm practically a published author now and about to be an editor in the biggest and best city in the world."

He smirks and slowly nods his head, soaking in my words. "You know, Margaret really likes you. You showed her something she hasn't seen in a while, and that's raw talent, Zoe. This job offer doesn't have to be decided on now, either. It's a big decision that'll take time to process and decide on. From reading your story and emailing you now what feels like years ago, I knew you were special. I knew you were different and had the confidence to chase whatever you wanted. But I can see that that confidence has shifted and tilted a bit... especially when we walked and talked the other night. And you deserve to grow and have all the confidence in the world, not have someone take it from you."

My smile fades and I soak in the noise and colors of the city all around us, this big beautiful city is full of chaotic dreams. Do I really see myself living here in the long term? Am I just feeling like I want to because it's *New York*, because it's the city that never sleeps, because it's what's always revolved around in those rom-coms I love so much? Perhaps that's only why I want it.

Because it's so adored and desired throughout all of those movies and shows. I feel myself shiver, but not from the cold air hanging about, from my jumbled messed up thoughts. I then look at Ben, his smile beaming wider as I turn to him. He's really something. He's got it all here in New York.

My cheeks warm up. "Thanks, Ben. I appreciate it." I then stand up, swinging my tote bag over my shoulder. "And shouldn't you be working right now? It's not even lunch time."

He stands, his head bobbing from laughter. "I suppose so, yeah. I just wanted to see you again before you head off. Make sure you're okay."

I can't help but smile. His words wrap around my heart as goosebumps trickle down my neck.

He continues, rubbing his neck, and I see just a smidge of pink painting his cheeks. It's sweet. "So what about you? What do you have planned for the rest of the day?"

I bite my lip and shrug, tugging at the hem of my blazer. "Probably call my best friend and tell her the good news. I think I'm going to head back to the hotel and maybe read, or do some writing. Getting all anxious and going on interviews really tires a girl..."

My voice trails as I look around and my eyes catch sight of James stepping out from the bar across the street, hand in hand with a redhead. He's beaming ear to ear and holding the girl so close to his side she's practically wearing his clothes. This is a totally different James compared to the other night. He looks really happy, as if he's head over heels for this girl, their arms swaying back and forth.

What the hell is going on? He's a pig, a lying asshole.

It's the most appalling picture I've ever laid eyes on. And I need it to vanish from my vision immediately.

I quickly look away as I scoot behind Ben, my fingers trembling as I yank his blazer to hide hopefully my face. He darts his eyes around, twisting his neck as if trying to look for Waldo.

"What is it? Are you okay?"

I shake my head. He is supposed to be gone from my life. I deleted him off my phone. Isn't that supposed to send the universe a signal like, *Hey, universe, do your thing and dispose of this person from my life ASAP*. Apparently I was wrong, because the universe keeps shoving him in front of me.

It's the fucking worst.

I inhale and exhale slowly, looking up at Ben. His golden eyes soften as they meet mine, his fingers brushing my cheek as a tear suddenly comes sliding down.

"James. He was there across the street, with a woman." I wipe my nose and dig in my tote bag for tissues. Ben gently dangles his handkerchief in front of me instead and I accept it, blowing my nose.

"It shouldn't bother me but, it's like his entire existence irks me now, you know? He should get hit by a bus or something."

Ben laughs, a deep laugh that echoes in my chest and swims from one ear out the other. It's a sound I'd like to hear more of.

"Zoe, it's okay. James is going to exist in this world and that's just it. Just like Melanie. We just have to try to let them exist and do their thing as we do ours, right? You know he's not worth it, and honestly, it kills me how much of your brain he's taken over."

I look up at him, fingers clenched around the handkerchief. His expression is careful, all concern and control—but then, it wavers. Just for a moment. He lifts his hand and strokes my cheek like he doesn't mean to, like he forgets he's supposed to be keeping things professional.

His eyes lock on mine, something tender and unspoken passing between us before he catches himself and pulls away.

"Hey... how about I get you a cab and have it drop you off at your hotel. You had a busy morning, and I can tell you need some rest."

I bite my lips and sniffle, handing his handkerchief back. He shakes his hand as he waves a cab down. "No, it's okay. Keep it."

I can't help but let out a soft laugh. Without saying it, he's right. I'm a mess and I shouldn't be. Fuck James and his existence.

Moments later a cab pulls up in front of the office and Ben walks me toward it, opening the door for me as I shuffle inside. I roll the window down and try to smile. "Thank you, Ben. Thank you for everything. Tell Margaret I'll be in touch soon."

He shakes his hand and ushers me off. "Don't worry about that now. Just get to the hotel and relax. Take it easy, okay?"

I smile as the cab drives off, making Ben become a blur of blues and whites and reds.

Chapter 36

Hours later, after dozing off in my hotel room, I wake to darkness still dressed in my interview clothes. But I couldn't care less.

My mind boggles thought after thought after seeing James with that woman. Why did he have to show up again? I thought deleting the message thread and his texts would have sent the universe a sign to not let him reappear. I guess it took that as a joke, and not a funny one. If James can move on, so can I.

And this time, I mean it.

I feel my phone on the nightstand buzz, and again, and again. Then it rings, but I shove the pillow over my head, ignoring it so hopefully it'll stop. I close my eyes and try to get some shut eye, but there's a knock at my door.

Can't a girl get some sleep?

I sigh and shove my feet into my slippers, slip on my glasses, and slowly walk to the door. After everything going on, I ask who it is.

"Room service, Ms. Donovan."

My eyebrows crinkle in thought. I don't recall ordering any-thing, unless I did on the way up to the hotel and my brain fizzled it out given the thoughts on James.

I open the door and a short stocky man rolls the cart in. He takes it to the other room and I follow, my blanket sliding against the floor. He places everything on the coffee table, organizing it with grace. He then takes a large bouquet of white roses and sets them in the vase.

Now that's what I call a bouquet.

"All right, Ms. Donovan. You're all set. Anything else I can get for you?"

I bite my lip and shake my head.

"I, uh, don't think so. Thank you very much." We stand there for a few moments and the awkwardness smothers the air. "Oh, right, sorry."

I quickly grab my wallet and take out a five dollar bill and hand it to him. He tucks it in the front chest pocket of his vest. He bows and heads to the door.

"Enjoy, Ms. Donovan."

I make my way back into the second room and sit on the couch, staring at the food and roses. Did I do this? Damn, I really can't remember. I smell them and smile. They really are beautiful.

I take a fork and pick at the plates: a giant cinnamon roll smothered in icing, a stack of French toast and syrup on the side in a tiny dish, grapes and slices of banana and mandarins on the second plate, and a small side of scrambled eggs. I don't think I can eat all this, but I guess I should eat. I didn't even touch the granola bar Ben gave me.

And that's when I notice a small card placed in front of the roses. I pick it up and open it.

Zoe, please accept this breakfast as an apology of sorts. I feel horrible for what happened earlier and felt the need to apologize. I hope I didn't come off as pushy for getting you a cab… and for the other night. You're a wonderful girl, and I don't expect anything. I hope you'll accept my apology.

Warm regards, Ben, aka Mr. Editor

I feel myself smiling as I read the card a couple more times. Ben apologizing, and he didn't have to. He really is so sweet, and kind, and caring. The way he came to my hotel the other night, talked to me and expressed his thoughts and just let me vent about James. The fact that he showed me around the office one-on-one. When he texted me safe travels before flying out here. And even when he invited me to have brunch with me as a warm welcome to the city.

And then… he kissed me. Almost, barely, a glimmer of something. And I can't—shouldn't—do anything about it. I told him we need to keep things professional moving forward, and he has done just that.

I sigh and rub the card between my fingers. I look down at it again and feel my cheeks burn. I feel my nostrils flare at the thought of his face closing in, his soft pink lips grazing mine, and for a moment, something was there. *Something.*

Damn, why is it me going through this?

I shake my head and set the card on the couch. Maybe I just need to figure out what I want? I don't want another whatever that was with James. I don't need to go through something like that again. Being lied to, cheated on, yelled at. No one deserves to go through that… not even me.

I grab a fork and immediately fill my mouth with a bite of cinnamon roll. It's ooey gooey cinnamon clogging my senses and I moan in happiness. And who says food isn't the key to a girl's heart.

I finish eating and bring the flowers to the desk. I spread the curtains back open and open the windows just a tad to inhale the city and all its wonderfulness. This place is for me. I know it. Like that woman at the park said. *You're exactly where you need to be.*

The breeze cools my face and fills the room. I stay by the window for a long moment, letting the night air soothe me, holding the lip of the curtain with one hand and the warmth of the room behind me brushing my back. The sounds of the city are muted up here, almost dreamlike—honking horns, distant laughter, a saxophone drifting from somewhere down the block.

I take another deep breath of the scent of the roses with the lingering cinnamon on my tongue. I even catch a faint whiff of Ben's cologne from earlier. It's slowly becoming my favorite smell.

I glance back at the card. It's still lying on the couch, waiting like a question mark. I walk over and pick it up again, reading Ben's words one more time. He didn't need to do this. He could've easily moved on, buried the moment and chalked it up to awkwardness and mixed signals. But he didn't. He tried. Thoughtfully. Gently. That means something, doesn't it?

And yet, why am I still afraid?

I press the card to my chest and close my eyes. I think back to the almost-kiss again. The memory of that plays in my mind like a silent film. The way his voice softened when he said my name. The slight hesitation in his eyes, like he was waiting for me to lean in first. And I almost did. I *wanted* to. And that's what scares me.

I've barely had time to figure myself out again. To heal. And here comes Ben—steady, kind, full of the quiet strength I didn't know I needed—and he sees me. Not just the writer, not just the girl who's trying to make it in a new city. He sees *me.* Even if I tried to pretend I'm just here for the job, for the fresh start, there's a part of me that craves something more. But I can't tell if that craving is for him… or for who I'm becoming in this city.

A ping from my phone pulls me out of my thoughts. It's Tish.

Did you die?? You haven't texted me back since yesterday. Spill everything. And don't even think about saying "I'm fine" because I know you're spiraling. It's these best friend senses.

I type back quickly. *I'm alive. I'll call you in the morning at the airport. A lot happened. Also… Ben just sent me room service. And roses!*

Her reply comes in less than five seconds. *OH MY GOD. YOU ARE LIVING IN A ROM-COM. I swear if you don't tell me everything tomorrow I'm flying myself out there!!*

I chuckle and lock my phone, feeling a little lighter now. Trust Tish to pull me out of my head.

I shuffle back toward the bed, picking up the abandoned granola bar Ben gave me earlier and placing it on the nightstand. I slide out of my interview clothes and into my pajama set, crawling back beneath the comforter. The sheets are cool against my skin, and my stomach is full for the first time all day.

The roses rest on the desk, gently illuminated by the city lights outside. The card is back on the nightstand, like a whispered secret. Maybe I should talk to him. Not to clarify or define anything, because there's nothing to define, right? It's just to *talk*.

And talking is good. That's all I have to do right now.

275

Chapter 87

After taking a well-deserved four-hour nap, I drag myself out of bed to fix myself up. And of course, James still paints my thoughts.

Gross.

I sit up and roll the blanket off me, staring at the roses. They immediately bring a smile to my face. I shove off my slippers and take a shower, scrub some of this morning off and cleanse myself. I change into fresh new clothes and glance at myself in the mirror, feeling brighter than this morning. I opt for a more casual outfit with a black babydoll dress, a lacey sheer long-sleeved shirt, my red Mary Jane flats, and flip the ends of my orange hair.

And who says getting dolled up is only for special occasions?

I slip on my silver hoops and head out the door. A short time later, I find myself immersed in the colorful Central Park. Yellows and reds and oranges smother my vision as they expand closer. I pull out my phone as I find an empty bistro table and take a seat. My thoughts tumble and twirl in my brain, and I tap my knuckles against my temple to knock them out.

Biting my lip, I hover my thumb over Tish's text from the other day. I scroll down to my deleted messages, recognizing James's thread instantly. I shake my head at the very thought of him. He confuses me, irks me, makes my chest shake and tumble with anger.

I'm not going to bend my life backwards for a boy who I thought loved me, when in reality, he loved himself more. He had the courage to take my feelings and so many pieces of me and have them permanently printed on paper. It might fade over time, but the memories are what'll last forever.

It feels like I am holding myself back for someone who's doing just that—holding me back in the past. Or... maybe I'm doing that to myself. I have the chance to live this new life that I've been wanting for so long, even through self-doubt and overthinking. This is my chance. I can't throw it away for someone who's... thrown me away.

That's not what I want.

My eyes wander over the crowd walking past me, in a hurry to get to work, appointments, friends, or shopping. My thoughts tumble back to seeing James walking out of the bar with that woman, that mystery redhead.

As if reading my thoughts, a man resembling James walks past. My breath catches in my throat like a frog. I shake the image out of my head. Why do I care? He's in my past and needs to stay there. When I see someone who looks like him, it's like a gut punch of reality. It's like a pile of laundry I should have left unfolded.

New York is basically welcoming me in with open arms, and I'm inches away all scared and worried. It's inviting me in and I'm second-guessing it all. If someone else was offered this opportunity, they'd take it in a heartbeat. But here I am over-contemplating it. Like I do everything.

Without another thought, I delete all of my deleted threads for good. No point in looking back. I scroll back over to my texts and start a thread with Margaret. She was kind enough to leave a sticky note with her cell.

All I need to do now is move forward. All I need to do is say yes. And suddenly my phone rings, just as I'm typing her number in.

It's Ben.

My nostrils flare and my heartbeat races. I answer on the third ring.

"Hi, Mr. Editor. I was actually going to call you. I got your flowers, and breakfast. Thank you."

I can hear him smiling, his hazel eyes probably creasing at the corners and the gold flecks deepening. "You're very welcome, Zoe. I saw them just outside the office and knew I had to get them for you."

"They're beautiful, really."

A few moments of silence pass. I clear my throat. "So, thanks again. You really didn't have to apologize though. You didn't do anything wrong, Ben. I promise."

He sighs. I can see him standing in a fresh suit, his muscular arms probably prodding and teasing underneath. His hair as perfect as ever, his smile wonderful and bright. Anyone can see how attractive he is, and yet, he kissed me. *Nearly* kissed *me*.

"I wanted to. It was sudden and selfish, and I truly do apologize, Zoe. I shouldn't have done that after all you went through... with your ex. I'm sorry."

I press the heel of my hand gently against my chest, grounding myself in the feel of my own heartbeat. My cheeks grow warm, but my voice stays soft. "It's okay, Ben. Really. We're good. More than good. Promise."

Just above, an airplane cuts across the sky, its silver body glinting against the deepening blue. My eyes follow it instinctively, and just like that, I remember: tomorrow. The return flight. The departure. I leave for Cleveland tomorrow. It came up faster than I thought, given all the chaos going on since I stepped foot in this city.

"Ben," I ask, hesitating only for a moment, "did you say you booked me a return flight for tomorrow?"

"I did, yeah. Your flight departs at 9:20 tomorrow morning at LaGuardia. I can book you an Uber to pick you up from your hotel too. And I'll be sure to send the ticket confirmation, don't worry."

"Thanks, Mr. Editor. You're really great, you know that?"

He chuckles. His laugh is warm and sincere. "All thanks to you, Ms. Donovan. How have you been since... you know what?"

His question catches me off guard. I didn't expect him to ask about that. I was kind of hoping he forgot. Seeing James for the millionth time in New York was not expected, but how could I have predicted that? Just like all the other run-ins with him, at the laundromat, at the pizza shop, at the airport, on the plane. The universe really has it out to get me, though I've come to realize it was really pushing him toward me for his stupid book. His stupid, dumb, doesn't-deserve-a-bestseller label.

"I've actually been pretty good. The breakfast surprise really helped, by the way. But really, I've been good. Like you said, he's just another person who's going to exist in this world, and that's okay. He let me down but that doesn't mean I need to let me down too, you know?"

He chuckles, and I can hear him smiling. "Well, I'm glad you enjoyed the food. Their cinnamon rolls are the best." His voice is low and warm and just—ugh—*nice*. "But Zoe, that's more than enough. You don't have to have it all figured out. There is no hurry. You got an amazing job offer, and sure, I say amazing because I work there, but you did that yourself. That takes a lot of courage, and you never let that go, even when life shoved your ex in front of you a billion times. You moved through it, and you'll move through this because you're you."

My heart catches and I feel myself blushing. A pigeon struts confidently near my foot, and even it seems to be nodding in agreement like, *Yes, Zoe, listen to the charming magazine editor.*

I laugh under my breath. "God, you really are good with words."

"Hazard of the job," he says lightly. "But also... I meant it. I just don't want to see you dim your light because of someone who never deserved it."

Tears prick at the corner of my eyes, uninvited but determined. I blink them back, breathing through my nose. "I should probably go," I say finally, my voice a little wobblier than I'd like. "I've got to start packing and, you know, figure out how to say goodbye to this New-York-City-girl version of me. The one who let him win."

Ben is quiet for a beat, then his deep voice hums through my ears. "I wouldn't say 'let him win.' Maybe... don't say goodbye to her. Maybe just thank her. She got you here, after all."

My throat tightens. God, who says things like that? How is he real? "Ben?"

"Yeah?"

I smile, small and shaky but real. "Thank you."

"Anything for you, Zoe."

We end the call and I sit there for a moment, my phone resting on my tote bag. I watch people pass, bicyclists speed past, and dogs dragging their owners as if taking them on walks instead. Red, yellow, and orange leaves all shimmer down, fluttering like autumn-themed confetti. I take a breath. A deep, grounding, *real* breath.

I know what I gotta do. It's time I say yes to me, yes to what I know I deserve. I grab my phone and pull back up my text thread to Margaret, but instead, I delete it. I dial her number and hear the rings thump in my ear.

"Poets & Writers, this is Margaret."

"Hi Margaret, it's Zoe. Do you have a moment?"

Chapter 88

"Zoe, hello! How great to hear from you."

Margaret's voice echoes through my ears and shimmers down my spine, making me smile. "Thanks, Margaret. I figured I'd give you a call rather than an email or text, it feels more comfortable for me. Anyway, I'd like to accept the Assistant Editor position. With every fiber of my being, the answer is yes."

"Oh, Zoe," she says softly, and there's a shift in her tone—like something gentle has bloomed open. "I can't tell you how happy that makes me. We were hoping you'd say yes, but not this soon!" She lets out a low, easy laugh—real and full of warmth. "You're such a natural fit for the team, and for what we're building here. I knew it from the moment you set foot in my office."

Tears sting the backs of my eyes. "To be honest with you, I was scared. Not because I didn't want it—but because I wanted it so much. It felt too good to be real, you know? But today... I don't know. I guess today gave me permission to believe in this new beginning."

"Well Zoe, I'm glad you called. I'm very much looking forward to working with you—we all are at *Poets & Writers*." She clears her throat. "So the next step would be to finalize your paperwork with payroll, and HR will be in touch with your onboarding schedule. I want you to know there is no rush for a start date. Ben and I can manage with the rest of the team as long as you need to get ready to come out, okay? You have his number I presume?"

I nod, realizing she cannot hear me nodding. "Mmhm, yes, I do."

I hear her smile. "Splendid! Oh, and when you arrive, we'll work a day in so all three of us can have a proper welcome lunch, okay? This is so wonderful, Zoe. Again, welcome to the team. Safe travels! Talk soon."

"Sounds good, Margaret. Thank you so much!"

When we hang up, the quiet returns—but it's different now. It's no longer empty and filled with tension. It's brimming with possibility. My eyes wander, the city dancing about as the hustle and bustle is still chaotic as ever.

This is it. I said yes to something I've never been so sure of until now, and I'm so glad I did.

It's about damn time.

♡

After some writing back at the hotel, my phone pings and I immediately yank it off the coffee table. I will never get tired of staying at such nice hotels, especially one with room service and such a pretty bouquet of roses.

I sit up on the couch and unlock my phone. It's the flight confirmation from Ben, and as promised, my flight leaves at 9:20 in the morning. It's not even six o'clock and I'm already sleepy.

Spending the afternoon walking through Central Park and window shopping at the Oculus really tired me out.

My phone vibrates and then pings once more. It's my mom. *Hey sweetie! Any chance you're available to call me? Your dad and I would like to talk to you. Love you!*

My heart skips, then gallops. Talk to me? About what? My brain does that thing it always does—fires off worst-case scenarios like a panicked bingo machine. My overthinking taking control as usual. Is she okay? Is Dad okay? Did something happen at the house?

Oh god, what if it's the roof leaking again? Or the car? Or one of them is sick and they didn't want to tell me while I'm away?

I don't hesitate. I open her contact and hit FaceTime, the image of her name swimming a little from the anxiety gathering behind my eyes. The call rings twice before she answers.

Her face fills the screen, brightened by the golden hues of sunset behind her. She's sitting on the living room couch in one of her paint-splattered tank tops—purple with a swipe of orange near the neckline—and her blonde hair is tied into a low ponytail. Her reading glasses rest halfway down her nose, as always. Dad leans in beside her, his arm draped comfortably over her shoulders, a forest green t-shirt stretched across his chest. His glasses are perched on top of his head. He's always forgetting where they wind up.

The living room looks exactly the same—light pouring through the windows, casting soft glows on the family bookshelf, the puzzle table cluttered with edges and corners. That little bubble of home I carry in my chest swells, warm and steady.

"Hi honey! That was quick," Mom says, already smiling. "Is now a good time to talk?"

"Yeah," I say, dragging my suitcase from the closet and heaving it onto the bed. "Perfect timing. So, what's going on? Your text kind of made my heart leap out of my body a little."

Dad laughs. "Hey, baby! Quit your overthinking, we know you're good at that. No emergencies. No car troubles. No roof caving in."

"No parrot?" I ask with mock suspicion, squinting at the screen. "Please tell me you didn't adopt a parrot."

Mom chuckles. "No parrot, promise. Although your dad did once try to teach a neighborhood squirrel to eat from his hand, so... never say never."

Dad shrugs, a smirk tugging at his mouth like he's not even a little ashamed.

They share one of those glances—the kind married couples have after decades of inside jokes and silent conversations. The kind that says: okay, here we go.

"Okay," I say slowly. "You're doing the thing. The something-big-is-coming thing. Just tell me."

Mom lifts a hand. "We've been keeping something from you. Not because we wanted to, but because we weren't sure when or how to tell you. And, well... your dad made a big decision."

Dad clears his throat. "I'm retiring. Early. From the firm."

My jaw drops. "Wait. *What?* Like—actually retiring? Not just taking a break?"

He nods. "Actually retiring. Fully. No more client dinners. No more suits, unless I *want* to wear one—which, let's be honest, will be never."

"But... why now?"

He looks at Mom, then back at me, his expression tender. "Because life is short. And full. And sometimes we forget to *live* it, baby. I want to spend more time with your mom, with you when we can visit, with... books. With peace. And quiet. And story."

His voice grows soft on that last word—story. And something in me tightens, then melts.

"Dad..." I whisper. "That's... really touching."

"There's more," Mom says, her smile widening. "He bought something."

My brain goes fuzzy. "Okay. If you say a boat, I might actually scream."

Dad grins, his pale blue eyes crinkling. "No boat. But close in terms of the adventure." He leans forward, like he's telling me a secret. "I bought a bookstore."

Silence.

"You *what*?" I laugh, nearly dropping the phone. "A real bookstore? Like... actual shelves and books and receipts and everything?"

He nods proudly. "It's small. Cozy. Downtown. *Your* downtown."

I blink again. "Wait. Waitwaitwait. *My* downtown? So it's gotta be the little bookshop Tish and I went to last week. Where I bought that journal and the two paperbacks I've added to my never-ending stack of books."

Mom beams. "The very one."

My breath catches. "Oh my god. You bought *that* bookstore? They're selling? Geez, I'm so surprised."

"Well, your mom and I checked it out and I got to talking with the owner, and one thing led to another... Closing finalized yesterday," Dad says. "We will open it early next week after some small renovations and decorating, which I'll leave to your mother."

I sit in stunned silence, hugging my phone to my cheek like it'll anchor me. I picture the wooden floors and shelves that leaned with time. The adorable lights spread across the entryway as if letting you into another world. The abundance of stationery, notebooks, pens, stickers. The scent of dust and paper and quiet dreams.

I immediately picture my dad behind the counter, in jeans and a cozy flannel, recommending his favorite classics like *To Kill a Mockingbird* and *Brave New World* to strangers who just want to feel something.

My voice cracks. "That's amazing. Really. I don't even have words, and you know how rare that is."

Dad smiles. "I figured you'd understand. It's where I've always felt closest to you, baby. When we read together. When we got lost in bookstores and went to all those book sales and came home with bags heavier than we could carry."

I nod slowly. "I remember, Dad. And I gotta tell you… that's still my favorite kind of ache."

Chapter 89

I set my phone on my nightstand and begin taking clothes out from my closet. Whites and reds and blacks smother my vision as I pull them off the hangers and fold them into my suitcase. I can't believe Dad retired early... and bought a bookstore. My mind can't even wrap around it and yet I am so utterly happy for him.

The thought alone makes me pause, a smile tugging at my lips even as my hands keep moving. My dad. The man who wore ties to breakfast, who taught me how to properly format an Excel sheet before I could drive. The same man who used to fall asleep with stacks of cases and pleadings on his chest, ink smudged on his thumb. That man bought a bookstore.

He's finally doing something just for him. And I'm so excited to see him in his sanctuary.

I continue packing my things, tucking and folding and constantly rearranging it all. I pause, glancing toward the windows where the skyline glows faintly under the streetlights. Maybe I should have bought some souvenirs, like a magnet or postcard. Something. But that would be so cliché. Everyone who visits New York leaves with the same small magnet or postcard, or even the same snow globe or t-shirt. They bring back proof they were here. Something to pin to a fridge or tuck in a drawer and forget about until years later.

I feel my lips curve into a smirk, feeling a smile sprout on my lips. What I have is something better. I have the memory of the moment I said *yes*.

Yes to *Poets & Writers*. Yes to Margaret. Yes to everything I never thought I was ready for.

I chuckle to myself and zip up my suitcase, finally finished packing. I haul it off the bed and roll it next to the entry table. After all this, I'm feeling I deserve a nice warm shower and to appreciate this amazing hotel room one last time on my final night.

I turn the shower on, warm water spilling from the faucet. Within moments, steam begins to rise, curling up around the mirror and hugging the walls like new wallpaper.

And then, as if on cue, my mind drifts. It feels as if the jumbled thoughts and noise in my head have been dulled to a manageable hum. And it feels like the world is quieter now. Not silent, of course, but... softer. Like the music you hear in a coffee shop but don't really pay attention to.

I think back to the email from Professor Hopkins. About finishing my story. About that strange, glowing pride that bloomed in my chest when I hit *submit* and those big, bold words congratulating me on finishing my degree that popped up on my laptop.

I think about James, too. The way his voice still makes my stomach tighten, not with love, no, but with memory. Like muscle memory. Old fears masquerading as feelings.

And how, for the first time, I didn't chase the familiar. I finally fucking let it go.

And then I think about Ben. The ever so charming and handsome editor.

I think about his quiet steadiness. How he told me about his father and him living his dream as a writer in the Big Apple. How he once admitted that his last relationship left him wary, but not closed off. How he always gave me space, even when I didn't realize I needed it.

He never asked me to be okay and have it all together. He simply waited for me to find my way there. And I think maybe that's what love looks like.

It's not fireworks or grand declarations, but the person who shows up anyway. Who tucks you in when you fall asleep on the couch. Who sends you a good morning text just because they wanted to, reminding you you're not alone. Who asks for nothing but honesty, and offers his own in return.

A smile tugs at my lips, feeling warmth rise in my cheeks and the fluttering of butterflies in my stomach. Who sends you your favorite flowers with an apology that wasn't really needed, just because he felt the need to.

The air in my room feels lighter suddenly. And suddenly my heart doesn't race the way it used to around James. It settles around Ben. I can feel that loud and clear rumbling through my chest and entire being, like my brain applauding for finally getting to this moment.

I inhale a deep breath, and exhale. And then I remember I need to get washed up. I start peeling off my dress, the zipper whispering down my back as if I am closing a chapter I've just started writing. My earrings drop into the dish with a soft *clink*.

I stand under the water and let the steam wrap around me, water rolling over my shoulders, down my spine. The tension in my muscles begins to melt, but my thoughts still swirl, like leaves caught in a current. I press my forehead to the cool tile and close my eyes.

Tomorrow, I board a plane. Tomorrow, I'm back home in Cleveland to celebrate Dad's new bookstore. Tomorrow hasn't even started yet, and I'm already mind-boggled over leaving New York.

After everything that's happened, it only feels like I just got here.

Chapter 40

The morning breeze flows through the window I left open just a smidge, dancing with the sun as its golden glow smothers the room. Honking and laughter and conversation seem endless in this city, but I wouldn't trade it for anything.

I stretch under the covers and rub my eyes as I straighten up. My eyes automatically dart to my now-packed suitcase by the door. I look at the roses on the desk and smile.

And then suddenly I feel my eyebrows creasing together as I bring my knees to my chest, resting my chin on them. It's not like they have the same meaning as the tulips James for me. Never. And it's not like Ben and I are going to become a thing. I can't just start something up, whatever this is, with a guy from another city I barely know. That's crazy. That only happens in those cheesy Hallmark rom-coms. I firmly told him we're strictly professional here on out, and I meant it.

But I came here to prove something, to myself, to P&W. But somewhere between the Uber rides, brunch, the argument, and the interview, something shifted. I eventually stopped keeping my distance. In this very moment, it doesn't feel like I'm leaving the city. It feels like I'm leaving someone.

Him. Editor Extraordinaire.

My cheeks warm at the thought of Ben, and my heart nearly beats out of my chest. I inhale a deep breath and exhale slowly, sliding my legs over the bed and shoving my feet into my slippers. I need to get ready for the day. After all, soon I fly back home and New York will be just a memory.

A wonderful memory...

I pick up my phone off the nightstand. It's just past seven on Wednesday. And it's my last day in New York. Well, my last morning in New York. Luckily I have just enough time to get dressed and head to the airport to get through security.

I tug my suitcase back up onto the bed and slip off my pajamas, folding them tightly in whatever space I have left. I change into the clothes I hung in the closet, my gray oversized sweater and black ankle jeans with my pink Converse, and dab a little makeup on in the bathroom. I bite my lip, nostrils flaring as I stare at my reflection. It's not like I'm trying to impress anyone or anything, I'm just getting ready for the day.

I scan the room and do a quick walk-through in all the rooms, making sure I don't forget anything. The roses still sit on the desk, mocking me. If only I could bring them. I walk over to them, brushing my fingers over one of the petals. It's still soft, still alive.

"I can't take you with me," I whisper, like they might understand. "But thank you for being here."

I take a photo of them on the desk, bathed in early-morning New York sunshine. For memory's sake. For proof that someone thought of me in bloom. When *I* finally bloomed.

I smile, taking one last glance over the room as I stand by the door. I decide to give Ben a call. Not as a goodbye call, more of an update kind of thing. Who knows, he might not even answer, being this early and all.

He answers on the first ring.

"Well, good morning, Ms. Donovan," he says. "This is quite an early call I wasn't expecting. Unless we had something scheduled..."

I chuckle, shaking my head as if he can see me. His voice has a slight grogginess to it, but I like it. "No, no. I just wanted to say I am heading out of my hotel now, about to check out. You mentioned an Uber picking me up. Is that still the case?"

I hear him smiling. His deep hazel eyes probably creasing at the sides. "Yup, you're all set to go. I'll forward you the confirmation, but a white SUV will be picking you up. I requested the driver to stand by the vehicle with your name in front."

"You didn't. Well thank you, again. I appreciate you, Ben, truly. I don't know what I'd do without you."

"You can say I couldn't help myself. Pleasure's all mine, Ms. Donovan." The line goes silent for a moment. "Hey... you still have some time until you need to get to the airport, right? How about we meet up for a quick coffee? Call it a going-away gift?"

I bite my lip, feeling my face and neck redden. *Going-away gift.* Now it's for real.

"U-um, yeah, I think so. Text me the place and I'll be there."

"Great. I'll see you soon."

We hang up and I realize I'm still just outside my hotel room. I haven't even made it to the elevator.

Shit.

I scramble my luggage behind me as I press the elevator button. The numbers count down above me as if counting down the minutes I have left in this city.

The doors glide open and I step inside to the empty shaft. As if it took a million years, I finally reach the lobby and make my way to the check-out counter. "Good morning! I'm here to check out. The room is under Cartwright, but my name is Zoe Donovan."

The woman beams a bright smile at me, nodding as she takes my ID, her fingers typing away. "Of course, Ms. Donovan. We hope you've enjoyed your stay at Warwick Hotel. Just a moment while I pull everything up and check you out."

Her words sound so rehearsed as if it's something she says to everyone, and she probably does. But there is something so final about checking out. Something so... done.

I glance around the lobby while she finishes typing, like I'm trying to memorize it—the giant floral arrangement by the windows, the polished marble floors, the faint scent of lemon cleaner and brewed coffee in the air. It's just a hotel. A place to sleep. But it's also where everything started. Where *he* showed up. Where I made the decision to come here, to take this leap. Where I said yes, and finally meant it. And now it's the place I'm leaving behind.

"Here you go, Ms. Donovan," she says, handing back my ID with a folded receipt. "You're all set. Safe travels."

I nod, swallowing past the lump in my throat. I open my mouth to say thanks, but it's only dead air. I step back and begin walking to the entrance instead, trying to photograph everything in my brain.

My suitcase wheels click softly against the tiled floor as I walk toward the revolving door. Outside, the city is wide awake—horns honking, footsteps shuffling, the aroma of bagels and roasted coffee drifting from the corner cart. I pause for a breath, hand on the door, feeling the press of the moment.

I'm really leaving.

Chapter 41

My phone buzzes in my pocket and I pull it out. It's Ben. "Ms. Donovan, it looks like you left something at the check-out counter. The hotel just called me."

I crease my eyebrows in confusion, circling back toward the hotel doors. "U-uh, forgot something? Why didn't they just call me? What about—"

And that's when I see him. He walks through the hotel doors like he's done it a hundred times, phone to his ear, calm and completely unbothered while my insides tangle themselves into knots. He's wearing a loose NYU sweatshirt—navy and soft-looking, sleeves rolled up to his elbows—and slightly wrinkled khakis. His sunglasses mask the hazel eyes laced with gold I've come to memorize, but with one effortless move, he pushes them up and tucks his phone away.

And then he smiles. The effortless charming smile that makes my heart shake at my ribcage.

"Coffee, Ms. Donovan?"

I let out a startled laugh, shaking my head as the corners of my lips curve up despite myself. The suitcase handle slips from my fingers as if my body already knows what it wants to do before I can stop it. I step toward him, arms wrapping around his waist as my head presses against his chest. I can feel the soft rhythm of his heartbeat beneath the cotton of his sweatshirt, steady and sure.

Oh my god, what am *I* doing?

I pull away instinctively, but he catches me, his arms winding around me like he can't let go—not yet. His fingers move gently through my hair, a touch so tender it stirs a shiver that trails down my spine.

Oh my god, what is *he* doing?

My heart races, wild and unsteady, and I feel my lips trembling. His hand lingers at the back of my head, and then I feel the faint press of his lips on my forehead—warm and smiling and so, so gentle. The kind of touch that says things neither of us have said aloud yet.

We finally pull apart, like we're both aware the moment can't stretch any longer without one of us breaking it. The city spins on around us—yellow taxis blur past the curb, a bell rings from a bicycle, a couple of children chasing pigeons bursting with giggles just a few feet away. But everything feels muted, like I'm under glass, sealed inside this fragile bubble where only Ben and I exist.

I fiddle with the hotel receipt in my pocket, trying to focus on the paper, but my thoughts are everywhere—on his hands, his voice, the way he looked at me. The way he still is.

He clears his throat, and my heart hiccups.

"Ben—" I start, but he cuts in at the exact same time.

"Zoe—"

We both fall silent, blinking at each other. And then we laugh. It bubbles up out of nowhere, this shared breath of nervous relief. From what, I'm not sure. I feel my eyes staring at him, my blue orbs against his gold-speckled hazel ones. He clears his throat once more, and I immediately shut off my brain to let him speak.

"Zoe," he says again, voice low and sincere, "please don't take this the wrong way, but... since you came to New York, I don't know what happened. From very text and phone call to every moment we met up in person. I've tried to make sense of it, explain it away, shove it in a box and forget it—but I can't. You're probably going to think I'm crazy." He pauses, rubbing the back of his neck. "And I've been trying to ignore it, and figure it out in any way I can, but I think I just need to be honest."

He looks straight at me now. No hesitation. My heartbeat pulsing in my ears.

"I love you. I know it's fast. I know this is messy and probably terrible timing, but I'm not saying it to complicate things. I'm saying it because it's true. I'm saying it because you walked into my life and suddenly every part of it felt clearer. More awake."

He breathes out, his hands open at his sides like he's offering up every raw piece of himself. "You make me feel like I've been sleepwalking in this chaotic city and didn't realize it until you showed up."

I stop fidgeting with the receipt and fold it in my pocket. I look at him again, feeling my nostrils flare, feeling the cool air tickle my neck. My chest is tight, like it's too full—of surprise, of nerves, of something that might be hope. The cool breeze plays with a loose strand of my hair as I feel the slight weight of his hand hovering near mine. Close enough to touch. Close enough to change everything.

And still, I don't pull away. I should say something. I *need* to say something.

Because he *means* it. I can feel it with every fiber of my being that he really means it.

I'm suddenly too aware of everything—how close we're standing, the way hand grazes mine, the fact that the city noise has dulled into background static. I can feel my pulse in my throat. I remember the conversation we had just the other day—me, clear-eyed and firm, telling him I needed this to stay professional. That I wasn't looking for anything more. That with everything going on, I needed space, focus, boundaries.

And I meant it.

But now, standing here in the middle of the city with his confession still hanging between us like a heartbeat, I don't feel distant or detached. I feel *drawn*. Pulled by something magnetic and warm and terrifyingly real. I look up at him again, at the way his gaze is fixed on me—hopeful, nervous, reverent.

The kind of look you only give someone when you're waiting for them to either change your life or shatter you.

"I know I said I wanted to keep things professional," I whisper. The words feel like glass on my tongue, fragile and sharp. "And I did. I just…" I trail off, because nothing I say will explain this electricity zipping through me like I'm standing in a storm.

"I remember," he says quietly, a quiet ache beneath his words. "I've been trying to respect that. I wasn't going to say anything. I just couldn't pretend anymore. Not when I feel this much. Not when someone, *you*, really gets me, Zoe."

He begins to lean in, slowly, his breath warm as a hint of cinnamon clogs my senses. A shiver trickles through my spine. My hands all of a sudden ooze sweat, but I don't rub them on my jeans. I want to remember this exact moment, this feeling, the words Ben echoed moments ago.

Then, gently—so gently—I feel his lips on mine.

At first it's slow, tentative. I lean into it, and something shifts. The kiss deepens, heat flooding between us in a wave so fast it nearly knocks the breath from my lungs. My hand slides up his chest, fingers gripping the soft fabric of his sweatshirt as his mouth moves against mine—hungry now, purposeful.

His other hand cradles the back of my neck, and I melt into him like I've been waiting for this without realizing it. And who am I kidding, of course I've been waiting for this.

God, he's warm. Steady. His lips mold against mine and he tastes faintly like coffee and cinnamon gum. And the way he kisses me—slowly, then hungrily, like he's trying to memorize the feel of my mouth—is enough to make the world fall away completely. There's a pressure behind the kiss, something aching and unsaid. It's not just attraction. It's *longing*.

When we finally pull apart, my lips feel swollen, my breath coming in uneven gasps. My heart is pounding so hard it's a wonder he can't hear it. We stay close, our foreheads nearly touching as I'm on my tippy toes. I feel his breath on my skin, warm and soothing, even though everything inside me is spinning out of control.

"Ben," I say softly, barely able to find my voice. "That was…"

He brushes his thumb against my lower lip, his eyes still locked on mine. "I know," he says. "Me too."

And suddenly, something in me cracks wide open. Because I can't pretend anymore, either.

Chapter 42

I feel my heart knocking against my ribcage, my lips now swollen and burning from the kiss, my nostrils flaring. I suddenly feel Ben's hand over mine, lightly squeezing as he holds me firmly against him.

Oh god, coffee. After all this, we still have to get coffee.

I clutch my suitcase handle and yank it next to me, clutching it even tighter than normal. He smiles at me and places his hand on the small of my back as we walk across the street to Starbucks. The same one he was at after the whole James fiasco.

After he came to my rescue.

Ben's voice is soft, careful, like he's testing the edges of a wound he doesn't want to reopen. "Zoe, I'm sorry if I made things... weird between us now."

Oh god, he thinks *he* made it weird?

He opens the door for me, and the moment we step into the Starbucks, the world changes. The hum of the city fades behind us, replaced by the low buzz of conversation, the hiss of steamed milk, and the rhythmic tapping of laptop keys.

The warm, roasted aroma of espresso and baked pastries curls around me like a blanket, thick and comforting. It smells like cinnamon and dark roast, vanilla syrup, and something buttery and sweet—maybe the blueberry muffins stacked behind the glass counter. I inhale deeply, letting it fill my lungs, letting it ground me.

But my heart is still hammering. Not from the cool, brisk weather. Not even from what he just said.

It's the kiss.

That fucking *kiss*.

I can still feel the ghost of it on my lips, like a heat that lingers long after the fire is gone. His mouth on mine—warm and searching—like he wasn't just kissing me, but reaching into something deeper. It wasn't rushed. It wasn't reckless. It was purposeful. Like he'd waited for the right moment, and when it came, he didn't hold back.

And there was feeling behind it—so much feeling.

There *was* something there. There *is* something here.

And now, standing here in line at Starbucks, it's like my body is still echoing from it. My lips are tender, my chest is too full, like my heart is trying to rearrange itself inside me.

Ben stands close beside me, just enough that I can feel the warmth of him at my shoulder. His hand brushes mine lightly. Every nerve in my skin seems tuned to him now, like my body knows something I'm still working up the courage to say out loud. These things aren't supposed to happen this fast. My head screams at me to pull back, to protect myself, but my heart won't listen.

I swallow, feeling the heat rise to my cheeks. My eyes flicker up to him. His profile is serious, thoughtful, his brows drawn together just slightly. There's a line at the corner of his mouth, like he's been biting the inside of his cheek. I exhale a breath I didn't realize I was holding and finally speak up.

"You didn't make it weird," I say. "You made it real, Ben. You didn't overwhelm me, either. You just reminded me what it feels like to be wanted. I don't mean just being liked. Being *wanted.* And you could say that I wasn't ready for how much I needed that. How much I needed that until you said it."

That gets his attention. His brows knit together, like he's trying to understand where I'm going.

But I already know.

I pause, grounding myself in the sterile floor underneath me, the warmth of the room, *him.*

"I tried to shut it down. To protect myself. But you kept showing up. Not with promises. Not with big declarations. Just with presence. You saw me, even the messy, overthinking, shut-down parts of me. And my favorite part? You didn't even flinch."

And as we stand in Starbucks, I feel myself leaning into him, my voice soft and raw. "Ben... I love you too."

His whole face stills. Like he can't believe it.

"I didn't expect it," I go on. "I didn't come here looking for this. And god knows I tried to stomp on these feelings. But I can't. I don't want to anymore. You make me feel safe. And alive. And challenged and seen. I admit I'm a little scared. But I can't help it. My heart settles around your name, and I'm not walking away."

Something flickers in his eyes, like wonder, maybe relief. He exhales a breath that sounds like he's been holding it since the moment he met me.

"Zoe," he whispers. He softly strokes my cheek and bends down to place a kiss on top of my head. His hand slides to cradle my cheek, and he leans down, pressing his forehead to mine.

"You do?"

"I do," I breathe, my eyes stinging. "I do, Ben. I really, really do."

The look on his face nearly undoes me. Like I just handed him the thing he didn't think he'd ever get. And then he lowers his lips over mine, warm and soft.

I let my hands take control as I lace them around him and pull him against me, our lips molding into each other. It's slow and deep. His hands pull me tighter against him.

We finally pull back, our hands still tangled and breath uneven. Butterflies swoon through my stomach, making me wobble like everything in this moment is a dream.

He smiles, warm and delicious, and nods toward the counter. "I'll get us coffee, and you can find us a table, okay?"

"Okay, Mr. Editor." I can hear him softly laughing as I roll my suitcase through the shop, finding an empty booth near the back. It's quiet, the light above the table trying to shine the best it can as it flickers every few seconds. I slide into it and exhale, sitting back as I close my eyes.

Ben kissed me. Really kissed me. Not a maybe-kiss, not an almost. A real, breathtaking, soul-messing kiss.

And then we said it—*I love you*. Both of us. I'm officially in love with a charming, steady-souled editor. All in a span of forty-eight hours, too. And he's in love with a chronic overthinking writer who almost ran from it all.

Almost.

Maybe Tish is right. I really am living a rom-com life, and I should be more ecstatic about it.

A few minutes later, Ben reappears from around the counter with two coffees in hand. He shimmies in across from me and slides one toward me. I take off the lid and let the strong smell of vanilla and cinnamon tickle my nose, letting the warmth brush my face.

I take a few sips when I feel his foot lightly tapping mine playfully. I glance at him, smiling as he lets his sunglasses cover his eyes. "I believe we have a flight to catch, Ms. Donovan."

And that's when his words practically rip my heart out of my chest. That's right. I do. A flight home to Cleveland. And if we don't leave now, I'll miss it.

Stupid LaGuardia airport. Ruining our rom-com moment.

Chapter 48

It feels like I was just here yesterday, and in a way, I was. These last few days flew by, and I almost wish they hadn't.

I yank out my suitcase and grab my tote bag, slinging it over my shoulder as Ben opens the passenger door for me. He ended up canceling the Uber he requested for me and hailed a taxi for us instead, mostly due to the unexpectedness of the kiss that occurred earlier.

I mentally kick myself. That damn kiss.

LaGuardia airport always seems to be bustling, even for being the middle of the week. They're right when they say the city never sleeps.

I take my phone out, checking the time. Just past 9:30. Shit.

I turn to Ben, who shuts the door as we stop in of the departure entrance. I know he can sense I'm freaking out just by the flaring-of-my-nostrils thing. It's been my thing since day one. He holds me by the shoulders and instructs me to take a breath.

"Hey, it's okay. So we didn't make it on time, it's going to be fine. Good thing for you is that I always have a company card on me at all times. It's for emergencies only, but I think we both know this counts as an emergency."

He winks a gold-flecked hazel eye at me, which sends a shiver down my spine. I simply nod and take another deep breath. "You're right, I'm sorry. I just... feel bad, you know, given what happened back there and everything."

He smirks and rests a hand over mine, which is clutching the handle of my suitcase. He softly rubs his thumb over it. "Don't fret over anything, I got you. Anytime, anywhere. Okay?" He begins to roll my suitcase a few steps in front of me toward the entrance. "Now, let's get you back home, Ms. Donovan."

Nodding, I follow behind him, pulling my tote bag close to my side. I can feel my face reddening, my hands suddenly clammy. *Anytime, anywhere.* He says the right things to put me at ease. And he makes it all sound so easy, so not complicated.

Why does he have to be so sweet?

♡

The automatic doors open with a soft hiss, and I follow Ben into the cool buzz of the airport. The noise swells around me—layered, chaotic, alive. Rolling suitcases thump by on the glistening tiles, the low murmur of conversations, and the occasional ding of announcements overhead. It's all so familiar and yet very different, almost surreal.

Ben walks a step ahead of me, my suitcase rolling effortlessly behind him. I can't help but take him in again, almost taking a mental picture. His NYU sweatshirt bouncing just below his elbows like it's almost too big for him. His sunglasses perched on top of his head twinkle against the sterile light fixtures above, and his golden hair is tousled. Somehow it's the perfect kind of messy.

And suddenly I feel a pair of eyes on me. He swings his head in my direction, his glowing brown sugar hazel eyes catching the light just right, warm and knowing.

"You okay?" he asks, voice low, almost drowned out by a large tourist group next to us.

I nod, my chest feeling tight at the sound of his voice. "I'm okay, yeah. I just wish I wasn't leaving yet, you know?"

He takes a step back until he's level with me, clasping his warm hand around mine and pulling it up to his lips. He places a gentle kiss, like he's telling me it's okay without actually speaking.

He doesn't say anything right away, the gold in his eyes somehow less intense than just moments ago. And he doesn't have to say anything—the way his lips press together tells me he feels the same way.

We reach the ticket counter, and he sets my suitcase gently beside the counter as if it's the most precious thing. And right now, I can tell it is to him.

I suddenly feel my fingers tremble as I realize I should have had my ID out. I rush to open my wallet and feel Ben's fingers softly graze mine. I look up at him, his eyes warm. A small smile appears. He mouths, "Take your time."

My breath slows and I nod, sliding it on the counter. The woman thanks me, and just after a few clicks and tapping away at the keyboard, she informs us a flight to Cleveland leaves in just thirty minutes.

Ben gives her his company card and the transaction is completed in just a few minutes. We thank her and begin to walk toward my gate. We're rushed through security like cattle, feeling the pressure of whether I should put my phone or shoes in the bin.

Once we get to my gate, a line stretches behind the podium and a few people begin walking into the small hallway leading to the airplane. A few people sit in the seats around us, scrolling their phones, reading a book, or just staring outside as the planes depart and land.

I notice he's still clutching my suitcase, his fingers drumming the handle. There's a pause, a silence between us now, and neither of us move. He slowly shifts in place as if he's not believing this moment is here.

As if he's not ready for this to be over either.

I fiddle with my boarding pass, folding it and unfolding it. The sound of the piece of paper slices through my body. I feel my nostrils flare, and I hear Ben clear his throat.

"I just want to say, Zoe... thank you." He rubs the back of his neck like it's a habit he has to break, his hair curling around his fingers. "Thank you for coming here. You were here for us. For... your story. So thank you, for being you."

I blink a couple of times as the sound of his words echo through my brain, jumbling around as I try to comprehend them. He's thanking me, for being here, and for my story. For writing it.

For taking a chance on myself.

I lick my bottom lip, slowly nodding in response. I look back up at him and smile. My smile widens when I suddenly feel myself crying. Warm drops of tears flow down my face, and my lips begin to tremble. I don't know if it was what he said, or what I'm thinking, but I can't help it.

Then all of a sudden Ben leans close and his fingers reach for my face to wipe away the tears. I swallow and feel more rolling down my cheeks. He smirks and wipes my cheeks softly with his fingers.

He leans closer and I feel his lips reach my cheeks, placing a soft kiss on each of them. And then one warm and soft on my forehead. His arms wrap around me, his hands stroking my hair. I feel my breath catch just a little and I inhale his cinnamon and vanilla cologne as I sink my head against his chest. I cradle my arms around his torso, and he squeezes me back tighter than before. I close my eyes and let myself stay there for just a beat longer than I probably should.

I can't help but melt into him.

"I'm proud of you," he whispers as he pulls back. "And not just for the story. For all of it."

When we let go of each other, we look at each other once more. His golden flecks shimmer, and he smiles. He nods toward the gate as more people walk past the podium toward the airplane. "You'll be okay. You have me in your corner. Whether it's for a phone call, text, email... a telepathic kiss perhaps, you have me." He chuckles, giving me another peck on my temple. "Safe flight, Ms. Donovan."

He grins and kisses me on the temple again, slower this time, like he's trying to memorize the shape of goodbye.

My face warms at his touch. I'll never grow tired of those lips.

I grab my suitcase, gripping the handle tighter. "Thank you, Mr. Editor. I'll see you again soon."

I walk toward the podium and tell myself not to look back until I am at the end of the line. When I look back, I see Ben still standing in the same spot. His eyes stay steady on me as if watching my every move. My cheeks flush at the sight of him, and my nostrils flare once more as I bite my lip. He must notice, because he laughs, a deep hearty laugh that echoes through my chest and ears.

And I swear, his laugh is my favorite of all the sounds in all the city.

312

Chapter 44

Two Months Later
Zoe's 29th Birthday

"We've been over this, Tish, you told me no surprise birthday party and no gifts or anything. You promised! Pinky swore and everything. Doesn't that mean anything anymore?"

Tish laughs as she gathers a couple of birthday bags and wrapped boxes in front of me. Two months have passed since my New York adventure in October, and another year of getting older has sprung by faster than every year before.

The fireplace is warming the apartment around us as Ollie bathes in front of it, stomach hanging out and all. What a time to be a cat. A fat cat, that is.

She happily claps and grabs her wine glass. "Oh, come on, Zo. You only turn twenty-nine once. Plus, this is the last year of your twenties! This is absolutely a major big deal, babe!"

I sigh and clink my glass against hers. "Fine, I suppose you're right about that. So, let's see what you got me, huh?"

She beams and gestures dramatically to the glittery bag like she's unveiling treasure. "Then start with this one. Open it already, before I explode."

With a laugh, I pull the tissue paper aside and peek inside. My fingers brush against soft fabric first—then I lift it out and realize what it is.

It's a vintage typewriter key necklace, the letter z gleaming in the center of a tiny brass circle. Attached to the chain is a small charm in the shape of a book, engraved with the words *Chapter One*. I stare at it for a second too long, speechless.

"I saw it on Etsy," Tish says gently, watching my face. "And I just had to get it. It immediately reminded me of you. Starting fresh. Owning your voice. Writing your next chapter—not just in your work, but your life, you know?"

"Tish..." My voice trails off.

She waves me off, like she's suddenly uncomfortable with the emotion in the room. "Don't cry. I swear, if you cry, I will too. And then we'll be sobbing into our wine glasses like old ladies in a Hallmark movie."

I laugh, but my eyes are already stinging. "I'm not crying. You're crying."

"Liar," she grins, topping off both of our glasses. "Now open the next one. That one's a little ridiculous, but very you."

I glance at the second bag, this one wrapped in layers of cat-themed paper. "Should I be scared?"

"Oh, definitely."

Ollie lets out a loud snore by the fireplace, utterly unbothered. Somewhere between the laughter and the soft clinking of our glasses, I realize how much I missed this. How much I missed being home.

♡

After opening the gifts and finishing off our wine, Tish practically yanks me out of the apartment. The smell of marshmallows roasting tickles my nose as squawks of birds hover above us. Tish tied a scarf over my eyes as a make-shift blind fold, and she's lucky I haven't fallen on my butt yet.

I try to flip the scarf up but Tish is quick to smack my hands away.

"Excuse me, miss ma'am. No trying to take a peek at where I am taking you, got it? Now just hold my hand and follow me. We'll be there sooner than you know."

I groan and nod in response. "You know, you're so bossy today. What happened to my perky best friend? All supportive and shit while I was in New York?"

Tish snorts beside me, her fingers tightening around mine as we cross what I can only assume is another sidewalk. "Oh, she's still here," she says, the grin in her voice unmistakable. "But today? Today she is Birthday Command Central. You're lucky I didn't make matching shirts."

I stumble slightly over what I pray is not a squirrel carcass, but Tish keeps me upright with a firm tug. "Matching shirts?" I repeat, adjusting the scarf over my nose. "God help us all."

The cool breeze flits under the collar of my coat, but it's not unpleasant. There's the distant sound of laughter—children maybe? A dog barks somewhere across the street, and I hear the gentle whoosh of a car passing. Everything feels a little too quiet, a little too perfect. Suspicious. Weird...

"Are we downtown?" I ask, suspiciously sniffing the air

like some kind of bloodhound. "Because I swear I smell The Bean's cinnamon buns, and you know that place has a special place in my heart."

"Nope. You smell nothing," Tish says quickly. "I think you have birthday brain, sweetie. That's a real thing."

"Uh-huh." I'm about to protest further when we come to a stop. Tish's hand slips from mine and I feel her step away. "Don't move," she says. "And no peeking!"

"Fine, fine, no peeking." I freeze dramatically, hands up like I'm being held at gunpoint by a very aggressive party planner.

I hear a door creak open, the tiny chime of a bell overhead, and then—

"Okay," Tish says, breathless with excitement. "You can take it off now!"

I pull it off, blinking rapidly as warm light spills into my vision. My breath catches in my throat. We're standing just inside my dad's new bookstore.

I take a breath, and it hits me all at once: the scent of fresh pages, warm vanilla, old wood, and citrus-spiced tea wafting through the air like the place itself is giving me a hug. The bookstore glows from the inside out—light pouring from the amber sconces and fairy lights overhead, reflecting off polished wood floors and glass display cases that sparkle like they've been dusted with magic. The whole space hums with comfort and quiet joy.

Tish grins beside me, smug in the way only someone who's just pulled off a double surprise can be. "Happy Birthday and Happy Graduation, babe!"

I spin around slowly, eyes wide as I take it all in. There's soft jazz playing in the background and the low murmur of conversation from little pockets of people scattered around the store. But this isn't just a birthday party.

This is something else entirely.

There's a sign propped up on an easel near the poetry shelves, surrounded by vanilla candles and pink tulips. In curly calligraphy it reads: *Celebrating Zoe — 29 & Mastered: Happy Birthday + Congrats, Grad!*

My breath catches. It's silly, maybe, but something about seeing it written out—something about the acknowledgment of everything I've worked so hard for these past few years—makes my throat tighten.

"You guys..." I whisper, blinking rapidly as a few familiar faces wave from nearby. A few friends from school and even my favorite high school teacher, Mrs. Everly, is here, her smile wider than ever. "You said no party," I murmur, half to Tish and half to the cosmos.

Tish shrugs, clearly pleased with herself. "Okay, but I lied. For good reason. I mean, c'mon—you finished your master's degree, had a short story published, survived a trip to New York, *and* fell in love with a hottie of an editor. Well, barely survived, with only one meltdown."

I can't help but feel my face warming up. "Hey, that meltdown was hardly a meltdown."

"Sure," she says, patting my arm. "And Ollie's only slightly overweight."

Before I can protest further, Mom sweeps me into a hug, smelling faintly like lavender just like always. "We're so proud of you, sweetie," she murmurs, brushing a loose hair from my cheek. "We thought—well, you've been working so hard, and your birthday's always been a big deal, but this? This felt like something bigger. I mean, you got your dream job in New York, honey!"

"Thank you so much… but I just thought we'd go to dinner," I say, still stunned, letting her hands hold mine. "I didn't expect *this*."

Dad steps forward, handing me a mug that's practically steaming with something that smells like mulled cider and honey. His eyes crinkle at the corners as he smiles. "You didn't expect it, but you earned it, baby. And besides, when your mom said she wanted to celebrate, I figured—why not do it here? You love books. We love you. It made sense."

"And," Tish cuts in, practically bouncing now, "I got to plan a party in a *bookstore*. How awesome, right?"

I can't help but laugh. I then glance around again, soaking in every detail—the cupcakes that have little frosted pink books on them, the table in the back where printed pages of my short stories are displayed like rare treasures, the twinkling pink lights strung through the ceiling beams. They have a copy of the magazine laid open with my published story and feature.

There's a large chocolate cake shaped like a stack of books, with the top one titled in pink frosting: *Zoe's Next Chapter*. They're too good to me…

My eyes sting. "I don't even know what to say."

"You don't have to say anything, honey," Mom says, pulling me in for another squeeze. "Just let yourself enjoy this. Let yourself feel it."

And so I do.

I let myself stand in the middle of the bookstore my parents built from their shared love of stories. I let myself be celebrated, not just for turning twenty-nine, but for becoming the writer, the woman, the version of myself I fought hard to grow into. I let myself laugh when Dad accidentally trips over himself, dropping not one but two cupcakes. I let myself be surrounded by people who love me enough to make space for every part of me: the tired, the triumphant, the scared, the still-dreaming.

It's all here. I don't feel like I have to prove anything. I just get to be.

Tish nudges me with her elbow, a small candle-topped chocolate cupcake in hand. "Okay, grad girl *and* birthday girl. Time to make a wish."

I take the cupcake, stare at the tiny flickering flame, and close my eyes. For once, I don't wish for something distant. I don't wish for success or certainty or some golden-ticket future. I wish for this feeling—to stay a little longer.

I blow out the candle, and when I open my eyes, everything is still glowing.

Chapter 45

It feels just like yesterday was my twenty-ninth birthday party. And now, one month later, I'm somewhere else entirely and a smile is practically glued on my face.

The cab moves steadily through the streets of Manhattan, weaving through early-morning traffic as sunlight slips between the buildings in narrow, golden beams. The city is alive in a way that feels almost cinematic—like everything is moving toward something. It feels so good to be back.

People rush along the sidewalks with purpose in their stride, and I press my fingertips against the cool window glass, taking in the way steam curls from subway grates and pigeons scatter near carts selling bagels and coffee. A man in a dark woolen coat cradles a bouquet of peonies. A young girl in bright red headphones dances at the edge of the crosswalk. There's something about this city—it holds stories in the cracks of the pavement, in the chipped paint of fire escapes, and the flurry of newsprint blowing down the avenue.

I tilt my phone so Tish can see the view. "You seeing this?"

Her face lights up on the screen. "Oh my god, babe," she breathes, eyes wide, "you look like the main character right now.

Are you having a movie moment? You're having *that* moment, I can feel it."

I let out a soft laugh, but it catches in my throat. I nod, and Tish's smile widens. "I think I am." For the first time in a long time, I say it out loud without hesitation.

"I am," I say again, quieter this time, like it's a secret I'm still getting used to telling myself. "I don't have it all figured out yet. But I know this much—I don't want to go back to the life I was living before. The waiting, the constant second-guessing, the shrinking myself down to fit into places that never really felt like mine. I'm done with all that."

Tish softens, her excitement turning into something quieter, something proud. "You're choosing you. And let yourself fall in love for real this time. I'll say it once more: it's about damn time, sweetie."

I can't help but laugh. "It's been far overdue, huh? I'm absolutely staying, and no one can say otherwise, Tish."

The truth is, I didn't come here planning to stay. It started with one email, one published story, one interview. I thought it would be a weekend, maybe a week—get in, talk about my writing, and get the closure I never thought I'd have.

But then I started walking the streets. I started writing again, even when I didn't have to. I started noticing things I'd forgotten how to look for—bookstore windows with hand-scrawled signs, the sound of someone humming on the subway, the way the city breathes in noise and exhales possibility.

And somewhere along the way, something clicked.

I remembered who I am outside of all the noise. Outside of James.

I still think about that day in the bookstore. I remember standing behind a display of newly released hardcovers, half-hiding, heart pounding, stomach twisted into a knot of disbelief and something dangerously close to shame. His name was everywhere—on posters, in window displays, across a table stacked high with copies of his latest novel. And there, right in the middle, was me.

Not my name, of course. But *my* words. *My* heartbreak. *My* fears. *My* voice. All repurposed, rewritten, rearranged so he could sell our story as if it had only ever belonged to him.

He took everything I had ever shared with him in trust, turned it into prose, and made himself the misunderstood protagonist. He stripped my story of its nuance, erased the parts where he lied and manipulated and walked away when it mattered most. He left only what he wanted the world to see: a woman who felt too deeply, who clung too tightly, who asked for too much.

But I'm done carrying the weight of his version of me. I've shed it like old skin, and what's left is someone real. Someone whole.

The cab slows to a stop in front of Poets & Writers. I look down at my phone. Tish is still there, watching me like she's afraid this moment might vanish if she blinks. "Well, babe, I have an inkling I'm going to need to let this call end, am I right?" she asks.

I smile. "I swear you can make a solid living as a psychic, Tish. I just pulled up to the office. I love you, thank you for everything. Wish me luck!"

"You don't need luck, babe. You got this! Love you always."

I step out of the cab and the wind catches the hem of my coat as I land on the sidewalk. New York air hits me—cool and alive, full of motion and familiarity—and I inhale deeply, letting it fill my lungs. The sounds of the city rush around me: footsteps, snippets of conversations, the distant wail of a siren, the thud of delivery trucks against pavement. I stand still in the middle of it all, and for once, I don't feel lost. I feel found.

I adjust my black boots around my ankles, clutch my tote bag, and start toward the steps—when I see him.

A familiar figure walks down the sidewalk toward the entrance. His stride is easy but purposeful, like he already knew I would be here. He's wearing a dark gray coat, collar turned up against the wind, and his deep navy scarf is slightly askew like he got too distracted to fix it this morning.

Ben.

He sees me almost at the same time I see him. His eyes crinkle just slightly at the corners. Those amber-gold eyes I once described in my journal as "sunlight trapped in honey," though I would never let him read that page.

"New York missed you," he says as he reaches me, a smile tugging at the corner of his mouth. Then, a pause—his gaze dips from my eyes to the grip I have on my bag, then back again. "Welcome back, Ms. Donovan."

And that's when I feel it—his fingers, warm against mine, curling gently, not demanding or pulling, just there. A quiet certainty.

My heart knocks against my ribs like it's been startled awake.

I look up at him and smile, tightening my hold on the tote slung over my shoulder. He's grounding me with just his presence, steady and sure, like I never really left and he's been waiting for my return.

"Why, thank you, Mr. Editor," I murmur, holding his gaze. "I guess you could say it'll be like I never left." I squeeze his hand back. "I'm glad to call this place my new home."

His eyes don't leave mine. There's something in them—something warm and searching, like he's looking for proof that I mean it. That I'm really here.

"Good," he says softly. "Because I was hoping you'd stay. Those late night phone calls and texts weren't enough for me, you know."

And before I can respond, he steps closer, and I feel it—his presence, his pull, the way everything else dulls around us.

His hand lifts to my cheek, fingers trailing lightly along my skin before settling at the nape of my neck. My breath catches, heart thudding so hard it feels like it echoes between us.

And then he kisses me. Real and rich and raw.

No hesitation, no holding back. His lips claim mine with a kind of quiet urgency, like he's been holding this in for too long and he's finally allowed to feel it again. I melt into him, gripping the front of his coat, anchoring myself in the heat of him, in the steadiness of the moment.

When we part, we don't go far. Both of us breathless but smiling, like we've just remembered something we never should've forgotten. And it feels like we never did.

He doesn't say anything right away. He just stands here with me in the silence, letting the city move around us, the noise muffled by this moment that somehow feels both inevitable and brand new. The beautiful and hectic city fades around us. All I know is the press of his mouth, the strength in his hands, the way I feel like I'm being rewritten in real time—line by line, breath by breath.

"Welcome home," he whispers, and I feel the words settle inside me like they've been waiting for a place to land.

Maybe I've found love again. The real kind that bends with you, holds you solid, and never lets you down. And maybe it's with the man standing next to me. I'm not sure yet. This man is charming, gorgeous, and oh so kind.

Love, I realize, isn't just about holding on—it's about knowing when to let go and when to start again.

I see it now. I believe in it now.

I've already chosen myself. Fully. *Finally.*

And this—this moment, this decision, this messy, beautiful unknown—isn't the end.

It's the beginning. A blank page. A fresh chapter.

And if anyone ever asks me when everything changed, when the story stopped belonging to someone else and started being mine, I'll know exactly what to say.

It all started with a rewrite in New York.

*The short story that first brought Zoe into the publishing world,
now for you to read.*

He left the note on the kitchen counter, and she almost didn't notice the blood on her hands. Not her own—just a small nick from slicing fruit too quickly, but it looked like proof, like a mark he had left behind for her to find. The apartment felt too large, empty in the way that hollowed her chest with every echo of her own footsteps.

The faucet dripped. *Drip. Drip. Drip.* Each drop struck the sink like a clock she couldn't read, a heartbeat she couldn't catch. She pressed her palms against the counter, letting the cold ceramic ground her, willing herself to stop shaking. But she didn't. The note sat there, folded neatly, impersonal, cruel in its casual departure.

Sunlight spilled through the blinds, catching dust particles that twirled like tiny stars. She watched them for a moment, thinking how fragile they were, how easily they would fall apart if a single gust disturbed them. She thought of him the same way—careful, bright, and suddenly gone.

The apartment made noise on its own. Floorboards creaked as if remembering the weight of him. The refrigerator hummed low, a tired engine. Outside, the wind tugged at leaves, whistling between the buildings. Somewhere, a bird called, sharp and desperate. She imagined it had a voice meant only for her, trying to tell her something she didn't yet want to hear.

She moved toward the window, fingertips brushing the sill. The curtains trembled, lifted by the breeze, and shadows fractured across the floor. Her reflection stared back at her from the glass, pale, small, uncertain. She blinked. He was gone, but she could still feel the weight of him pressing into the space she had given him for so long.

The notebook on the table called to her. She hadn't touched it in days. Now she picked it up, the spine warm beneath her fingers, the pages slightly curling. She pressed the pen to paper. Words came, jagged and unpolished at first: fragments of mornings spent in disbelief, nights replaying every laugh, every small betrayal. She wrote for herself, not for him, not for anyone, because for the first time in weeks she needed something tangible—something real that she could claim as her own.

Water ran in the sink, forgotten, spilling over its edge, splashing onto the tiles. *Drip. Drip. Drip.* She did not count. She did not need to. Each sound echoed like a memory she hadn't wanted, a truth she had ignored: he had never belonged to her the way she had thought, the way she had hoped.

The words poured from her, cascading across the page. They spoke of love she had given too freely, trust she had lent without guard, of nights that left her hollow and mornings that smelled of smoke and regret. She wrote about anger, sharp as broken glass, rising from her chest into her fingertips, turning her hands raw and alive.

The world outside went on. Leaves tumbled across the sidewalk, scraped against windows, fell into gutters. Children laughed in the distance. A dog barked somewhere too far away to matter.

She noticed all of it, the way a distant observer might, but it did not touch her. She was in the room, alive in a way that no absence could erase.

A cup clinked against the counter, unnoticed. Steam rose from a kettle she had never turned on, curling into shapes she could not name. She could smell it anyway: hot metal, stale air, faint sweetness. The small, ordinary details wrapped around her, grounding her, reminding her that she was here, fully, entirely, despite the chaos he had left behind.

She stopped writing eventually, leaning over the table, forehead resting on her crossed arms. *Drip. Drip. Drip.* The faucet had slowed. Sunlight shifted, catching on dust motes that danced lazily in the air. A bird landed briefly on the windowsill, cocked its head, and flew away. She imagined it watching her, curious, judgmental, indifferent. She smiled slightly, a small acknowledgment that she had survived him.

The note remained on the counter, innocuous, almost laughable. It could not erase her. It could not undo the hours she had spent writing herself back into existence. The pen rested beside the notebook, poised and ready, but she did not need it for a while.

She walked to the window again, hands pressed lightly against the glass, feeling the sun warming her fingertips. The wind tugged at the curtains once more, and she let it. She breathed in the scent of rain and dust and possibility. She could feel her pulse, steady, her heart stubborn in its rhythm. She was alive. She was here. She had words. She had herself.

And for the first time in months, that was enough.

Acknowledgements

It feels surreal typing out my first acknowledgements page for my very first novel. I've had the dream placed on my heart for years, and here it is, as real as can be.

I want to thank my family—my mom, dad, stepmom, brother, and sister. They have known my passion for reading and writing has been alive for years. Supporting me through college and the uncertainty of not knowing what to major in. Through it all, their support never dimmed, but rather pushed me to go for it. Even when I'd drag them into bookstores "just to look", they'd follow along with no complaints. I love you all.

I want to thank my closest friends, Hope and Katelynn. Hope, thank you for sticking around this long and sharing my love for reading as we grew up. I'm surprised you're not tired of me yet. From reading my fun little stories back in high school to my college essays and stories, you were cheering me on. I'll never forget when we were sitting in my bedroom, both of us still in community college, and I was unsure about what to major in. You simply said to me, "Just do what you love. Do what makes you happy." So, I did, and I never looked back. You're such a real one for that. You've given me your full support and love, and it's more than I could ask for. You're more than a friend. Just like Tish, you're my best friend and platonic soulmate.

Katelynn, thank you for sharing your love for reading with me and for being one of the first people to cheer me on when I started writing this book. From sending endless TikToks with book recommendations and sales to being my go-to book shopping buddy, your support has meant so much. I'm so grateful for how close we've grown over these last few years. Your encouragement and shared love of stories have made this chapter of my life even more special.

I'd also like to thank the booktok and writertok communities on TikTok. This might seem silly, but it's true. Ever since joining and posting my writing and publishing journey a year ago, I've received nothing but encouragement, support, and kindness. From cheering me on in the comments to sharing my content, every little thing means the world to me.

Lastly, I want to thank the person writing this: me. I've always wanted to write a book, and whenever I'd get so close, I'd toss it aside, losing my confidence. And yet, over the years, while it's diminished and blossomed all at once, I can proudly say I made my dreams come true.

You did it, now smile. It's about damn time.

Holly Lipovits resides in Cleveland, Ohio, with her two boy cats, Alfie and Pretty Boy. She holds a BA in Creative Writing and English from Southern New Hampshire University and is an editorial assistant for a medical journal. *A Rewrite in New York* is her debut novel.